50ᵈ
HR

Girlfriending
A Collection of Stories

Christopher T. Werkman

Dedication

This collection is dedicated to my sweet lady and poet, Karen Wolf, who offers me wonderful advice and suggestions for my writing. She knows me better than anyone, and loves me regardless. She puts up with me and is still here (as of this writing).

I also must acknowledge my fellow writers in my Monday night online writers' group at Allwriters' Workplace & Workshop, and Kathie Giorgio, my writing mentor and the director of Allwriters' for all the input they offered to help me craft the stories collected here.

CONTENTS

SAFE HARBOR

The bottle danced an erratic jig. Otis saw it floating near the stern of *Bubble Watcher* as Andre backed the fifty-five footer into its mooring slip. Otis decided prop wash caused the motion, but even after Andre shut down the grumbling diesels, the clear-glass beer bottle continued to jiggle, bottom-end-up. While other divers off-loaded their gear, Otis watched the bottle continue to wiggle and bob amongst the Styrofoam cups, plastic bags and other harbor flotsam. He realized there had to be a creature hooked on a line tied to the bottle's neck, engaged in an unending struggle for freedom. The work of bored teens, he figured. Bait the hook and toss it in the ocean—a floating gallows. Otis grabbed the gaff, climbed out of the cockpit and shuffled along the narrow deck-space between the cabin and the gunwale, hoping the bottle would come within reach.

"What's up?" Andre called down from the flying bridge.

"Not sure," Otis shouted back. He could snag anything inside ten or twelve feet, but the bottle was out of range. It submerged, then popped to the surface again. Whatever the line held was too small, or weakened, to take it under for long. "C'mere," Otis hissed, in his raspy whisper. Instead, the bottle moved closer to the algae-coated jetty, green as ripe spinach. Just as Otis decided to get off the boat and try to recover the bottle from the pier's walkway, it made a break for open water, giving *Bubble Watcher* wide berth.

Diving in to swim after it was Otis' only option. He noticed a tampon applicator floating in the coffee-with-cream colored shore-water. A mile or so out to sea, he could count the planks in *Bubble Watcher's* hull from a depth of a hundred feet, but in the marina, all manner of waste found its way into the water. Not only that, he had no idea what was hooked on the line. Getting bitten or being speared on the dorsal of a panicky fish was even less appetizing than a leap into the murky water. So, the bottle skittered away, leaving Otis as angry at his own inaction as he was with whoever set the trap.

He jumped down onto the main deck, stowed the gaff and picked up his gear. He dove the summer-warmed ocean in his swim trunks and a tee-shirt. Since Andre, the owner, supplied him with a tank and regulator, he had only to off-load his buoyancy vest, weight belt, mask, fins and snorkel.

Andre climbed down from the bridge and tilted his head toward the jetty. "No treasure?"

Otis hoisted his equipment onto the pier, then glanced in the direction the bottle took. He wanted to tell Andre about the bottle, but the words hung in his throat. "Nah, turned out to be nothing."

"How was the dive?"

"Spec-tacular. One of those little gals and I found a sea turtle with a wad of fishing line tangled around her flippers. We cut it loose, and she followed us around for most of our dive." His smiled. "Neat."

"That 'little gal,' the tall drink of water you surfaced with?" When Otis nodded, Andre did a once-around to make sure she wasn't nearby. "Man, Otie. I was you, I'd be on her like spar varnish."

Otis winked. "She probably already has a grandpa." He stepped up onto the stern, then to the pier. "Same time tomorrow morning?"

"Sure. Eleven spots reserved. Probably some walk-ins. Castin' off at ten sharp."

"I'll fill the tanks and have everything good to go." Otis picked up his gear, walked into the dusty gravel parking lot and discovered the girl they were talking about was parked next to his car. Her shiny red SUV wore New York plates. She was toweling off her robin's-egg blue aluminum tank. A large woman with olive skin and long raven hair, she was fleshy, but athletic. He judged her to be in her thirties, and imagined she might look at home on a soccer field or a basketball court.

"Hey, Otis." Her smile came on like high beams. "I really enjoyed the dive. That poor turtle seemed *so* happy when we cut off the fish line."

"Yeah, glad we ran across her. Damned monofilament line is

ruining the ocean." The jittering bottle did an encore in his memory as he opened his car's trunk and laid his gear inside. He almost mentioned it, but as he turned to face her, she stooped to remove the regulator from her tank. Instead, Otis watched the top of her Day-Glo pink swimsuit strain to contain her breasts.

She stood and gave him a knowing look. "I bet you'd like one of these." She stowed the regulator in the back of her car, and pulled two cans of beer from a cooler.

"There's the way to my heart, girl. Thanks."

"What makes you think I'd want your heart?"

"You wouldn't." He opened the can and took a sip. "It's old and worn out, just like the rest of me."

She laughed hard. "I work with guys half your age who will never be in the shape you're in."

"Then they have my sympathy. And what is it you do up there in…?"

"Schenectady. Marketing."

Otis grinned. "Convincing people to buy what they don't know they need?"

She wrinkled her nose. "Sometimes. Or what they bought from me a year ago isn't as good as what I have to sell them today. Companies though, not people." She closed the SUV's back hatch and leaned against it, her reflection on the window doubling her beauty. She explained she was a refugee from the dot com collapse of the late nineties and she'd sold software for six years. "The company is moving into a new building in late August, so I bumped my vacation up a few weeks. I get a corner office with a great view of a park, and I need to be there to make sure it's arranged the way I want."

"Well, if you have to work, it sounds like you've got a great situation."

"Have to work." Her laugh rolled. "That's right, you said you retired. What did you do before you became a dive bum?"

"Michigan State Patrol. Was a trooper for thirty-two years. My wife, Jayne, died a few years back after ten rounds with breast cancer. Right after that, I had a bout with the big C myself."

For the first time, a serious expression cleared away the woman's smile. Her dark eyes brimmed with concern, making her even lovelier. "Oh, Otis." She touched his arm lightly. "You're okay now?"

"Seem to be. Had surgery and some radiation." Radiation scared him, especially because he believed radiation exposure from traffic radar caused the cancer in the first place. When the course of treatment ended, he was declared clear of disease, but lacked confidence in his body. To his way of thinking, nurturing cells bent on his destruction amounted to treason. As a trooper, he relied on his body to safeguard his life. Its dalliance with cancer shook him to his core. On the way home from his final radiation treatment, he saw a mid-sixties Pontiac GTO gleaming beneath the wind-tickled plastic flags on a used car lot. Half an hour later, he was writing the chain-smoking salesman a check. The car took Otis back to the time when he was young, strong and healthy. At another level, the control he exerted over such a powerful machine transposed into a feeling of mastery over his body. Otis liked to think of the GTO as an outgrowth of his psyche, although the reverse was probably closer to the truth. "But, yeah," he told her. "I've been clear since."

"And you had it…where? Do you mind my asking?"

Otis shrugged. "Not if you don't mind me telling you. My testicles. They took the right one. Managed to save the left." He raised his eyebrows, amplifying his grin. "Easier to cross my legs, now."

Dark as she was with a tan compounding her complexion, her blush ripened. "I'm sorry" She laughed. "I deserved that."

Otis shook his head. "No. You really didn't. I should watch my manners. I'm the one who's sorry."

She waved off his apology. "So, Mr. Trooper-man, if I was boogying on down here to Florida and you pulled me over, would you give me a ticket?" she asked, challenging him with a quirky lopsided grin.

"Damned betcha!" He enjoyed her obvious surprise. "If I stopped you, you'd have been doing at least five over. I let a few folks off if their story was creative enough, but never a good-looking lady."

"Well, I suppose that's a compliment, but why not the pretty ones?"

"Because lookers get breaks all their lives. They *expect* to get off easy. I always enjoyed disappointing them."

She finished her beer. "You're a study, Mr. Trooper-man. But today was wonderful. You're a great diver."

"Oh, you're pretty good yourself. Do you have much chance to get deep, up north?"

"Quite a bit. In the warm months, anyway. I've dived Lake George lots of times, and the Finger Lakes. The water's beautiful. Clear as a crystal, but cold. You wear a full wet suit, or you stay in the boat. That's why I love it down here, diving in just a swim suit. I'm surprised you wear a tee-shirt."

Otis chuckled. "Tracy, at my age, the more you wear, the better people like to see you."

"So, you *do* remember my name. I was beginning to wonder."

"Sure." He took the empty can from her and started for a trash barrel. "You told me on the boat. Tracy Walterman. Cops remember names."

She laughed. "It's *Welter*man."

"Well, I'm a retired cop with old ears."

"Mr. Otis Trooper-man Cop, I head back north tomorrow, and I'm going to my favorite seafood joint tonight. If you'd be my guest, I'd leave Lauderdale feeling like I've evened the score for a terrific dive."

Otis wished he was twenty years younger, and that he didn't already have plans for the evening. "It's nice of you to offer, but I have a gal friend I promised to take to dinner tonight."

Tracy's smile lost its usual symmetrical balance again, pulling itself higher on the left and forming a shallow cleft in her cheek. "I feel silly. I should have figured a man like you was busy, if not spoken for."

"To be honest, I've been wondering the same about you. A fine looking lady like yourself can't get one of them New York boys to tear himself away from the office long enough to come along to Florida?"

"I think I intimidate a lot of them. My height." She shrugged and turned her palms to the late afternoon sky. "I've dated some guys as tall as me, and even some who were shorter. I don't have a problem with it, and it always seems okay, at first. But it's like, somehow the reality catches up when the newness wears off. They stop calling." Her hands rose gracefully to rest on the smooth curved cliffs of her hips. "That, and I'm pretty independent, probably on the pushy side, which might put some of them off. It's nothing for me to pack my gear and drive down here alone. The right guy will eventually stumble by, or I'll stumble across him. In the meantime, I just do what suits me." Her smile straightened.

Something about the way Tracy punctuated her final sentence with a jut of her chin made a memory flicker. Otis recalled an evening on the patio-deck of a house in Ann Arbor, Michigan. He and Jayne were drinking wine while their steaks grilled. Earlier that day, Jayne told him about the lump her doctor found in her breast. "Don't worry, Otie. I'll beat this," she told him, cocking her head with her typical spunk. His awareness slipped back into the parking lot, and he smiled at Tracy. "I think you're doin' it all just right."

She extended her hand. "I'm so glad we rescued the turtle. I'll always remember that. You're a good man. And a great diver."

He gave her hand a gentle squeeze. "You drive careful tomorrow. Watch out for those bad old cops, and good luck with your new office."

Otis allowed himself some wistful fantasy as he watched Tracy drive off. "Might haves" and "could haves" swirled in his mind like scuba bubbles. Kate, the lady he was taking to dinner that night, was a close friend, but neither of them had a lasting relationship in mind. A quick phone call could have smoothly extricated him from their plans, with no hard feelings. However, the way things played out with Tracy was for the best. That's what Otis decided to believe.

Just as he relaxed into reluctant acceptance, however, the specter of the wriggling bottle returned. "A good man," he muttered, walking back to the pier. Andre was gone, the area deserted. Most of the slips were occupied now, with boats tied at rest for the night. Wavelets slapped at *Bubble Watcher's* hull as he peered into the space between the boat and the jetty, where he first noticed the bottle. Only an iridescent petroleum slick rode the gentle swells. He ambled a short distance along the pier, watching for any movement not associated with natural wave action. After searching unsuccessfully around several moored vessels, he walked slowly back to his car. The bottle and Tracy were both gone.

~ * ~

Otis got into his GTO and fired the big engine. Neither the bottle, nor the beautiful girl from New York would stop looping through his mind. Those two unrecoverable losses nagged at him all the way to his townhouse. As he idled past the fastidiously maintained and almost identical dwellings in the gated community, he traded waves with several of his elderly neighbors. At fifty-eight, Otis was the junior resident of the neighborhood, and the object of a lot of gossip, he learned. The fact he was considered a mystery man amused him. There were no dark secrets. After a couple months alone in the house he once shared with Jayne, he decided he would be happiest if he clung to the memories, but changed his surroundings. Early on the morning he set off from Ann Arbor for Ft. Lauderdale, Otis paged through an album of photographs chronicling his marriage. Jayne assembled it while she fought for her life, and her swoopy feminine script titled or commented on every picture. Other than the album, his clothes and his car, the only other possession he brought south was a set of golf clubs his co-workers at the patrol post gave him as a retirement gift. He enjoyed golf, but made up his mind to expand his interests when he came south. He met Kate, another transplant from the north, playing tennis. Scuba led to his part-time job, which offered free diving and some extra walking-around money. There was nothing for his neighbors to discover, but he enjoyed fostering their speculation by volunteering little about himself in chats out on the lawn.

After cutting the sea salt with a steamy shower, Otis dressed in khaki shorts, a Hawaiian shirt and sandals. He'd just picked up his keys and started for the door when the phone rang. "Hi, Kate," he said. "I was just on my way over." He glanced at his watch. He wasn't late, so he knew something else was going on. "Everything okay?"

"Oh, Otie." Kate's voice dropped into the apologetic range. "Charlotte called this morning. We have a problem at one of my stores, the one in Cicero. I don't know, some kind of big blow up with the new manager. The groomer there, a man who has prepped dogs for Westminster, is threatening to quit."

"That isn't good."

"Not even a little bit. Charlotte could probably handle it, but I want to be sure that groomer knows I think enough of him to take care of it personally." She paused. "God, it sounded so simple. Put the business in competent hands, bask in the Florida sun and collect checks."

"Except for a hiccup here and there, it's gone pretty well."

She chuckled, and Otis pictured the way her deep smile lines framed her lips. Jayne had true dimples, but Kate's smile lines did close impressions. "I guess you're right. Well, anyway, I'm flying to Chicago tonight, in about an hour and a half. I admit it's an excuse to see my grandkids, too. There was no way to let you know sooner. Char didn't call until after you'd cast off." Kate clicked her tongue. "You won't carry a cell. Anyway, tonight's a no-go, Otie. I'm sorry."

He smiled his tight smile. "Don't give it a thought. Go take care of business."

Otis scooped up his keys and walked out to his car. On his way back to the marina, he peered into the parking lot of every seafood place he passed on the chance he'd spot a red SUV with New York plates. His imagination refused to leave Tracy's sumptuously upholstered body alone.

Tide's Inn was no tourist hangout. Its shabby yellow exterior had a "needing maintenance" look that repelled snowbirds, and attracted locals who preferred not to mingle with them. The restaurant/bar sat in a cluster of similar businesses, only a few blocks from the slip where *Bubble Watcher* was tied off, and Otis ate there often. He loved the sea, but preferred beef to fish. Sid, the owner, named an open-faced steak sandwich in his honor.

Sid whisked Otis' empty plate away. "OT Special met your exacting standards tonight?"

"I don't know about any 'exacting standards,'" Otis said through a wry smile, "but it tasted plenty good."

Sid laughed. "Another beer?"

Otis stood and dropped several bills on the shiny dark bar top. "Thanks anyway, buddy. I've got a lot of tanks to fill tonight."

Andre's dive shack was so well insulated from the locomotive-like commotion of the huge compressors in the back, Otis didn't have any trouble hearing the Rolling Stones on the tiny transistor radio dangling from a ceiling joist. Sweat wallpapered his shirt to his back while he stood in the yellowish light leaking from the single bulb hanging like a noose from the ceiling. He swatted at the occasional mosquito, waiting for the air pressure gauge to reach three thousand pounds. Then he shut the valve, hit the switch to kill the compressors and disconnected the final four tanks from their supply hoses. Pulling them out of the cooling bath, he stacked them with the others.

Otis got a cold beer from the dingy refrigerator, stepped out into the humid darkness and locked the door. He already decided to spend the night on *Bubble Watcher*. Including the beers with Tracy and at dinner, the one in his hand made six. He didn't feel affected, but any thought of a DUI overruled a drive home.

Otis walked to the edge of the pier. He looked into the water where he first spotted the bottle that afternoon. The surface was smooth. Nothing stirred outside the frequency of the water's gentle rise and fall, the ocean's heartbeat. He boarded *Bubble Watcher*, climbed the ladder to the flying bridge and settled into the comfortable captain's chair. Sipping his beer and gazing into the star-speckled sky, he awaited the moonrise. Although it was quiet for a Saturday night, muted music and laughter made the drift across the water. Otis fantasized about what entertained the unseen merrymakers.

He thought of Kate and of Tracy. Although female companionship was a tempting notion, Otis didn't believe he was lonely. He accepted being solitary as a carryover from his former career. The job of a patrol officer was, after all, to ride alone and observe the behavior of others, something that was second nature to him. If he walked back into Tide's Inn, it was a good bet someone would call him by name and offer to buy him a drink. However, he would be just as happy to sit by himself and watch people argue with, seduce, and entertain each other. Besides, there was no one in that bar, or anywhere on Earth, whom he could tell about the bottle.

When he finished his beer, Otis let his head loll against the high seatback. His awareness soon dissolved into slumber, and a dream formed in which he floated close above the ocean, his body rising and falling in harmony with the wave action. The full moon glowed and he watched his shadow dance on the sparkling breakers below. He soared off like Superman, toward the beach where the restless swells rolled and broke against the sand, their roar evaporating into a foamy hiss.

Then, through luminous curtains of mist, he spotted the silhouette of a figure in the distance. Zooming off in that direction, low over the broken water, Otis rose to hover above a woman wading hip deep in the roiling surf. The hem of her dress swirled about her on the turbulent indigo surface like light-colored paint. Just as Otis realized the woman in the midst of the surge was Jayne, he noticed the bobbing bottle, riding the swells near where she stood. "Jayne!" Otis called out several times, but she couldn't hear him.

Then, just as he hoped, she saw the bottle and reached to grab it from a frothy roller. Otis held his breath while, hand over hand, she gathered the line until a silvery fish, less than a foot long, emerged from the water. She deftly unhooked the struggling creature and let it slip free.

A departing freighter's horn roused Otis from his sleep. He glanced at the clock on the pilot's console. 9:45. He had only napped a few minutes. Regardless, he felt more refreshed than he would have expected. Moreover, Otis awakened into a soothing calm, much the way he felt when *Bubble Watcher* made safe harbor with all its divers. He remembered dreaming, but as often happens, he lost any distinct images in the fog bordering consciousness. He recalled something about the moon reflecting on the sea, but in seconds, even that slipped into his mental mists.

He picked up his beer and the warm glass reminded him it was empty. He tipped it up, but only a trickle made its way down the bottle's long neck. Thirsty, he climbed down from the bridge, jumped onto the pier and started for the dive shack where the old refrigerator held some cold ones.

Otis changed his mind. What the heck. It's still early. I'll head for Tide's Inn. Or maybe even someplace else.

CRASHING

Lacey flipped her pillow and savored the cool underside of the case until it warmed against her cheek. It was going to be a sizzler. Not Iraq-hot, but blistering for Ohio. She just knew.

Tyler was still asleep, awash in crisp sheets. The night before, he invited Lacey to a family picnic and she said she wouldn't go. No family meet-ups. Just friends. Fuck buddies. Not ready for a relationship. Having enough trouble rediscovering her civilian-self and easing back into everyday Midwest America. Now, she lay looking at him, wondering how her decision would affect the day. His face had a thousand freckles. Little sepia spatters. He pawed his dark tousles into orderly eddies after showering and his hair never changed once it took its set and dried. Even his helmet didn't affect it. The idea of permanent helmet-hair crossed Lacey's mind and the thought coaxed a smile just as his eyes opened. "Hey," she said.

He smiled back. "What?"

"Your hair. It's like a sculpture. Looks the same as when you went to bed. Even wind doesn't faze it."

"You jealous?"

Lacey rolled onto her feet and picked up her panties. "No. Well … yeah. Maybe," she said, slipping them up over her hips and letting the elastic snap.

Tyler turned onto his back and nodded toward where his erection tented the sheet. "Hey, what about this?"

Lacey shrugged. "Morning wood. Take a squirt. It'll go away." She dropped a loose sleeveless shirt over her slender-but-muscled torso and smiled. "Don't trip, though. You'll pole vault."

"Aw, come on." He cradled his head in his hands and rested chin on his chest. "I'll be fast."

Lacey buttoned her shorts, jerked at the hem to get them on her hips where she liked them and padded barefoot around the bed. She bent and planted an open-mouthed kiss, enjoying the wetness of Tyler's lips while she wrestled his tongue into submission. Standing abruptly, she turned for the door. "Bummer," she said, over her shoulder. "I've got to be at the Haverhills' house by eight-thirty."

He grabbed for her, but missed. "Jesus, are you a cruel woman," he bawled theatrically. He slid out of bed and started for the john.

She used a scrunchie to fashion her hair into a short, straw-colored ponytail and winked. "You got it. Cruel and unusual. Not someone you want loose in polite society."

Tyler thought to set the timer, so the kitchen steeped in the thick aroma of coffee. Surrounded by her troop of cats, Lacey spooned food into their bowls, rinsed her hands and pushed a thumbnail through the cellophane of a package of English muffins. She split one and dropped each half into the toaster. By the time Tyler walked in, his coffee was poured, the toaster had popped and Lacey was nibbling a boiled egg.

"How do you eat that without salt?" he said, hot-handing a muffin and slicing off a pat of butter while simultaneously stoking Bahrah, Lacey's fluffy blond cat, with the bottom of his bare foot.

Lacey smiled. "What? You put salt on deviled eggs, too?"

His eyes clouded over and he shifted to stand on both feet. "I guess you'll never know."

"Shit." She rocked her face to the ceiling and shook her head. I go and mention picnic food. I'm such a dumb ass.

"Eating a hamburger within a hundred feet of my parents doesn't constitute common-law marriage or anything," Tyler said. "Not in this jurisdiction, anyhow."

She stepped on the pedal that opened the lid and let the wastebasket consume the rest of her egg. "You know what it means when you bring somebody around. Family immediately assumes there's something going on." She paused. "More than just, you know, casual."

He started to put his arm around her and she stopped him with a look. She could eye-Taser anyone into submission. He stepped back. "And that's all this is? Casual? 'Cause I've been living here with you for a while."

"Crashing." She stooped to gang-pet her cats, then walked over to get a container of yogurt from the refrigerator.

He smiled thinly. "Never say 'crash' to a biker." He spread butter on the other half of the muffin, then gave her a piercing look. "So, I've been saying it wrong? I've been crashing, not living with you? Because I thought you crashed for just a night or two, not for four months."

She spooned some yogurt. "What *did* you tell your parents?"

"Them? I just said I had a friend with a house who was letting me stay."

She flicked out her index finger like a switchblade. "There you go. Crashing."

He turned, put his hands on the sink and looked out the window. "I think I'm way past that."

"Past what?"

He looked into her eyes. "Past the friend part."

She slammed the yogurt down and tossed the spoon into the sink. "Well, that's your problem, Ty. I told you from the git-go, N-S-A. No strings attached. I have one business, and I'm trying to get another one up and running." She looked at the clock. "Christ, now I'm late." She started for the door, remembered her shoes and scurried back across the kitchen to the utility room. "I got an attic full of crap I dragged back from Iraq, and my work. I don't have the time or the emotional ammo to be your little girlfriend." She alternated hopping on one foot, then the other while she pulled on her ankle-high walking shoes. "Girlfriend experience," she said, tying the laces. "Isn't that what expensive whores call it? Sweet talk and hand-holding, too."

He rolled his eyes. "I wouldn't know. I was never with an expensive whore, 'til I crossed paths with you."

She patted his cheek as she passed by on her way to the door. "Nice try, but that's not going to empty my magazine. I've been called worse, hon. I'm still locked and loaded." She crossed the living room and dropped to her knees, caressing, and cooing to each of her cats. They rolled like big dust balls and pawed gently at her hands. She stood and opened the door. "You and Jett are going to practice stunts today?"

He nodded, then leveled a pretty impressive stun-gun stare of his own. "Afterwards, maybe I'll pack my shit."

She exerted control. She *had* to leave, with no time to let this death-blossom out of control. "Over a picnic? Don't be a wuss." She started to go, but wavered. "Besides, I might be horny tonight. You want to be here for that." She blew a kiss, grinned and closed the door.

Outside, she keyed her van and it clattered to life. She slammed the lever into drive, side-glancing at the house as she pulled away. Her house. Rent-to-own, maybe, but it was her world. She loved the house and her cats about as much as a human could. Tyler's cycle crouched on the sidewalk near the porch, its silver stripes carving big shiny breaks in the hot red paint.

Man, could that boy ride a bike. Not ride, really. He danced with the monster. Romanced it. Watching him move with that cycle was sexual. High compression porn. A Kawasaki Ninja has more horsepower than most cars, but he could make that thing stand on either tire and waltz like a debutante during the daddy-dance at her coming out. Some girls she hung with at a local bar were going to the county expo one night last spring, and Tyler and his team of crazies performed a stunt show for the grandstand crowd. Lacey had never given a motorcycle a second glance until she saw Tyler with his legs wrapped around one. On the spot, she knew she had to meet him. Careful what you wish for, she thought, as she guided her van onto the highway, eleven weeks later. She'd been so certain he'd just want to play; use her like some biker-boy groupie. That was the idea. Not a date to meet and greet Mom, Dad and the sibs.

Five summer morning miles later, she pulled onto the driveway of Dr. Brent Haverhill and family. The blacktop gently twisted and curved through a good quarter mile of heavy woods, with little areas cleared to display wood, stone and metal sculptures along the way. The driveway finally made a circle in front of the house, which was centered on a couple acres carved out of the forest. The white brick McMansion was dwarfed by the surrounding trees, so it wasn't until you let yourself into the twelve-foot ceilinged foyer and looked down the cavernous central hall that you realized the size of the place. Lacey had been cleaning for the Haverhills for nearly a year and their apparent wealth continuously amazed her. Sure, she'd poked around in drawers and snooped a little. Ms. Haverhill, who was never anything but pleasant, and "call me Suzanne" friendly, had a closet the size of Lacey's living room, and more jewelry than a mall kiosk. The children, Avery and Adrianne, were grounded and not at all bratty. They always called her Miss Lacey, and told her little stories about school and their activities.

Dr. Haverhill was the only one who made her uncomfortable. For a cardio-pulmonary surgeon, he seemed to be around more than Lacey would have expected. His flirting was subtle at first, but as time passed, he was more and more overt. She never felt the least bit threatened; on the contrary, she could easily cross-hawk him into a world of whoop-ass. No, it wasn't a matter of fear. Just discomfort knowing he disrespected his wife and family enough to make obvious verbal passes. He was a rich, middle-age jerk who figured his wealth and position of power would wow a twenty-something. Sure, like I really want that big doughy belly slapping away on me while you prove you can make cookies with a woman half your age. Sign me up!

When Lacey mentioned to Suzanne she'd started pet sitting, in addition to her housecleaning business, the woman's eyes went dinner plate. Now the family was in Switzerland for a month, and Lacey was embarked on thirty-two three-a-day visits at sixteen bucks a pop. Over fifteen hundred dollars was a substantial hunk of cake. The fact Lacey loved the Haverhills' adorable little cockapoo was the icing.

"Hey, Zoober," Lacey shouted, as she opened the door and coded into the security system. "Let me hear ya!"

The dog's happy yaps and barks echoed through the huge rooms separating them. Lacey hurried to the utility room to let Zoober out of his crate, his "house," as Suzanne and the kids referred to it, and knelt to rub and pet his soft curly white fur. He made chirp-like whines and licked Lacey's face and hands. Having a routine with each animal she sat for was important, and Zoober's first activity that morning was a quick trip to the small fenced area outside the utility room door. After a couple leg-ups to pee, he was ready for breakfast. "Come on, Zoob," she said, slapping her thigh. "MREs in the mess hall."

While the pup scarfed his canned food, Lacey wrote an entry in the daily log she kept for the Haverhills. After Zoober licked the last morsel from his sterling silver chafing dish, she walked him back to the utility room. The Haverhills had a circuitous path cut through the surrounding woods, and both Lacey and Zoober enjoyed the walk. She hooked the leash to his collar and grabbed a poop-bag. "Time for a little recon, trooper."

They walked across the back lawn and around the half-acre pond to where the trailhead opened into the trees. It was still morning-cool in the woods, so Lacey didn't expect mosquitoes to be a problem. Zoober was good on walks. He'd stop to sniff around, but Lacey could maintain her pace and the leash rarely went taut. They hadn't gone far when, just as they rounded a turn in the trail, Zoober growled and Lacey caught a flash of black and white in motion, a few feet into the low brush.

A wall of stink hammered her with nearly the effect of an IED. Her eyes, nose and throat went red-hot with pain. She stumbled back, tripped on a root or a branch and landed smack on her can. More pain shot through her shoulder and she realized Zoober had run out of leash, ending his headlong dash back the way they came. His tortured barks and coughs ripped her out of her sensory agony and she fought her way to her feet. Reeling in the leash as she trudged in Zoober's direction, she gathered him into her arms and managed to jog a few yards. She turned to see what the skunk was up to and realized it was locked in a struggle of its own. She ventured a few steps to confirm her suspicions. Yes, the poor animal was tugging against a leg-hold trap. Jesus God, what the fuck do I do now?

Lacey fell into a dead run with the dog in her arms. When she got back to the pond, she tied Zoober's leash to a bench and pulled out her cell. Tyler's phone went to voicemail. He was no doubt riding, so there was no way he'd answer. She hoped he had it on vibrate because she knew he couldn't hear it over the baritone of his bike.

During his away message, she told herself she would be calm. "Ty, I need help. We got hosed by a skunk. Me and the little dog I'm watching. Oh, shit, Ty. You wouldn't believe it. The poor skunk's in a leg-hold trap, and I don't know what the hell to do." She actually started to laugh. The thought crossed her mind that emotions converge in unusual ways. This was a crisis, but comedy was its Siamese twin. She couldn't separate the two. "I stink. I can't set foot inside the people's house. I'd goddamn destroy the place with skunk smell. Call me." She gagged, almost vomited, but she managed to gulp it back. "Please, Ty. I don't know what the hell I'm gonna do." She put the cell in her pocket and sat down next to Zoober. He was rolling and writhing on his back in the grass.

The skunk. A wildlife officer with a tranquilizer gun would simplify things, but even if she 411-ed a number, how long would it take to get someone out there? She wasn't used to this. In the sand hole, she was always part of a team that worked as a unit. "Army of One" was recruitment bullshit, not how the infantry worked. Now, she would have to go it solo, her only weapon a cell phone. Wait for Tyler? *Christ*, I can't wait. Ty might not check his messages for hours. Zoober was whining and wiggling around in the grass, but seemed to be breathing okay. She stroked him gently, which seemed to settle him. Damn, do we stink. She didn't know if the skunk had a second shot of spray chambered and didn't much care, considering she was already thoroughly layered with stench. Another shot of skunk juice wasn't going to make any difference.

"You sit tight, Zoob. I gotta deal with this."

Lacey booked it back down the path into the woods. At the turn in the trail, she slowed and advanced quietly so the skunk wouldn't get riled again and try to pull free of the trap. She scanned the area where she last saw it. Nothing. Oh man, did it get away? Another thought occurred; it might have yanked the trap loose from whatever held it in place. The image of the skunk running through the woods dragging a leg-hold trap taunted her for a moment. Then, she saw it. It wasn't moving, but she could see the rise and fall of its belly. She had to free it. Now. Ty wouldn't let her down, but how long would it be before he got her message?

She planned to leap onto the chain near the trap with her left foot so she could jam down on the spring to release the jaws with the other. She didn't care about getting sprayed again, but she worried the skunk might panic and bite her.

Just then, her cell ring-toned. "Oh, damn!" Sure enough, the skunk immediately began screaming and yanking against the trap to get free. However, what seemed bad turned out to be good. The chain was taut, now, and Lacy stomped on the spring. The jaws clattered open and the skunk skittered away.

"What can I do?" were Tyler's first words when Lacey answered.

A dizzying clap of relief hit her hard and she stumbled to a nearby tree for support. "Oh, Ty." She began to giggle. "What a freaking mess this turned out to be. I … I handled it though. The skunk's out of the trap. Couldn't have been hurt too bad because it ran okay." Time to think. To gather her thoughts. "I guess all we need now is something … oh hell, Ty. This little dog and I, we both stink to high goddamn heaven."

"Tomato juice? That's what I've always heard."

Lacey thought. "No. You know what? I just remembered. Some gal in basic told us. Massengill." She blotted her face with the hem of her top and giggled. "Honest, Ty. That's what this trooper said. Supposed to work better than anything."

"What the hell is Massem-what?"

"Massengill." She laughed heartily now. "It's douche. Massengill douche. Go to the drugstore and get a bunch. Buy all they have."

Tyler laughed. "Are you some kind of stink-induced nut case now?"

"No. Honest. This chick was somebody I'd believe. Please hurry."

She gave him directions to the Haverhills' and hung up. When she got back to the pond, Zoober was rolling on the grass like his coat was on fire. She lay down next to him and he seemed to relax. She patted his head and smiled. "I called in reinforcements, Zoob. Relief is just a douche away."

The stench was so heavy, it felt like she and Zoober were buried in a haystack of reek. And it never seemed to get better. Her eyes no longer burned, but she was as close to a stomach-twisting retch as she was the instant the skunk first sprayed. Lying in the soft grass, stroking the whimpering pup, she found herself repeatedly flashing on Iraq. Better skunk stink than rotting corpses, she decided.

She knew Tyler would bullet, but the minutes seemed to creep. His alarmed voice rumbled through her memory. "What can I do?" That, even after she'd told him she didn't want to meet his family the night before, and gave him a raft of shit that very morning. Lacey rocked onto her back and looked into the azure sky. It looked the same from Toledo as it did in Iraq, and even surrounded by manicured grasses, foliage, and boisterously chattering songbirds, she couldn't pull her mind out of the sandpit. Not entirely, anyway. Months of reining in emotions and cutting off feelings to keep fellow soldiers detachable, in case they got wonked, were hard to overcome. On top of that, Lacey's experience as female infantry on deployment had two choices—make yourself a clearing barrel for any horny trooper in the unit, or be the nastiest, surliest, most repellent man-bitch you could be. Lacey chose the latter, and the hard, coarse, don't-screw-with-me persona she'd perfected to keep gender out of any and all interactions zombied back into existence every time she thought she'd finally pronounced it dead. How can Ty care for someone I hate so much?

Her head was a repository of horror. She'd narrowly avoided a general discharge or worse because, during her second tour of hell in the sandbox, she finally lost it, big-time. Went ballistic when some Iraqi soldiers they were training began using dogs and cats—any animal having the misfortune to happen by—for target practice, and no one in the stream of command seemed to give a shit. She tried to reason. She tried to ignore. In the end, she could no longer hack it. She went off on a big trooper from Texarkana, symbolically fragging him with fifty caliber shell casings hurled as hard as she could throw them. When he only sneered, deflecting her fusillade with his sirloin-sized hands, she put him on his back with a smooth Jujitsu move he never saw coming, didn't have time to react against, and was no doubt still trying to live down. He came off the ground angry, and she drew down on him with her sidearm. Lucky for Lacey, her chief warrant officer liked her stuff and came to the plate. Ordered her into "counseling," which set the stage for a psychological intervention. Her C.O. testified her previous service was exemplary, and she got an honorable discharge, full benefits.

She heard the whoop of Tyler's cycle as he ripped it through the gears, the sweet yowl of the big engine getting louder by the second. He was flying. Then, downshift, downshift, downshift—she could picture him slowing to make the turn—then another big howl from the motor as he picked up speed on the driveway.

"Just chill, Zoober," she said, giving the pup a soothing tap on the head. She got up and jogged toward the front of the house, rounding the corner just as Tyler pushed the kickstand down and swung his leg over the seat.

He pulled off his helmet and smiled. "You're all good?"

She held her nose. "Take a big whiff. Good, but very freaking ripe. I went back and freed the skunk 'cause I figured even if I got waxed again, I couldn't smell any worse." She shuddered and made a bitter face. "I wanted it out of that trap. The way it took off, I guess nothing was broken."

Tyler gave her a facial ataboy, then wiggled out of his backpack and riding leathers. Stripped to a pair of shorts and a tank top, he dumped the contents of the pack onto the driveway. Eleven four-pack boxes of Massengill, and a plastic garbage bag.

"What's in the bag?"

"Fresh clothes. Didn't figure you'd want to drive home naked." He stooped to pick up one of the boxes, pulled out a six-ounce bottle and looked at the label. "No instructions for getting rid of skunk stink," he said, grinning. "I hope this shit works."

The house was surrounded by acres of woods and she shucked her clothes right there on the driveway. The sun felt like a wash of warm butter on her skin. "We have to hurry. Zoober is really miserable, but you won't be able to help wash him down until we take care of me. My hair will be the worst. My arms and legs got it, but my clothes took the rest. We can just bury them." She spread her arms. "Hit me with your best shot, big boy."

Tyler dribbled douche over her hair and she reached up to work it in, shampoo-like. They kept moving from spot to spot when they realized the smell lingered where it washed onto the grass. Several bottles later, they could tell the treatment was working. "I need a rinse, then I think I'll be halfway decent," she said. "Let's grab the rest of the douche and head for the swimmin' hole. You up for a skinny dip?"

"I think I could be persuaded."

They picked up the remaining boxes and bottles and started for the back yard. She held up a container. "You didn't tell me, how'd the drugstore clerk handle the run on douche?"

"You'd have died. Some guy about my age. He kind of gave me a look, so I leaned close and whispered that I was having a party and this is the latest drink craze. Massengill and Grey Goose. Douche-drivers." He cackled. "Christ, I think he believed me."

Lacey took a breath. "Maybe we should make up a batch to take to that picnic, next Sunday." Tyler froze in mid-step, tilted his head and his eyebrows shot toward his hairline. "Look," Lacey went on, "I can't even believe you're still hanging in with me, what with my crazy mood swings and bullshit."

His face drew into an exaggerated smirk. "But the sex is so damned good."

She dropped the containers she held and gripped his loaf-like biceps. "You could have any woman, and probably one with better tits." Her face drew into a lop-sided smirk, but it vanished quickly and her eyes moistened. "I'm broken, and I know it. The deploys to the sandbox screwed my head around good. I thought I could Frankenstein myself back together without anybody's help," she shook her head, "but I can't. I'm going to find a good V.A. shrink, soon as I lose this stink." She chuckled.

Tyler dropped the douche he was holding and pulled her into his arms. "I've smelled worse." He kissed her. "But she did have better tits."

Lacey gave him a play-slap, and they stooped to pick up the boxes and bottles scattered at their feet. They started around the pond. It was getting hot, but a freshening breeze put ripples on the water. Lacey loosely wrapped her arm around his waist. She liked the way their hips bumped together as they walked.

"So, I guess I can still crash at your place?" Tyler asked.

She shook her head. "You were right. Crashing is for a night or two. We're living together."

Zoober barked and they both looked over at him. He strained against his tether, made a series of miserable bird-like cheeps and coughed. Tyler grunted. "He's a wooly little shit. This is going to be a long process."

"That's what life is," Lacy said. "One step at a time. First, we'll get me rinsed off, then we'll douche that doggie down."

MISTRUST, JEALOUSY AND OTHER GOOD JUNK

"I'm tellin' you, JD, ain't nothin' going on between me and Moke," Rita says, staring straight into Jed Dudak's stormy eyes. Red veins shoot across the whites like tiny lightning bolts. She sucks on her Marlboro, exhaling a blue cloud toward the bar's water-stained ceiling tile. When the azure fog clears, she's still locked in the monsoon of his glare. He's good at ciphering a lie. She damn well better have all the lug nuts on her story torqued down right. A loose one and he'll know she's spinning a tale with a wobbly wheel.

He takes a pull on his Jack Daniels and Rita can sense the storm breaking. Jed loves police dramas on TV, and the liquor seems to propel him into an alternate state of being. Now he's a suspicious police detective, with a surly streak.

"So why was his hand on your shirt, I come walkin' 'round that Plymouth?"

"Like I told ya, Spud sent us out to pull a starter off that Buick. Moke dropped the damn thing in a puddle on the intake manifold and splashed rusty water on me." Rita nervously fingers the pocket of her work shirt, where 'Tater's Auto Recycling' is embroidered. Just south of that it reads, 'Parts Reclamation Specialist.' "He went to wipe it off. You saw me slug him," she adds, pointing an index finger grayed with a patina of grease directly at Jed.

'Detective' Dudak pauses, probably to assess her story. "Yeah, you busted him one all right, *after* you seen me." He grabs her wrist, jolting the cigarette free of the crook between her fingers. It lands on the bar. "I jus' don' buy it," he says, in a voice that rumbles low, like a gate on a jail cell sliding closed. "No man would have his hand that close to your titties, 'less it'd been there before."

"Oh, shit, JD," she says, twisting her wrist from his grip. "You think Moke's gonna try to cop a feel with a shop rag in his hand? Get real," she adds, picking up her smoldering Marlboro and smearing the scattered ashes across the bar's sticky surface with her hand.

Jed gives her a once-over as she raps her cigarette on the ashtray. She throttles up her smile. Sure, she knows she's plain and thin. Okay, skinny. But she's got a great set of headlights for a chick her size, and Jed loves her eyes. Says they're the same blue-green as the stone in his authentic Navajo belt buckle. Jed told her the mole on her cheek reminds him of some movie star's, but he can't remember the actress's name. And he likes that Rita understands the ins and outs of a small-block Chevy engine as well as any man at Tater's. Jed dogged old Spud about hiring her, until the day she dropped the transmission out of a Chrysler New Yorker and dragged it all the way to the office by herself.

But the main thing is she pays attention to Jed in ways no other woman ever has. She loves to get it on, something he never experienced before. Jed tells her he always believed sex was something women merely endured. She's a gal who really loves it. Wants it all the time. Unfortunately, that breeds mistrust. Maybe she likes it too much, Jed tells her. Maybe even with more than one man. "I ain't nothing special," he says. "Why only me?" Says he looks at her mouth and wonders where else it's been.

Rita picks up the long-necked bottle of Bud she's drinking. She sees 'Detective' Dudak watch her encircle the rim with her lips. She finishes her swig, winks, then slides her stool closer to his. She bookends his arm with her boobs and lays her head on his shoulder, letting her wheat-colored hair, cascading from under her Delco ball cap, waterfall down his shirt.

Again, Rita brings the bottle to her lips, but she doesn't drink. Instead, she flicks the tip of her tongue against the opening. She takes the bottle away and whispers, "You know you're my special guy … the only man for me, JD." She kisses his ear lobe. "Come on, let's cut for your place. We said we'd swap out the carb on your Camaro after work, right? Then I'll whip you up some dinner, and…" She concludes the evening's menu with a smile she's confident leaves little to Jed's imagination.

The bad-ass detective appears to close his investigation and go off duty. Just like that, she can feel Jed is back in reality now, idling on his bar stool in The Overtime Lounge.

"OK," he says. "Just lem'me finish my drink, here. A Marine don't leave no man behind, 'specially not ol' Jack Daniels." Jed tips up his glass and Rita watches the ice avalanche against his mustache, just as the door slams behind them. Travis Mochrie saunters past, nods to Rita and gives her a wink. "Hey, Rita," he says.

"Hey, Moke," she deadpans, quickly gathering her cigarettes and lighter, knowing she has to get Jed and herself out of there, fast.

It's too late. Jed's eyes flash like an arc welder's spark as he trains them on Moke. The big man steps around the corner of the bar, waves the bartender over, then fires Jed a nose-wrinkling smile that looks like a sneer.

"Come on, Hon, let's go," Rita says. When she grips Jed's arm, it's rigid as a header pipe. She gives him a look. The veins in his neck bulge thick as battery cables. Jed's face is approaching a shade of candy apple red. "JD …" Rita hisses. Jed begins to ratchet himself off his bar stool. "No!" she shouts.

"I'm gonna rip you apart," Jed growls at Moke.

"Did you hear me?" Rita screams. "I said *no!*"

She slaps him hard, but she can see Jed's already catapulted into a new reality. He vaults the bar and tears into Moke like a junkyard dog.

SUNOCO NIGHTS

Jake Gaines hated gassing his car. If this sucker had a hundred-gallon tank, I could go weeks between fill-ups, he thought. He squeezed the lever on the pump handle like the trigger on a semi-automatic handgun to wring every drop he could into the tank. When the readout showed even money, he replaced the nozzle, tightened the gas cap and headed inside. Benny, the owner of a station that still did repairs, was busy cutting the exhaust system off a Buick dangling on an overhead lift.

"Thirty dollars even," Jake yelled.

The sharp hiss of Benny's cutting torch accompanied a shower of yellow-white sparks exploding from under the Buick. "Go ahead and make your own change," he hollered. A section of exhaust pipe that looked like a mutant tree branch dropped onto the shiny, painted concrete floor with a resonant clang. Benny shut the gas valve, and the flame vanished with a loud snap. "Hey, you wanna buy a gross of rubbers?" he asked, pulling his safety goggles up onto his sweaty grease-smudged forehead. Benny had a burgeoning under-the-counter business, his back-room office stocked with pornographic magazines, DVDs, and sex paraphernalia.

"Rubbers?" Jake said, pulling a ten from the cash drawer. "What the hell am I gonna do with a gross of rubbers?"

"Use 'em up, I 'spect. Sensual Sensations. Ribbed and lubed for maximum satisfaction. That's what the box says. You're still a newlywed, ain'cha?"

Jake slammed the register closed and coughed out a one-syllable laugh. "Two years in October. But hell, a gross might last me the rest of my marriage."

"Ow!" Benny yelped, doing a take like he just caught a muffler on the noggin. "Took my ex *three* years to go frigid."

Jake joined Benny under the Buick and looked up at the fresh-cut end of the exhaust pipe, still glowing yellow-orange through a filmy waft of smoke. "Not what I meant," Jake said. "She's on the pill. That aside, things are a bit chilly at home right now, anyway."

"Yeah?" Benny shook a Marlboro out of its pack and stood on his toes to light it on the still-glowing exhaust.

"Summer vacation just started," Jake said, stepping from under the car to escape the blue fog of cigarette smoke. "We saved some cash, and I was going to paint a couple rooms and landscape the front yard." He shook his head. "My summer off didn't bother her last year, but this summer her nose is out of joint because I'm on vacation and she has to work."

"Yeah, but it's gotta be tough, rolling out of bed to go to work when hubby's snoring."

"But I don't. Hell, I get up before she does. Made her pancakes this morning." Jake leaned against Benny's tool chest. "I'm not going to just sit on my ass. And she has no idea what it's like to teach special ed. Second year teaching, and my class was two over the state maximum. Next year might be worse. I need time to recharge the batteries." He picked up a piece of exhaust gasket and tossed it into a trash barrel.

"I got work," Benny said. "My night-man quit me yesterday. Midnight to six, Monday through Friday. Work six hours and I pay eight. Can't beat that for a shift premium," he concluded, smiling with the seamless confidence of a pitchman suckering a hapless mark. "Eight bucks an hour."

Jake worked gas station/convenience stores all through college, his memories of swabbing floors and the odor wrinkly hot dogs twirling on rollers were warehoused in the same mental closet with his recollections of all-night study marathons and the smell of cafeteria food. His senior year, he worked a Shell station open to close on weekends, and weekday mornings from six until eight. The job forced him to attend Principles of Teaching in a shirt with his name on a patch and black oxfords, while the other guys sported Starter jackets and running shoes. However, that indignity paid for necessity and caprice while he ricocheted through the hallowed halls of Kent State University. "What's your night-man do?" Jake asked. He knew Benny better than the average customer would, and liked what he knew. Benny was friendly and seemed like he'd be an easy-going boss.

"Clean the bays, is the main thing," Benny said. "Get done, the rest of the night's yours. Pumps are self-serve. Work on your car. Hell, look at the magazines in back if ya like, long as you don't leave the pages sticky." He nudged Jake's arm and winked. "Shit, sleep if you feel like it. Just so you wake up to collect money and make sure there ain't no drive-offs."

"I'll have to talk to Gayle," Jake said. "She'd be home all alone."

"Tell her I'll be happy to stop by, she needs any company," Benny said, leering lasciviously.

"If you do any good, make sure you use one of your damned Sensual Sensations," Jake said, laughing. "I'll get back to you."

"Make it soon," Benny said, stooping to pick up the amputated Buick exhaust.

~ * ~

Jake drove straight home. He loved having the house to himself until Gayle got out of work. Quiet, or noise. TV or stereo. Chores or relaxation. Choices. Marriage turned out to be encompassed in compromise, which caught him off guard. To a naive college student, matrimony sounded romantic and easy. Together every day and night. No more good-byes at her dorm. Going out to dinner and coming home to make love. He never dreamed they might be too strapped to go to a restaurant, or that Gayle might say, "Not tonight, babe, I've had a rough day."

He read a golf magazine until he fell asleep, but awakened in plenty of time to have burgers sizzling when Gayle came through the door. He wondered how it would go. The night before, they argued like teamsters when she told him she thought he should find a job for the summer. Blindsided, and more than a little miffed she implied he wasn't doing his fair share, he'd stood his ground. That next morning, the atmosphere was just south of arctic. He took a breath in anticipation of the worst and hoped for the best. "Hey, doll. How you doin'?"

"Great, Hon," she answered, whisking a kiss across his cheek. Her former irritation seemed to have vanished. "Anything I can do?"

"Not a thing," he said, sliding the patties into sesame buns. "Just sit your pretty self down."

By anyone's standard, Gayle was beautiful. She'd played tennis at Kent, and her body was athletic and willowy. Her butterscotch complexion contrasted nicely with her dark brown hair, and her eyes seemed to project more light than they could possibly take in. The trade-off? She was strung as tightly as her tennis racquets, and her demeanor could match that of a line judge. Jake usually placated her—hence, his new summer job at Benny's.

The table was replete with baked beans, potato chips, and the usual condiments. Gayle washed her hands and slid into her chair. "Beer, or pop?" Jake asked.

"A beer would be nice." she said. He pulled two cans from the refrigerator, poured them into glasses and they began their meal. "M-m-m, this is good," she said after swallowing a bite. "So, what's new?"

Jake couldn't believe she fed him such a perfect set-up. "My job," he said, smiling as he put his burger down.

Gayle looked at him as though they never argued about a summer job. Enough of a disagreement that when he fell asleep in his recliner and never made it to bed, Gayle never mentioned his absence when she awakened. He had her breakfast on the kitchen table when she came in from showering and dressing. She ate it, thanked him and gave him a sister-kiss on the cheek as she left for work. Now, she was cordial and friendly, but doing a great impersonation of someone who had no idea where this "job" idea came from. "What?" Now she put her burger down, too. "I thought you just wanted to work around the house this summer."

Jake sipped his beer. "You made it abundantly clear last night it was going to go a whole lot better if I got a summer job." She started to say something, but he raised his hands to head her off. "You did. And I listened. And so today I got an offer, and I think I'm going to take it." Gayle tilted her head and shot him the half-smile she used for inquiry. "Benny, down at the Sunoco. One of his guys quit him and he needs somebody to take the night shift."

"Nights?"

Jake felt like a gambler, turning up a card and watching her eyes. "Midnight to six, Monday through Friday."

She didn't fold. "And you're going to take it? I mean, you didn't want to work at all. Now, nights?"

"It might not be a bad deal. You go to bed about eleven, so we'd still have our evenings. I'd get home while you're getting ready for work, so I'd be here to see you off. I'll catch some sleep and have the rest of the day to paint and landscape, the way I planned."

"So, you're going to do it?" Gayle always chewed exactly twenty-five times, something her parents ingrained in her as a child. It was automatic. She took a bite of her burger, giving Jake lots of time to answer.

"Yeah. We could use extra money, and I think I can still get a lot done around here in the afternoons." He swirled the last inch of beer in the bottom of his glass. "This is a safe neighborhood, so I won't worry about you being alone. I'm not doing this because I'm pissed or anything. I understand how you feel. You work year-round, so there's no reason I shouldn't carry my weight in the summer, too." He finished his beer and set the glass on the table. "Benny's is different enough from teaching that I can still psych up for the fall. Heck, a summer at a gas station will make the classroom look a hell of a lot more inviting." He finished with a thin laugh.

She tilted forward. "Benny creeps me out," she said, in a staccato whisper.

"Benny?"

"Yeah. I think he deals in…" she gave Jake a mischievous leer, "pornographic stuff."

"Girlie mags?" Jake asked, as though it was news to him. He wondered why he felt compelled to play dumb.

"Not just that," Gayle said. "I walked in to pay for gas last week, and when I glanced into his office, there was some stuff in there. Not just pictures." She leaned forward a few more degrees. "Devices," she breathed, the corners of her mouth curling into a hint of a smile as her teeth put the bite on the final "s."

"Really?" Jake rolled his eyes like a man without a clue. "Well, I don't know about that, but he's got work. I thought I'd worked my last station when I got out of Kent, but I'll do it again, until September.

~ * ~

Jake's first night at the station went smoothly. He cleaned the bays in about an hour of earnest labor, then settled in with a *Time* magazine to while away the rest of the shift. Traffic through the station slowed as the night wore on, with the exception of a flurry when the bars closed. He waited on several customers who smelled of alcohol, and one who probably shouldn't have been driving at all. "Careful, now," Jake warned, handing the man his change. He strafed Jake with twitchy, red, rodent-like eyes, and nodded before disappearing into the night. The rest of his shift, half an hour or forty-five minutes might pass between customers. Jake decided this was easy duty. Over three hundred a week to clean the floors and read.

Benny's station faced west and, as dawn arrived, the glass facade of the large office building across the street was like a drive-in movie screen. The feature that morning was a sailor-take-warning sunrise. At a quarter to six, Jake closed his magazine, rubbed his eyes and walked outside. Traffic was picking up on Monroe Street, the four-lane artery which burrowed into the heart of downtown Toledo. He experienced a weird kind of jealousy, hating to relinquish possession of the streets. Everyone had been delighted to go to bed and leave Jake in charge. Now, they wanted to renege, and retake control. It was similar to the feeling he got when Gayle came home from work. The house was his, then she returned to reclaim half ownership. Jake owned Monroe Street until alarm clocks began to sound across the verdant suburbs. Daylight's return demanded a quit-claim.

A few minutes later, Benny wheeled in. His souped-up motorcycle's raucous exhaust sounded like a heavy-metal drum solo. He keyed the concert to silence and dropped the bike on its kickstand. Benny was rangy and muscular. His face could go from dead serious to clown silly in an eye-blink. His light brown hair formed fashionably unruly spikes, and he didn't wear a helmet, so they stayed that way. "So, how's my new night-man?" he asked, sauntering over with his thumbs hooked into the front belt loops on his jeans.

"Okay, Benny. No problems," Jake said, polishing his employee-to-employer tone. "You look bright-eyed and bushy-tailed this morning."

"Fuckin-a," Benny said, his index finger making a hollow sound as he thumped it against his chest. "Responsible businessman, here, my friend. I was in bed before nine o'clock last night."

"No kidding?" Jake said, surprised.

"And home by midnight," he added, nudging Jake mirthfully, before firing up a Marlboro. "The bays look great," he said, his eyes making a fast sweep of the floors. "This job gonna work for you?"

"Yeah, I think it'll be fine."

"And the wife? She's okay with the hours?"

"I think so. We're only apart when she's asleep."

Benny flicked his thumb against the filter of his cigarette, even though the ash was short. "I'll be honest, I really didn't think you'd take it. A night shift can make things rocky."

"Well, she's the one who wanted me to work. She can hardly complain." Jake dug around in his jeans for car keys. "Right?"

Benny clapped him on the shoulder. "Yeah. Now go home and give her a big kiss."

On the way home, Jake wondered how he would get to sleep with the whole world waking up. He was pretty certain it would be more difficult than staying awake when the whole world went to sleep. He let himself in through the side door and Gayle was in the kitchen, wearing only a bra and panties as she made instant coffee. She seemed happier to see him than he anticipated. "Hey, it's only been seven hours," he whispered, nuzzling her damp hair. He savored the lingering smell of her shampoo as she embraced him.

She stepped back, grasped his arms, and tunneled into his eyes with an unsettling stare, the same look he remembered from when she found out her closest friend at the branch Gayle managed was stealing. "There was a hold-up last night at the BP station on Jackman Road."

Jake spooned some instant into a mug for himself. "Really?"

"They took the attendant."

Jake knew where this was going, and he smiled while he plotted a way to cancel the trip. He decided to try humor. "They stole the attendant and left the money?"

"No, they took the money, but the attendant is gone, too," she said, her voice rising. "Someone stopped early this morning and the station was deserted. Nobody there."

Jake figured the way he handled the next several minutes would determine how the rest of the summer would go. "Maybe the attendant just unloaded the cash drawer and hightailed it," he offered, hoping his choice was the correct one. "He could be on his way to Vegas by now." Gayle's look indicated Jake might have taken the wrong fork, but was past fail safe. "Hey, I probably had a hundred in my cash drawer last night. We could have made it as far as, I dunno, the casinos in Detroit?"

Gayle turned and strode down the hallway to the bathroom. "Hey, I'm sorry," Jake said, but before he could turn the corner into the bathroom, his apology was met with the howl of her hair dryer. He couldn't argue over that decibel level, so he walked back into the kitchen and switched on the little portable TV above the stove. "...body was found an hour ago in a field off Smith Road, just north of the Michigan border," the scene reporter, a comely brunette, said with perfect enunciation. Several police officers stood in the near-background, talking and looking off-camera as she continued. "The attendant, whose name is being withheld pending notification of his family, was discovered, lying face down a short distance from where I'm standing, with a bullet wound to the back of the head. Officials are mum concerning the amount taken in the apparent robbery. As of now, police have no suspects. This is Sally Reynolds, WTTL News live. Back to you in the studio."

"Oh, shit," Jake said, and snapped it off.

~ * ~

"I wish you'd just quit the damned job." Gayle stood with her head pillowed on Jake's chest, picking at the name patch on his borrowed Sunoco shirt. "Fletch," it read. Hollis Fletcher weighed every bit of three-hundred pounds, and wearing his shirt, Jake was just two poles short of a small tent.

He gently pinched what little there was at Gayle's waist, and kissed her ear. "If I thought there was anything to worry about," he whispered, "I wouldn't be going. Robberies happen. That wasn't the first one in Toledo, and it won't be the last. But Benny's station is on *Monroe* Street. Lots of traffic. Nice part of town." He stepped back and tapped her chin with his finger. "No problem," he said, full voice. She sighed, clearly dissatisfied with his argument.

When Jake arrived at the station, at quarter to eleven, Fletch seemed as happy to see him as Gayle was that morning. "I'm outta here!" Fletch said, passing Jake in the open service bay door.

"Jesus! What's this?" Jake asked. "You all shook up, too?"

Fletch stopped dead and looked at him quizzically. "Shook up?"

"Yeah, you know, about the robbery."

"Robbery?" Fletch let his big head loll to one side as he processed the question. His acned forehead wrinkled. "Somebody got robbed?"

"Ah, forget it," Jake said. "What's the rush?"

"Race tonight. Some guy's trailering his Mustang down from Royal Oak. Thinks he's gonna smoke my ass. Five hunnert big ones on the line." He grinned large and homely and got into his Corvette, causing the car to sag visibly. Revving the motor and laughing maniacally, he popped the clutch and laid two wide strips of rubber all the way onto Monroe Street.

Watching Fletch's tire smoke clear was about the most interesting thing Jake did until around two forty-five, when a green P.T. Cruiser rolled slowly onto the driveway and stopped between the pumps and the building. Jake could see a portion of the driver's silhouette, but couldn't tell if any others were in the car. His stomach tightened when the door didn't open immediately. Was it another holdup?

The interior light came on and a sleek, graceful woman got out. She strolled into the station, her hips rolling provocatively in tight hip-hugger jeans. Jake decided she had to be in her early thirties. Her hair glowed white under the fluorescent lights. Her skin, on the other hand, was deep sienna. As she drew near, he could see her tan was an amalgam of multi-hued freckles that reminded him of a box of Fanny Farmer chocolates. She appeared tentative. Nervous, maybe.

"Hi!" Jake said, lighting up his friendly professional gas station attendant smile, to put her at ease. "May I help you?"

When she placed her hands on the podium-like desk Jake stood behind, he noticed at least one ring encircled each of her fingers. She sported multiple earrings and necklaces, too. One necklace, in particular, caught his eye, a slender gold chain linked to the script words, "Bad Girl," which lay on her tan, just above the halter-top straining to contain her breasts.

"I want...need," her voice dropped to a whisper, "...a vibrator."

"Excuse me?" He tried to look into her eyes, but couldn't get past the soot-black mascara caking her lashes.

The corners of her glossed lips made an upward turn. She tilted her head to point behind him, in the direction of Benny's office. "In the back room there. Doesn't Benny still sell," she paused and her finely drawn eyebrows rose, "...dildos?"

Jake watched closely as her pouty red lips crafted both of those last two syllables, in what seemed like slow-motion. Immediately, he felt his ears warm and redden, and his embarrassment over his obvious embarrassment pushed yet another unit or two of blood in their direction. Unable to contain a transfusion of that magnitude, the overage flushed out across his face until his head began to feel like a hot red boil.

"GOTCHA!" Benny yelped, so loudly even his Kewpie-Doll accomplice startled. He'd slipped in through the back door, and jumped from around the corner of the service bay.

"Jesus Christ!" Jake shouted, as the three of them formed a huddle of unrestrained laughter. Several times, they almost stopped laughing, then one of them would catch a second wind, and the other two would be swept up, again.

"I'm sorry, but I just couldn't resist," Benny finally managed. "Trina and I were headin' for her place, and, well, once I got the idea, we just had to do it. She really had you goin'."

Jake reached to shake her hand. "Trina, is it?" She nodded. "Trina, I have to admit, you suckered me in, big time."

"She *was* great, wasn't she?" Benny said, stroking her neon-white hair. "What an actress." He glanced at the clock above the battery display. "Well, we better git," he said. "Christ! I gotta be back here in three hours."

34

Trina stepped forward and gently gripped Jake's upper arm. "Just remember," she whispered, "if another chick comes in looking for a dildo, it'll probably be the real deal." She gave his biceps a gentle squeeze, then she and Benny walked out, laughing all the way to her car.

~ * ~

In the early hours of the following Friday morning, another station was hit. This time, the attendant, described in news reports as a twenty-five year old married grad student, was found face down in a field off Summerfield Road, a few hundred yards north of the Ohio/Michigan line. He'd been shot twice in the head. The Gas Station Murders had its own lead-in music on at least one of Toledo's news programs. City notables waded in with their opinions regarding who the perpetrators might be. Crack heads...serial killers...gang-bangers. The portraits weren't pretty. Gayle was convinced they were homing in on Benny's Sunoco, and Jake would be the next victim.

The two of them debated and argued. Jake wasn't certain of his motivation, but he stood his ground. Was it twenty-four-year-old invincibility, coupled with some macho need to confront danger? Loyalty to Benny? Or just the desire to assert himself, and maybe punish Gayle for wanting him to work that summer, as icing? Some mixture of those? Regardless, he decided he wouldn't retreat.

Benny called Saturday morning and asked Jake to stop by. Gayle wanted to go along, too. "My God," Jake said. "What if your boss called you in for a meeting and I demanded to be there?"

"But this is different. This is life and death!"

"This is a meeting between me and my boss," Jake said. "Case closed."

At the station, Bart, the weekend day-man, pointed his thumb at the office. Finding the door open, Jake stepped inside. Benny was flipping through a magazine featuring women who apparently enjoyed squeezing their ample breasts upward so they could lick their nipples.

"How we doin', sport?" he asked, tossing the magazine aside.

"Okay, Benny. You?"

"Been better." He opened the lower drawer of his desk and pulled out a pint of Jack Daniels. He carefully poured some into the opening in the top of a Coke can, then held the bottle toward Jake and raised an eyebrow. Jake waved it off. "Fletch shut the station down about two o'clock this morning," Benny went on.

"Shut it down? Why?"

"Hell if I know," Benny said, running the words together as one. He took a swallow of his drink. "I stopped in about eleven. He was droppin' a new motor in his 'Vette. It was all good. His only bitch was customers interrupting his engine swap." Benny rocked back in his chair, ran his hands through his spiky hair, and fashioned a headrest with his interlocked fingers. "Guess when he got it running, he locked the place up to take it for a test drive. Never came back. A buddy of mine stopped by about two-thirty. Called me. Said all the lights were on, doors locked, and no Fletch. I came right over and we poked around." He pushed some packaged sex gadgets out of the way, and rested his muscular arm, encircled with a barbed wire tattoo, on the desktop. "I wasn't worried about Fletch. I mean, the station was locked up just right, and all the money was still here. Turns out, the bastard just decided to go home." Benny shrugged at the inexplicability of it.

"That's crazy," Jake said. "So, you talked to him? What was his story?"

"He was pissed that I woke him when I called to make sure he was okay. Said he started to get edgy about the robberies and decided to close. He always hated working the night shift on weekends, anyways. Cuts into his street racing." Benny crossed his arms on his chest. "Like an asshole, I lost it. Told him he was fired. Now, *I* have to cover weekends *and* the week nights until you come in." He lowered his chin and looked at Jake from under his brushy eyebrows. "You *are* planning on being here Monday night?"

Jake smiled. "Not if Gayle has anything to say about it."

"She's worried?"

"Just south of hysterical. Wanted to come with me today."

"You should'a brought her." Benny tossed his arms sideways. "Look, I'm tryin, to find another man to work the overnight with you 'til they find these douche bags. All the stations hit so far, they've been one-man operations. But, especially right now, it's hard to find anybody. I'd do it myself, but with Fletch out of the picture…"

Jake nodded. "I understand."

"Well, anyway, the cops stopped by. They got a couple of units assigned just to patrol gas stations. They really wanna catch these sons 'a bitches, bad." He paused. "On top of that, I just bought you your very own security team. Meet Mr. Smith and Mr. Wesson," Benny said, opening a drawer to reveal a muscular blue steel revolver. He glowed like a new father as he picked it up and held the butt end out towards Jake.

The gun was heavy. Its smooth angularity insinuated lethal precision. The barrel was long. It had been fired recently, and the smell of the cordite and gun oil resurrected long-forgotten memories of Jake's deceased father and the rust-red hair on the backs of his porterhouse-sized hands. "Jesus, this is a fucking cannon," Jake said.

"Forty-four magnum, my boy. Dirty Harry approved. Can put a hole clean through an engine block. That's the beauty of it. Keep this son-of-a-bitch in the top cubbyhole, somebody fucks with ya, just blow a round straight through the damned desk."

"You don't have to hit 'em, either," Bart added. He'd come back to join the fun. "You miss with that monster, the noise alone will paralyze 'em."

Jake made certain it was empty and held it in both hands, combat-style. He sighted in Miss June on Benny's Snap-On Tools calendar.

"Go ahead," Bart said enthusiastically. "Let her have it!"

"I caught a shot in the chops for dry-firing one of my old man's guns once," Jake replied, picking up a shop rag to wipe the finger smudges from the blue-black finish. He laid it on the desk and gave Benny a wink. "See you Monday at midnight."

It wasn't the gun. It wasn't the increased police presence, or the promise of a co-worker. Jake believed this tug-o-war was pivotal because it was early in their marriage, and if he didn't win this one, he stood every chance of losing them all.

When Jake pulled into the driveway, Gayle stood on the porch, arms akimbo. "Well?" she said, her chin jutted high, the way she challenged line calls in her tennis days. Jake felt like he was walking into a spinning propeller, but wrapped his arm around her shoulders and guided her into the house. "The cops talked to Benny," he began. "They've got special units to patrol gas stations all night. And he's going to hire another guy to work with me until they catch these people." He decided against mentioning the big revolver, but gave her a hearty smile. "Everything's going to be fine."

As he expected, Gayle gave him a weary look and wiggled out of his embrace. "I've said all I'm going to."

True to her word, she had little to say after that. She sulked. Responded if Jake spoke first, but conversation was at a premium. He questioned her point. On one hand, she loved him and was afraid she might lose him; so, why let him leave for work with few words, and only a brusque kiss? If he did wind up planted in a Michigan farm field, wouldn't she feel even worse?

Jake questioned his own position. Even to him, jeopardizing day-to-day marital happiness in an attempt to control the power structure in the future made little sense. Also, he had to admit some measure of his decision to stay on at Benny's was a bit of thrill-seeking on the part of a twenty-something male. Of course, in the light of a warm summer afternoon, it was easy enough to discount the danger of working a night shift with killers on the loose. But, in the dark of early morning, with nothing to listen to but the chirp of a cricket and the hum of the fluorescent light fixtures, it became increasingly difficult for Jake to allow his attention to stray. Reading was out of the question. Evil possibilities derailed trains of thought books or magazine articles attempted to keep on track. Alert as a sniper, he tested his surroundings, and kept his hand near the cubby where the big cold pistol resided like a pet rattlesnake.

Patrolmen Charlie Moore and Joe Baker were assigned to Benny's Sunoco. As the nights wore on, Jake got to know them as friends. Sometimes they drove around the pumps and waved, but often, they stopped for a few minutes to drink coffee and talk.

If Benny ever tried to find a second night-man, he wasn't successful. Jake only inquired once. "Uh...oh yeah. No luck yet," Benny stuttered. Later that night, he stopped by the station with a woman who made Trina look like a Girl Scout leader. They were both quite drunk, and she appeared to be quite pregnant. She all but humped Benny's leg like a spaniel while he told Jake he was getting a raise.

"Come *ON*, baby," she kept whining, rubbing her pendulous breasts against Benny's arm. He responded the way a parent might with an unruly child, gently chiding her and flashing Jake whacha-gonna-do looks with his glassy, red spider-webbed eyes. "So, I decided," Benny slurred, "you're workin' a dangerous shift, and I appreciate it, my man. You get two more bucks an hour, eee-ffective right now. Tooo-night!" he added, steering his cranky date out the door.

Jake watched them stagger to Benny's car, awash in waves of disbelief. Benny was drinking with a pregnant woman? Their body language left little to the imagination, and it was obvious Benny was screwing her, a woman wearing a gleaming wedding set on her ring finger. Disgusted, Jake decided they deserved each other as much as he deserved the promised raise. He hoped it was Benny talking, and not Jack Daniels.

~ * ~

Increased police presence at gas stations worked so well, the robbers hit a carryout pizza place the following week. A forty-year old woman and an eighteen-year old male high school senior were working that night. Their bodies were found in a wooded area north of the Michigan line. The woman had been raped. Until then, the perpetrators only struck where one person was on duty. The tension in the city of Toledo, and in Jake's bowels, increased exponentially. To his surprise, the tension with Gayle eased. She apparently accepted the fact he wasn't going to quit. For his part, Jake was amazed at how little pleasure he found in being the victor.

Early in his shift one Friday night, Gayle stopped by the station with a girlfriend. Jake showed them the gun, which he'd held secret until then.

"My God! It's huge," Gayle murmured, touching the long barrel gently, almost sensuously. She aimed a stare at Jake. "Could you actually shoot someone?"

"I've had a lot of time to bat that one around," he answered, staring her back. "If it comes down to me or them, bet on me."

June melted into July, like butter in summer sun. There were no more robberies after the pizza shop hit. Jake, and the city at large, held their breath. Was the nightmare over? Then, shortly after two on a Thursday morning, a big Ford sedan screeched into the parking lot and skidded to a stop, its tires barking against the pavement. The doors jackknifed open and two men, angular and hardened and wearing military fatigues, were out of the car and charging through the open garage bay doors like storm troopers. Jake was nodding and nearly asleep, but he jolted into full-alarm and braced himself against the desk. Is this it? He wondered. Are these the guys? Is this how it happens, rushing in to swarm the attendant? Swarm me? "What?" he shouted, his hand found the .44 and his fingers wrapped around the grip, testing to make certain one found the trigger.

The men stopped abruptly. "You been fucking my wife, Benny Hartzell," one of them growled, grinding the words out through teeth that never unclenched, his lips pulled into a steely grimace of hatred. Jake could almost feel the man's emotion spool like a turbo, feeding on the energy of the words he snarled.

Jake began to shake his head. "Wait a minute. You got it wrong, buddy—"

"You fucker!" the young man shouted. "I'm dodging rounds in Afghanistan, and you're banging that whore bitch." Almost unbelievably, the Rambo-tough soldier melted before Jake's eyes as tears released and raced down the man's chiseled cheeks. "Does that seem right, you fucker? I loved her so much," he wailed, his shoulders heaving. His friend stepped to the man's side, both of them sagging as the anger dispersed amidst torrents of sadness the soldier couldn't contain.

"You have to listen," Jake said, his voice surprising in its steady forceful evenness. "Benny Hartzell owns this station, but he doesn't work the overnights. My name's Jake." He shook his head and shrugged. "I don't know who your wife is, buddy. Never met her." He paused. "I'm truly sorry about your troubles. Honest. But, I'm not your man."

Shock hit Jake like a thousand volts when the weeping soldier suddenly pulled a small automatic handgun from behind his back, waving it like a flag. "I was gonna shoot you, but you might just as well shoot me." He tossed the gun in Jake's general direction and it clattered on the shiny concrete floor. "I'm good as dead anyway," he cried, jamming the heels of his hands into his watery eye sockets.

Jake realized he'd reflexively yanked the big .44 out of its hiding place, but it wasn't in the soldiers' lines of sight. He pushed it back into its cubby. "I'm sorry for you, man," Jake said. "Leave and we'll forget the whole thing." The sobbing soldier's friend looked at Jake, nodded, then started for the gun on the floor. "Uh-uh," Jake said, loud enough to make the man stop and look at him. "You guys make Afghanistan safer, but I think Toledo will be a better place if you leave without the gun." The big soldier gave Jake a 'screw you' look and took another step. Jake pulled the big revolver, aimed it at the ceiling and cocked the hammer. It made a pleasing, loud click that stopped the soldier mid-step. A thrilling shot of adrenalin-fed testosterone surged, and Jake enjoyed the rush. "That wasn't a suggestion," Jake said. "Hit the road and it's all good. Give me trouble and I call 9-1-1." He lowered the .44 and aimed it at the soldier combat style, the way he had Miss June on Benny's calendar. "Touch that gun and I trigger this piece. Your choice."

The soldier scowled, but gathered his friend, who could barely walk on his own, and helped him to their car. Jake walked to the garage bay door, gun still in both hands, but drooping low, like a flag in a light breeze. "Hey," he shouted to the weeping soldier as the other one started the car. "I really am sorry, man. I hope it all works out."

Jake was sorry. He had the rest of his shift to think about how sorry he was. He was sorry for the soldier. He was sorry he'd gone in-your-face with Gayle over the job. He was even sorry he was going to quit Benny and leave him without a night-man, but he couldn't work for him anymore. Benny was a sleaze, though Jake chose to ignore that from the time he started working for him. Seeing him with a drunk and pregnant woman was troubling, but seeing the total effect it had put the finish on his employment.

"There's a soldier out there who wants to shoot your ass," Jake told Benny when he rolled in later that morning. "You've been balling his wife, and you better sleep with an open eye. Good luck, and thanks for the work."

"But Jake, she's hornier than a nympho-rabbit. Somebody'd be hittin' her if I wasn't. At least I'm good to her."

Jake just shook his head and walked to his car. The drive home that morning was the best one of the summer. He was done, and he couldn't wait to tell Gayle. He couldn't wait to see the look on her face when he told her the Sunoco nights were over.

To celebrate his unemployed status, as well as to grovel for what he put her through, Jake took Gayle to the fanciest steak house in Toledo. "How long do you think it will take Benny to replace you?" she asked as they passed the Sunoco station.

"No idea, but that's his ride," Jake said, nodding toward Benny's chromed-out cycle. "He must be working the clock around." Jake laughed. "At least he's not screwing anyone's wife, tonight."

Jake and Gayle dined at a table in a quiet corner of the restaurant, then sat holding hands, arms resting on the freshly cleared table linen, with flutes of Frangelico between them. Jake thought the candlelight was hypnotic. He wondered if there was ever a time when he was happier, or more in love with Gayle.

"I'm glad the whole thing's over," Jake said, deciding to abandon a speech he'd spent hours fine-tuning. "I was a complete jerk about that stupid job at Benny's. I love you more than anything, but I put you through a lot. I'll never do anything like that again."

Gayle's damp eyes gleamed in the candlelight. "We both have lots to learn," she said. "But, nothing bad happened, and we have the rest of our lives."

They danced to slow romantic music until after midnight in the restaurant's piano bar. On the drive home, the warm late-summer air washed over them through the open car windows. Gayle leaned across the console, resting her arm on the back of Jake's seat, and they necked like teenagers at every stoplight.

Jake slowed as they neared Benny's. Five police cars were skewed across the lot, doors open. The sharp chatter on the police radios hacked through the early morning silence like chain saws. Red and blue spots of light from the cruisers' blazing overheads swarmed the station's façade like angry bees. Charlie Moore stood near his patrol car, looking north toward Michigan.

SPEED

"Hello." She reaches to offer her hand across the table. He takes it and she grips his, shaking it with authority.

"Hello right back." He grins down at her, showing surveyor-straight teeth. "If you had to describe yourself in one word, what would it be?" His eyes twitch in their sockets, irises ricocheting like ice-blue dice. His face remains placid, but she feels he's trying to sink into her head and audit her mental process like an IRS agent. He's peering like she's a lab rat, obviously so far into his analysis, there's little chance he'll notice her appraisal of him.

He's no George Clooney, but he's easy on the eye. A young Clint Eastwood? Close. Has a scar echoing the smile line on his left cheek. She likes that. Handkerchief tucked into the pocket of the tailored sport coat that fits like it has him memorized. Earlier, in the parking lot, as she lowered her Harley onto its kickstand, he pulled in and parked his silver Maserati GranTurismo, blipped the throttle and cut the ignition. A man should know better. Leaves raw gas in the cylinders. Washes oil off their walls on the restart. Sounded good, though.

She notices his eyes cruising her body. Checking out her tribal tattoos? Wondering whether her leather vest enhances or flattens her breasts? He is obviously wealthy, probably a country clubber. What's his take on a woman who rides in on a big V-twin bike? Risk-taker? A wild ride? Someone who will be easy to take down, physically and mentally? A little smile begins modifying the corners of his lip line. On some men, that's a turn-on. Suddenly, every cell in her brain case begins to author rejections.

"Well," he says, "have you come up with your word?"

She rolls her eyes to meet his and allows the faintest of smiles. "Complex," she says, at slightly above a whisper.

"*Attention, speed-daters. Fifteen seconds left.*"

He grins and pulls his business card from an alligator wallet, places it on the shiny tabletop like a winning lottery ticket and gives it a gentle push. She reaches, her eyes unwavering and her smile more pronounced. Her fingers find the card, only to push it back.

"*Time's up, daters. Next station.*"

"Too complex for a man who wants a one-word description," she adds.

His eyebrows climb his forehead like Sherpas. He cocks his head as though he expects her to let him in on the joke. Instead, she turns to smile as the next man approaches. Meanwhile, the one in front of her scrabbles to pick up his business card, but his manicured nails can't catch an edge.

She notices his difficulty, flicks it into her fingers like a blackjack dealer and holds it out to him. "Cool Maserati, though," she says.

He fumbles the handoff and his card flutters to the floor. Before he can bend to retrieve it, she scoops it up and presses it into Mr. Maserati's hand.

BELIEVE IT

Paige first saw Tanner at the tennis club. Average height. Muscular, but not overly. Former high school and collegiate athlete, she heard. Quick with a smile. Always appeared posed, as though he was modeling whatever he wore. One of those swarthy men whose neatly trimmed onyx beard and generous carpet of body hair made him appear even darker. Tanner. She giggled when she made the connection, but that wasn't until after she heard his name a couple times. The body hair; she wasn't so sure about, but she found herself harboring fantasies of how her pale skin would look against his toasty-brown.

Paige was interested in Tanner's relationship status, but hoped to keep her curiosity on the low.

"They make a strange couple," Paige casually allowed, when Tanner and his mixed-doubles partner walked into the club's 40/Love Lounge one Saturday evening. She dipped a pita chip into some tasty hummus and waited to hear what her three friends would volunteer. The four of them just finished playing a few sets and were enjoying some wine and munchies.

"Millie and Tanner aren't a couple," Shay said. She barked a laugh. "Lyudmila," she added in a hushed voice, putting her hands on the table like she was going to push away from it. "Lyudmila Beckmann. Came over from Germany with her husband ten or fifteen years ago. He's some kind of engineer."

"Does he ever come around?" Paige said.

"He doesn't play," Trudy, one of Paige's closest friends, answered. Trudy and Paige were often mistaken for sisters. At twenty-six, Paige was a good five years younger than Trudy and when someone mentioned their Nordic resemblance, Paige always referred to Trudy as her prettier sister, never older. Trudy wrinkled her nose. "Look how much larger than him she is."

She was. Paige thought Millie was rather butch. Swung her arms like an athlete when she walked—a male athlete. She wasn't unattractive, but her face was wide with a strong, square jaw. Her coffee with cream hair only brushed her neck, but she always played wearing a headband. And man, could she rifle a tennis ball.

"She doesn't have a backhand," Paige said. She took a finishing sip of her Chablis, waved to Caitlin, the bargirl, and held up her empty goblet to ask for another. "I drew her for singles in a play-with-the-pro last week and she's one-handed, no matter where you hit it. Right or left, she just switches hands and pounds it back at you."

Paige watched them walk to a table. Each pulled out their own chair, and sat across from each other, Tanner constantly camera-ready. Nothing in their body language led her to believe they were anything but friends. Playing partners. She did notice Millie's ruddy complexion was close in shade to Tanner's.

~ * ~

Paige went to the club to practice early one Tuesday, several hours before she was to meet a client to show her a property. At 6:45, there were some people hitting the weights and jogging on treadmills in the exercise room, but Paige had the courts to herself. She dialed the ball machine up to seventy miles an hour and positioned it so she could take serves. She alternated between low cross-court returns and high deep lobs. She just hit a beautiful one that skimmed the rafters and dropped onto the far-side baseline when she heard a voice behind her and startled.

"I'm sorry," Tanner said, smiling broadly while holding up his hands as though he was stopping traffic. "You were so into hitting and I didn't know how to approach you." His teeth looked almost luminous against his dark complexion and manicured beard. His eyes danced like those of a happy child. "That was a terrific lob off such a fast serve."

The ball machine continued firing balls at seven-second intervals. One rocketed into the service square and bounced against Paige's fanny. She could feel her face go hot with a blush. The butt ball was apparently the last one in the hopper. The machine dropped to an idle.

"Thanks," Paige said, rubbing the spot where her skin still stung. She flicked her head toward the spot where the lob landed. "I want to play more mixed dubs, and a lot of men come to the net when they hit a hot serve. Lobbing it over their head can be pretty effective, but putting them up takes practice."

"That's actually why I came down here." Only then it registered, Tanner wasn't carrying a racket. "I wanted to ask you if you'd like to play in the mixed dubs tournament Saturday night."

"You're not playing with Millie?"

He rocked his weight onto his right leg and dropped his left hand into his pocket as though he was displaying the warm-ups he was wearing. "She sprained her ankle pretty badly last night, I guess. She texted me this morning and said no-go."

Paige fought to hide her excitement. Tanner and Millie usually won the tournaments they entered. Of all the women in the club he could choose, Tanner selected Paige. Not only that, a win with Tanner would cement her position in the club hierarchy as a player with cred.

"I'd love to fill in." She fired off her best smile and used her racket head to roll a ball against her shoe, flicking it into the air with a quick toe-kick. She caught the ball on her racket and bounced it a couple times. "I'm so flattered. I hope I don't let you down."

Tanner grinned. "Mill said you play strong." He put his cupped hand to his mouth and leaned in as though sharing a secret. "She's actually the one who recommended you. We tossed a few names around, but she said I should ask you first."

Paige was surprised. She went out of her way to be friendly when she played Millie in singles, yet the woman barely spoke. But as Paige well knew, liking someone and respecting their game are two different things. Millie won that day, but Paige made her sweat for it. She was disappointed it wasn't Tanner who chose her, however.

"Well, I'd love to play." Paige grabbed a pickup hamper and began slamming it down on the practice balls scattered on the court. "Do you want to get together and hit it around before Saturday?"

Tanner nudged balls toward Paige with his foot. "I could shake loose from the office for the Friday morning play-with-the-pro. Think you could make it? Give us some dubs time together to learn each other's moves."

She held up her palm for a five-slap and Tanner clapped it.

"See you Friday," Paige said.

"Believe it," Tanner replied.

~ * ~

Paige and Tanner won their way into the championship match. Paige thought it was over when the other team, a 40-something husband and wife who'd mastered the art of intermediate-speed placement shots interspersed with blistering-fast hero slams, took the match into a third set tie breaker. Paige and Tanner were one point from losing when Tanner walked up to Paige and said, "You're not Millie."

Paige thought her knees would buckle.

Tanner smiled. "So, don't try to play like her. You have a sweet game. Just play it." Then he put his hand on her shoulder and pulled her close. She looked into his eyes and it was like staring into high beams. "We lose this, the world's not gonna end, you know? Relax and have fun. Believe it."

Tanner was serving to their male opponent. Paige started for her place at the net, but Tanner took her arm and guided her back to the baseline.

"I'm trying to serve to his backhand, but stay back here in case I miss and he gets hold of this one."

Paige felt a lot less tense. It was amazing how just a few words from Tanner allowed her to relax. She wasn't Millie. She was Paige. And she was ready to take this guy's return. But it never came. Tanner curled a fast serve into the guy's left hip, jamming him up so he couldn't put a stroke on the ball. He tried to block it back, but it hit the net. They were tied, but had to win by two.

Tanner's first serve to the woman was long. "Second," he called, tossing the ball up again, then slamming it hard to her backhand. It hit the corner of the service square and her racket never came close to catching it. Up one.

Now Paige would receive serve from the male opponent. He could put some heat on it, and he had the control needed to get it to her backhand. She ran what Tanner told her through her mind again as she walked to the baseline. Play your game, she thought.

Tanner walked up, staring as intently as an ER doctor. "Tense?" he asked.

"Not too." She winked. "Just playing my own game."

Tanner spun his racket on his finger like a gunslinger. "Relax your tongue."

"What?"

"Just before he serves, let your tongue go limp. Your whole body will relax and it'll seem like you have forever to hit the return." He let his spinning racket cartwheel into the air, grabbed the grip and banged the strings against his palm. "Believe it."

Relax your tongue? Paige never heard that before, but what the hell, she figured. When the guy made his toss, she let her tongue fall into her lower jaw and watched the ball. When he hit it, she flashed on the way the balls came at her from the ball machine. He followed his serve to the net, and it seemed to Paige she had more time than she needed to position her racket and toss up a deep lob. It was the first one she'd thrown that match and it caught both the man and his wife by surprise. By the time they turned to chase it, the ball dropped just inside the baseline for a winner. Match point. Paige and Tanner high-fived, then embraced.

~ * ~

Several weeks and a couple dates later, Paige walked through Tanner's house the first time like Dorothy in Emerald City. Colors. Textures. More tile than a Roman bath. Vaulted ceilings. A screened-in hot tub overlooking the river below. A billiard room. A stainless steel and granite kitchen. Turned out Tanner was a gourmet cook. He also had a closet the size of an average bedroom, with all his clothing arranged by color and occasion. And his bedroom. A sixty-inch flat screen with a remote control curtain to cover it when it wasn't in use. A custom-built bed that looked like a throne with a mattress. Carpet so sumptuous, Paige felt like she should wear snow shoes to keep from disappearing into it. Sliding glass doors opened onto a deck overlooking the water. His speedboat bobbing at the dock. His motorcycles and his Cadillac CTS-V coupe in the garage.

Paige wasn't easy and she made that fact plain from the start. As alluring as Tanner was on so many levels, Paige told him an invitation to his home wasn't going to be rewarded with a roll on his high thread-count linen sheets. Not the first time. Or the second. Not for a long time. She took STDs seriously and if they became intimate, it was going to be an exclusive deal, or no deal. Tanner looked into her eyes and said, "Believe it."

~ * ~

Paige believed him. He gave her every reason to. He treated her with respect and never pushed, letting her set the pace at which the relationship progressed. And it did. He loved to treat her to candlelight dinners on the terrace overlooking the river. When cold weather set in, they took tennis trips to Florida. They didn't play dubs together at the club, however. His partnership with Millie was a "pre-existing condition." That joke was rooted in the fact he was in the medical field, an executive with a major pharmaceutical company. But other than tournaments, practice sessions with Millie and work, Paige and Tanner spent much of their free time together.

Tanner was an incredible lover. Talented, unselfish and inventive. He was a good listener. He asked Paige what she liked or didn't like, and followed what she told him like a map. What she enjoyed most was that sex with Tanner constantly evolved. As they grew to know each other and develop their intimacy, their lovemaking changed as well. She never felt so free to experiment before. She felt safe with Tanner, and that security allowed her to enjoy sex with him as she never did with any of the men in her past. The result was the sexual part of their relationship never became stale. Every encounter sizzled.

But as with all relationships, it wasn't perfect. There was an aspect to Tanner Paige found bewildering. She first discovered it by accident when she was waiting for him to finish dressing to go to a movie. She sat on the bed and looked at the beautiful blown-glass candy dish on Tanner's night stand. It was always there, but she'd never paid particular attention to it. She lifted the lid, expecting it to be empty, but it wasn't. She thought they might be breath mints or candy, but when she picked one up, she realized it was Viagra.

"They say they'll work for women, too," Tanner said as he came in from his dressing room.

"What?" she said. Even to her, it sounded like she screeched.

Tanner laughed. "For real. Increases the blood flow to the clitoris, just like with a penis. Increased flow, increased sensation," he added, sounding like a biology prof.

Paige dropped the pill in the dish. "Wow, I'm surprised you have ED issues." She sucked in a breath. Should she have said that? "You know, not in your thirties, I mean."

Tanner appeared completely unfazed. He continued to button his sport shirt, and shrugged. "I don't. It's like … guys who have ED are lucky to have the little blue pill." He reached out and when she took his hands, he pulled her to her feet. "The ones of us who don't are even luckier." He kissed her forehead. "Viagra's like a supercharger. A free supercharger when you're in my line of work."

Tanner took Paige's hand and led her into the hallway. At first, she was stunned, but his nonchalance over the issue and her discovering it washed that away. Recreational Viagra, she thought. I guess there are worse things.

~ * ~

There were. Tanner's penchant for lifting weights and fitness was coupled to drugs, as well. And as with the Viagra, Tanner never volunteered that information, but when he was carrying a large box in from his garage one day, Paige casually asked him what it was and he didn't hide anything. "Just some steroids and growth hormones," he said, as though he was listing grocery items.

"Aren't those illegal?"

"Ah, in the strictest sense, I guess so." He put the microwave-sized box on the kitchen island and leaned against the countertop like a car salesman. "But, it's not like dope or anything. I use them very lightly so I don't wind up looking like a gorilla," he said, doing a snorting impression. "Just occasional tune-ups. And some friends use them. I have access to sources they don't." He picked up the box and opened the door to the basement. "No big deal," he said over his shoulder.

As soon as Paige got home, she was on the internet, gathering as much information as she could. Everything she read convinced her Tanner's description of what he called "Annies and G-mones" was nowhere close to reality. Diabetes, elevated blood pressure, high cholesterol levels and psychosis were just a few of the negative effects she read about. And the possibility of reduced sexual function made Paige wonder if Tanner's use of Viagra was truly recreational.

She didn't sleep very much after she shut the computer down. By the time the night sky began to brighten into dawn, she was more conflicted than ever. She didn't love Tanner, but she was on her way. Now sirens were wailing in her head and she couldn't see him the way she once did.

There were so many positives about the man. Could she make herself overlook this scary aspect?

Could she Carmella Soprano her knowledge of Tanner's dark illegal side? At least, unlike Tony Soprano, Tanner wasn't a big ugly womanizer. On the contrary, when she walked into the club or one of the restaurants they frequented, she was proud to be the woman on Tanner Lynch's arm. All the girls at the club envied her and told her how lucky she was to be dating such an attractive and wealthy man. Every friend she introduced him to immediately liked him. He was warm and engaging; and when Paige talked with him, he always seemed to listen to understand, not merely to prepare an answer.

What she finally decided was to let things ride. She would hold her emotions in check, as best she could, and act as though what she'd learned changed nothing. Eventually, she figured, something would happen to convince her to stay or to leave. Tanner deserved that much. And in Paige's mind, so did she.

~ * ~

"Why not stay the night?" Tanner asked.

Paige wanted to. A look through the window at the snow blowing off the white mounds skirting Tanner's driveway was enough to make her want to stay, notwithstanding her desire for more time with him.

"Thing is, I have to meet the same couple I took through a house this afternoon for an early-early tomorrow." She made a gawky face. "Probably wouldn't impress them much if I showed up in the same clothes."

"I guess," he said, as his cell brrr-inged its text message tone. He picked it up, looked at the screen and smiled. "Just Mill," he said, laying it down. "About our next match." He kissed Paige, handed her coat to her, then texted back.

Usually, she had to argue her way out of his place when he wanted her to stay. This was new, but she was happy he understood. She worried he'd try to get her to stay the night and leave extra early to change at home before her meeting, something she didn't want to confront on a cold snowy morning.

"I could stay a little longer," she said, looking at the clock on the stove.

"Truth is," Tanner said, setting down his phone, "I have some paperwork I really should get into. I was going to put it off, but if you can't stay, I should get it done." He took her arm and walked with her to the door. "Want some help brushing snow off your car?"

Paige flicked the switch for the outdoor floods. "It isn't bad. The wind already blew most of it off," she said, before initiating a long tonguey kiss. "Thanks for dinner," she whispered, letting her lips brush his as she spoke. "And dessert was spectacular, as always."

Tanner gently touched her cheek with his fingertips, then opened the door. "Believe it. And we're meeting at Table Four 4 tomorrow at noon, right?"

Paige nodded, pulled her coat tight around her body and walked out into the frigid wind. When she got to her car, she waved before realizing Tanner wasn't standing at the door. That's when she reached into her purse for her keys and remembered she'd tossed them onto the chair she laid her coat on. "Damn," she huffed, starting back to the house. He usually locked the door and she hated second goodbyes.

She almost knocked, but decided to try the knob, hoping she could sneak in and out without him knowing. The door opened and she heard water running upstairs. The shower? Good, she thought. He'll never hear me. The keys were there, although they'd fallen down between the cushion and the arm bolster. As she hurried to leave, Tanner's cell brrr-inged again. She froze, waiting to see if he heard it. No interruption in the sound of the coursing water told her he didn't.

Paige was hit by an overpowering urge to look at the text, something she never did. Couldn't imagine doing. Privacy. She wanted it. She gave it. But the glowing screen was face up. Three short steps and the words would be legible. She couldn't stop herself.

WILL P GO 3 WAY? I LL STRAP GOODBAR ON AND FUCK U BOTH. LOL

Paige's mind went into hyper-drive. What the fuck? Was Millie merely joking with a close friend? Tanner and Millie were tennis partners with a special bond between them, so they made fun. Screwed around, figuratively. Paige wanted to believe that. But Millie didn't just say dildo. She called it by a name only an intimate friend would know. Goodbar. Not only that, friendly jest would allude to more normal sex, not Millie wielding a dildo. Paige read and reread the text. Every time she tried to wrestle up another meaning, Millie's wording pinned her.

Paige scrolled to look at the first text Millie sent. P STILL THERE? YES BUT LEAVING. COME GET IT, was Tanner's reply.

A bullet couldn't have intensified the white-hot pain streaking through Paige's stomach. The chicken cordon bleu Tanner served for dinner began to volcano up her esophagus, but she managed to swallow it back. Her brain whirred like a food processer, anger and heartbreak pureeing into a froth of misery. It was four or five steps from there to the door, and she managed to make her legs work. She opened the door, closing it behind her as noiselessly as she could, made it to her SUV, opened the door and flopped inside. It took her several tries to get the key into the ignition. Can I even drive? She wondered, giving the key a twist. She would. She had to. She jammed the Lexus into gear.

~ * ~

Paige cried out of hurt. She cried out of rage. Sometimes, when she almost stopped crying, she purposely rehashed thoughts that brought more tears. She looked at the clock. She looked out the window at the moon. Flipped her pillow over. Rolled onto one side and the other. No position was comfortable. The sheets felt like sandpaper.

The bastard. The son of a bitch. He lied to her. Exclusive relationship. He swore it. And Paige felt stupid because she never suspected Millie. Lyudmilla. That fucking bitch. That married dykey bitch. Paige tried to imagine the two of them together and she couldn't. Not Tanner. Not the man who, through occasional comments about women at the club or ones they ran into socially, always made it plain he was attracted to women like Paige. Athletic, but feminine. Not like Millie.

The worst for Paige was not knowing what she would do. Would she meet him at Table Four 4 and risk a public scene? Should she stop by his place before her showing in the morning and tear into him privately? Either way, since both of them were regulars at the club, she'd see him there. Maybe there would be a blow-up on the courts, or in the 40/Love Lounge. Could she even keep her membership there, having to see Tanner and Millie together?

By the time she drifted off, the only plan she formulated was to go to get a full battery of tests for STDs. The thought made her retch. She'd taken a shower when she got home from Tanner's, using the hand-held shower head to douche all of him she could down the drain. She considered another. Instead, she drifted into fitful slumber.

~ * ~

Paige needed to pull herself together. The couple she'd been working with really liked the house she showed them yesterday afternoon, but they were eager to see the one she was showing this morning. Paige doubted they would put an offer in for today's house because it was a good twenty grand higher than they said they could go. Yesterday's was right at their price-point. Today's might spur them to put an offer on yesterday's house, or best case, make an offer on today's. Win/win either way, but Paige had to be on her game to score. She studied her face in the bathroom mirror when she finished doing her makeup. Nope, she didn't look like a woman who'd been up most of the night, crying.

What she wasn't certain of was what she was going to do about Tanner. The motherfucker. She'd made the mistake of getting involved with someone firmly rooted in an important aspect of her life; the tennis club. That was all well and good while the relationship thrived, but now it was dead. Paige loved tennis. She loved the girls she played with at the club. There was no way she was leaving it, but Tanner was an influential and pervasive member. What the hell would she do?

On her way to the office, she just began to put her thoughts back on the couple she was going to meet at nine when her cell chimed. She knew it was Tanner, but she checked to be sure. His number was on the screen. Christ. She pressed "ignore" and kept driving. At the next light, she picked up the phone and considered listening to his message. Before she could decide whether or not to do it, the phone chimed a text announcement.

WILL BE LATE TO LUNCH MUST PICK UP A PACKAGE LOVE YOU—T

It was like a bolt of lightning struck Paige. Probably the closest analogy would be the day back in elementary school when she finally realized a number added to nine was one number less than the number added, but with a one in front of it. Whoa! A shipment. The answer to Paige's problems just pixilated on her iPhone. Hot damn.

She checked the clock on the dash. There was time. She flicked her turn signal and darted into the left-turn lane. Walmart loomed through her driver's-side window. Perfect.

~ * ~

The showing with the young couple went better than Paige could have hoped. They liked today's house better than the one from the day before, and some extra money mysteriously materialized, allowing them to make an offer that was five grand less than the owners were asking, but fifteen higher than the couple claimed they could go. Happened a lot. People low-balled what they could afford to their realtor, and suddenly offered more than they said they could afford. The world was full of liars. But unlike with Tanner, the lying bastard, in this case the couple's lie worked in Paige's favor. Paige was looking at seven per cent of a bigger purchase price if the sellers took the offer. They were eager to move. Paige was certain they would.

She arrived at Table Four 4 a half hour early, got a window seat and ordered a merlot. She glanced around. She didn't see anyone she knew, but she wouldn't have been surprised to see a former client or a fellow realtor.

Tanner said he would be late, so she sipped her wine until ten minutes before their original meeting time before she pulled out the pre-paid cell she bought at Walmart. She dialed 911.

Paige was surprised to find herself using a faked-up raspy voice. "In the next fifteen or twenty minutes, a man will pull into Table Four 4's parking lot. He will be driving a silver Cadillac CTS-V coupe. License plate is 1 ST SERV. He will be speeding, and his trunk will be full of steroids and growth hormones. So is the basement of his house at 77222 Riverview Trace. He is a dealer."

The 911 operator's voice never wavered. "And what is your name, please?"

"Just believe it," Paige replied.

Paige keyed off and dropped the cell in her purse. She would wipe it down and drop it in a dumpster somewhere, later. She sipped her merlot and readied herself for the show.

Minutes passed. She didn't see any police, and began to wonder if the dispatcher believed her. Maybe they only took tips seriously if the caller gave a name. Paige couldn't see the whole parking lot, but she thought she could see enough to know if the police moved in. Nothing obvious.

Tension set in and it felt like her traps were pulling her shoulders toward the ceiling. She relaxed her tongue, the technique Tanner taught her. It really worked for her in tennis and it seemed to work now. The pressure in her neck decreased. But what if the police blew off her tip? What would she say to Tanner if he came striding up to the table? What would she do?

Paige saw Tanner pull off Airport Road and accelerate down the service road toward the restaurant. He drove the way he played tennis, fast and hard. He was flying. Then she saw a marked police cruiser come out of a side road. The cop's light bar came on immediately, and both cars coasted to the curb. Tanner was out of his car and walking toward the cruiser almost before the cop could pull to a stop. Tanner's arms were splayed, hands turned upwards—the same gesture he used when questioning a call on the tennis court. The cop was out of his car, motioning Tanner back into his, but Tanner stood his ground and they wound up toe to toe, each speaking in what looked to Paige as a heated exchange. Another police car pulled up behind the first, and that officer exited with a dog. In less than a minute, the dog was barking and straining against his lead, lunging at the Cadillac. Paige watched in fascination as, just like on TV, the first cop pulled out a slip of paper and read while the other cop opened the coupe's trunk. Tanner kept looking toward the restaurant, almost as though he expected Paige to run out and intervene.

"Would you like another merlot, or would you like to see a menu?" the waitress asked.

"No thank you," Paige said. "My friend just texted and she won't be able to meet me. I think I'll just pay for the wine and be on my way." She pointed through the window and widened her eyes. "My goodness," she said, with faux alarm. "What do you think is going on out there?"

The waitress looked, just as two more marked police cars sped onto the scene.

"Looks like a bust to me," she said, as one of the uniformed officers led a handcuffed Tanner to a cruiser. "I'll have to tell my dad. Looks like there'll be a nice looking Caddy at the next police auction." She ended with a giggle.

Paige looked at the waitress. "Really?"

"Oh, yeah. Happened to a guy down the street. They found

marijuana in his car when they stopped him for running a light, then they got a warrant and found a big grow operation in his basement. He lost his house and his car." She nodded. "They can take everything you've got, for sure." She turned and started to walk away. "I'll ring your tab."

The car carrying Tanner was pulling away.

"Wait," Paige said. She pulled a twenty out of her purse and handed it to the waitress. "We're good on this."

"But it was just a seven dollar glass," the waitress said, when she saw the twenty.

Paige patted the waitress's arm. "You're excellent at what you do, and I'm pretty sure I just closed a sale on a very expensive house. Enjoy, and if you know anyone in the market to buy or sell, mention my name." She slipped the smiling girl her business card.

Paige decided passing her card to the waitress would be the last business she would conduct that day. She called in and told the secretary to mark her out-of-office and headed for the club. Paige might work out, take some steam, or she might find someone to hit balls with. While she did that, she would rehearse the way she needed to react when she heard the horrible news about Tanner Lynch. She would appear surprised and brokenhearted. And Millie, the fucking bitch, would have to look for a new mixed dubs partner. She might even look for a new club. That thought put a smile on Paige's face.

"Believe it," she said to her reflection in the rear-view mirror.

ARRIVAL

Didn't make many Ds doing lube and oil at Grease Monkey, but I scored some from my co-monkeys, rolling dice between lube jobs, and moneyed my pay check-a-roo after clocking out. Seven o'clock, cold November Friday night, and I decided to chow some lobster. It was a max-spend, but damn if I didn't have a big pull for sweet, flaky-white candy-meat. To hell with rent. Hoof to work when the 'tane needle bottomed. Yep, I was going big hat.

In the full-ride Mom and Dad days, we used to go to fancy-raunts every week, and the Dad-man never flinched if I ordered lobster. Drawn butter. Never cognated that. Who drew what? For that matter, who was the first hu-noid to stare a lobster down and say, "Yeah, I'm eatin' you, brother." I was awake in class that day and know in Maine they call them bugs. The one left in the tank at Kro-gaires looked like an insect gone all 'roid. Regardless, whoever chomped that first lobster, I'm like, thank-thank-thank you, man.

"I think he looks sad," a lilty little voice came from the other side of the tank. She sounded like the small holes in a harmonica.

"What makes you think it's a he?" I said. "Only another lobster could tell."

It wasn't diffy for me to tell she was super-glam. A menu of everything I wantoned for. Tall. Wide hips. Oh, yeah. Great grab-handles when you're doing it doggy. She looked at me and her face held stories I wanted to know. She stepped forward and pressed her fingers against the glass, like a visitor in a fed-pen flick.

"Is it cold?" I said. Her answer was to pull her hand back and put it in the pocket of her pea-coat. She got this look like I stole from her, so I smiled up some innocence. "That's what they need. The Atlantic's always cold around Maine, even in the summer." Sounding like my old teacher, Mr. Crothers, made me laugh.

At that moment, a gray-mane came around the corner of one of the aisles. I didn't see her at first, but her cart had that wiggle-wheel thing going. Next, I heard she slapped her face on the linoleum. Hollow thwack, like somebody back-handed a fresh turkey. Her uppers shot out and clattered over as if they wanted a bite of my foot. I looked at pea-girl and her eyes were ga-ga.

Ever wonder what you'd do? Someone else's old wrinkled grandmom? Neither did I. Odds on, without a gorge-o-glam who worried about nasty-look lobsters watching, I'd have let her be, but I figured it might make me look all Eagle Scout if I did something. "Hey, you k?" I yelled, fast-footing. I shook the grey and she felt like a sack of broken parts. I rolled her over and some spit broke for her ear, foamy white across her rougey cheek. That queered the deal on mouth to mouth. They say that's old school, anyway. Compressions are the thing. I heard a little pop and felt something give deep inside on the first one. I was revved on 'drenalin and the gray-mane's ribs were like dry twigs. I eased up on the next few, but she was flat-lined. Her pupils looked like portholes to eternity.

"Hurry. The Krogers at Detroit and Byrne," pea-girl celled. "Seafood department."

I stood, raised and dropped my arms to show her it was no use. She listened, snapped the phone closed and started to eye-gush, so I walked over to throw an arm over her shoulder. Instead, she locked onto me. Her face was hot and wet against my neck.

"Not coming," she burbled, then pulled away to splash me with a little horror. "Some kind of outbreak, the 911 lady said," she went on. Shook her head, maybe to make it go away. Her green eyes ricocheted around like a sniper's.

"What you mean? It was all good when I came in," I said, checking my watch in the name of accuracy, "ten mins back."

At that moment, a thirties-dude stumbled and headered into an open-top prepared-meals freezer. His legs stuck up like the stern of a sinking ship. One foot twitched a couple times. It would have been funny if it wasn't so fucking weird. People I couldn't see were hitting the floor too, making hollow thuds like dropped watermelons.

Some guy in a Kroger apron ran up. He looked like he'd seen too much—irises zigging like he was watching a swarm of locusts. Just stood there, mouth open like it would take a good old Heimlich to bust a word loose, his arms and legs controlled by a hyped puppeteer.

"What?" I said, always good for incisive interrogation.

Kroger-guy just turned and ran off, shoes slipping on the shiny floor like he was trying to lay leather.

Pea-girl was back on me, then. Arms around my neck like she was drowning. "First the lobster." She wailed like a siren. "Now this."

I looked at the lobster, who seemed cool. Had this leg-tap thing working. Just one of the ten. Tap, tap, tap. Antennae waving. What did she mean? "The lobster looks k to me," I said to gauge her heading.

"Okay?" It came almost like a squeal. "He's in a tank at a grocery store."

I never got scritchy with a glam-girl. Okay, I didn't have much happening after college shit me out and Dad-man gave me the key-don't-work. I nighted in crash joints, wondering if the Tontogany State pennant was still above my old bed. Did Dad-man repo my room for a den or home theater? Point being, not many hotties are looking for a dude with 10w-30 hair oil. Then, when it looked like an apocalypse might be on us, here I was in a Kro-gaire with bustin' glammer. If this was the end, at least I stood a chance for a happy one, if I caged it right.

"I think we should turn him loose," I said.

Her eyes went lioness-wild. "Loose?" she sopranoed. "In Toledo? They need salt water. He'll die."

Pitch on the way. "That's what I mean. We'll take him to the coast."

Her face blanked out like a dead flat screen. "Now?" she squeaked.

"I have no idea what's shaking, but if it's going the way it looks, there won't be anyone around to feed little lobby, here, or keep his bubbler gizmo churning." I pulled my mouth into my best heart-warmer. "I mean, if the world's gonna end, what are *your* plans?"

"You were here to buy him, weren't you?" She began to nod, doing her best Lisbeth Salander, sans the facial tackle box. "You were going to eat him, right?"

"None of that matters anymore," I told her. "If the world's sicking out, we have to fast-act. Stay here," I said, turning for the seasonal aisle.

I was a trackie in high school, and I vaulted bodies like low hurtles. First a twenty-something with a couple young kids, the little boy still clutching his open box of animal crackers. Then a phys-fit about my age. Looked like he could lift my car. All dead. What the fuck? Why weren't pea-girl and I ghosting, too?

I yanked a Styrofoam cooler off the top shelf and started for the ice freezer. My heart slammed my ribs like they were bars on a xylophone. From fear? The hype of fast-footing? Or was I the next to bag out? I whapped a bag of ice on the floor to make it back into cubes, filled the cooler halfway and dead-ran for the lobster tank. Pea-girl was still alive and hanging when I got back. I had no idea how much future was left, but the rescue gig might cast her as my co-star 'til our show finally closed.

I grabbed the lobster and lifted it, like a cold, wiggly plastic model. I eased it onto the ice and it looked like it was waving its claws at us when I started to close the lid.

She stopped me. "Take the rubber bands off his claws," she said. "They're cruel."

I snapped them off and the lobster began to open and close its claws. I looked at pea-girl. "Let's head east," I said, firing off a wink for added logic.

My plan sounded all good, I guess, because she tagged at my heels, out of the store and into the parking lot. The 'scape out there tied me tight. Hu-noids on the ground everywhere. A few falling out of cars and SUVs. Or into them. Then, a milf-glam about forty came past, looking pract'ly spastic. Shrieking. Arms spread like a songster hitting a high note. She looked at pea-girl and me, shrilled again and stumbled away.

I know you're wondering, so I gotta tell you. The more every other hu-noid freaked, the calmer I was. No sense to it. I'm not a brave-heart and I can't afford drugs since the parentals gave me the bye-for-now. No, I was straight as a dipstick that night, I just wasn't panicky. Maybe somebody with so little future doesn't care if it's cut short. Pea-girl, on the other hand, broadcast fright like a transmitter and I knew I had to keep her gray matter busy to maintain her mellow.

"C'mon," I said. Talking low and moving slow, sort of molester-luring-child. "We gotta get Kurtz to the ocean," I went on, rattling the ice cooler just a tad for a soothing shoosh effect. "My car's over here," using my chin to point.

"Kurtz?" Her eyes were vacant.

"From *Apocalypse Now*." I was walking backwards to keep her locked in. She shook her head.

"One of my fav flicks. Colonel Kurtz went rogue and formed his own army. The way things are rolling, Kurtz seems appropriate." I sloshed the ice in the chest again. "I think Kurtz is gonna hit the Atlantic, get his buds together and march 'em out of the sea to straighten this mess out." Figured a hopeful image would keep her in a soothing zip code.

We got to my old crapper, but parked next spot over was a new Lincoln Navigator. The door was open and the chime was gonging, so I knew the key was in it. I motioned pea-girl over to the Linc with a toss of my head. A gray-mane was lying in the d-seat, cocked against the console, so I pulled him out and onto the ground. Would have tossed him if I was alone, but went easy-down for pea-girl's sake. Put Kurtz's cooler on the back seat. Then I noticed a case of Pabst in a close-over shopping cart. Grinding out eight hundred miles from Toledo to the coast was a stupid idea, assuming this deal ever went that far, but beer was always smart luggage. I grabbed the brew, opened it and put a few in with Kurtz. I scored a smile from pea-girl when I told him to keep his claws off 'em. Then she got into the p-seat.

"We're really going?" she asked.

I mean, she's piling into a hoopty with a stranger she met less than a quarter-clock ago and she's not solid with the premise?

"I do what I say," I offered, spider to fly, patting her wrist. "But, before we kick it, we got Kurtz sorted out, and I'm Zak. So, you're...?"

"Annie."

"And if order is reestablished, I'm not gonna get bonked with a felony underage rap?"

Her head swung. "Twenty-three next week."

"Well, Annie," I said, trying for true-tone, "I'll do my best to get Kurtz to the coast, and you to next week."

~ * ~

The Linc was dry, so I went looking for 'tane. The scene on the way to Speedway was straight George Romero, 'cept the bodies weren't getting back up. Yet, anyway. That scary thought slammed me, but I tried to stay safe-zone, head-wise. I swerved around several wreck-ups and skidded up next to the pumps. I switched on the radio to keep Annie amused.

"...reports from all over North America. Many hundreds of people, perhaps thousands, are dying. It's still too early to say exactly why. Kathleen Sebelius, Secretary of Health and Human Services, is collecting information and plans to issue a statement soon. In the meantime, please remain calm. The best guess right now is this is some type of virus that attacks the heart muscle, so avoid contact with others. Its origin is unknown. Terrorism has not been ruled out. President Obama is monitoring the situation ..."

I snapped it off. Fuck. I gave the gray-mane at Krogers cardio. Contact. I jumped out and washed my hands in windshield cleaner. Annie went wild-eyed. "Get out and wash up, 'specially where I touched you." I said. "If it's a virus, we have it or we don't, but we're not croakers yet." I walked to the pump while Annie scrubbed. "Gonna tank up before we head for the coast. Meantime, nobody gets near us, comprende? No truck with foreigners equals no virus, right? You and me." I loved that thought. Me and a super-glam. "Kurtz is depending on us." Nice touch.

The 'tane station scene was crazy. Looters were snatching anything they could eat, drink or smoke. I shoved my credit card in the slot, figuring I'd never have to pony up. I mean, civilized order was pretty much long-gone.

"My cell doesn't work!" Annie shouted, coming around the back of the Linc.

"Get back in and lock it," I said, trying to stay easy-talk while I watched three creepoes eyeballing her. The pump was taking forever. The three stooges were on the move now. Their faces said jackpot.

"Get in and lock-tight," I growled, pointing at them.

She looked, fright-noised and jumped inside.

"Wayback," I shouted, holding my hand up, cop-like. I looked around for something, anything. I couldn't hold 'em off with a fucking window squeegee. The Linc was still sucking 'tane. I thought about a cut 'n run, but I wanted to be full-tank. If the cells were going shitty, no telling how long there would be juice for another fill.

"How 'bout a lift," one of the 'proachers said, his eyes lost in the shadow of his ball cap.

The pump finally shut down. I triggered 'til it clicked off again.

"Yeah, we got a ticket," another said, his teeth glinting in the lot-lights, bright as the large caliber gat he'd yanked.

I'm no genius, but sometimes ideas come. They were no more than ten feet off, so I jerked the nozzle from the tank and hosed them with 'tane. "Now trigger that, bitch," I said. "Go on and light yourself up. I'll watch you flame."

They spit and swore. Swiped at their eyes. The gat slipped loose as they dead-ran. I tossed the nozzle and grabbed the heavy cold .44. I popped the clip and it was loaded up, so I slammed it back in, wiped the piece with a towel and got in the Linc. Now I had heat, a tanked off speed-easy and a max-glam. If the end came down, at least I'd go style-right.

~ * ~

I hit the turnpike and vectored east. The Linc came with Sirius. That went first. Local radio was crapping, too. We found one station with a jock playing The Doors moaning *The End*, over and over. Breaks for news, all of it bleak-like. Same shit. The White House is monitoring. When that station broke bad, we scanned a time or two, then shut it down for a while. I never felt so alone, even with Annie in the p-seat.

She cried for a while, then stopped. "It's all a movie," she said, waving her hand at the windshield. "The End of Time, in Lincoln widescreen," she hooted. "Wish we had some popcorn."

The roads weren't what I 'spected. In the doomer flicks, cars were chocked in piles like bungalows after an earthquake, but the cruise was on eighty, and rare I had to brake or steer around trouble. We drank a couple Blue Ribbons, and Kurtz still waved when we put more brews on ice. Just on the skirts of Erie, Pennsylvania, there was a crashed airliner blocking the westbound. Still smoking. Bodies in seats, their ride over. I told Annie to close her peeps.

We rolled all-way to Rochester, New York before the Linc needed a guzz, just into Saturday morning. I kept flashing on the Speedway-scene in Toledo and wasn't into it, but this stop was good-way crazy. Almost like the Sunoco was open. People getting snacks, but it wasn't a hellhole. No cashiers, but no thrashing and looting. People at the pumps kept their distance and some masked their noses and mouths, but just the same, some talked.

"Where ya headed?" a woman asked me as I pumped 'tane.

"The coast," I shouted. "Mission of mercy." By that time I was down with the idea. Anything to joog it up with Annie. The woman couldn't know what I meant, but she grinned me up like she did. Winked. Gave me the feeling we were still a nation. Made me slobbery.

I rapped and Annie opened the window. "I'm going shopping," I said, nodding toward the store. "Whatchu want?" She shrugged. I knew her from nobody. She could have been a veggie or something. "You eat regular stuff?" She nodded. "I'll find you something—good as they got. Keep that gat ready, you need it." I started, then turned back. "Things get hot, key this bitch and go. 90 east'll get you to the ocean. I'll be k."

That made her face go scary, so I fast-footed. Grabbed sandwiches and chips, and a big bag of popcorn. I mean, my aim was to get scritchy before the end. The Linc had lots of room in back, and I had visions.

Annie was crying again, I got in. "Here's your popcorn," I said, pointing to the windshield. "For your movie."

"I think Kurtz is dead," she said, wet-eyed. "Look." She yanked the top off his cooler.

It was dark, so I domelighted and went knees-on-seat. Kurtz looked okay to me. Color was the same. Still smelled like moldy wet pillow.

"See? He's not moving," Annie shrilled. "He died before we could take him home." She reached into the cooler and stoked his back.

As she was taking her hand away, Kurtz opened his big claw and closed it on her hand. She froze and went all eye-pop. I started to grab Kurtz, or maybe Annie's hand—had to do something. Kurtz snapped at my hand with his other claw. He missed and it clicked like a dry-fired gat.

"No," Annie said, putting her other hand on my shoulder. "He's not hurting me." She laughed. "He's holding my hand." Kurtz opened his claw then and Annie petted him again. "He likes me, Zac. Don't you, Kurtz?" Kurtz clicked his big claw twice and Annie giggled little-girl. "See? You tried to grab him and he snapped his small claw once. No. Two with his big claw is yes. Right, Kurtz?"

Nothing. His antennae fish poled, but no clicks.

Noise outside the Linc cut through and I looked around. Things were crazy-up, now. Biker-dudes rolled in and one of them got off his steelhorse and started punching some necktie. No reason I could see. Just went whackwhack on the guy.

"We're outta here," I said to Annie. "Get me a beer, splash some water on Kurtz and put the lid back on."

Annie popped the top on a brew. It sounded almost like Kurtz's claw. I took a pull on the PBR, then put it in the cup holder and fired the Linc. "We got another six or seven hours," I said, gassing out onto the road. I could feel the spizz leaving me. Six or seven hours to put a fucking lobster in the ocean. I mean, the whole point was to get this glam naked, started out. Figured some Jack Hanna might cinch the deal. Then the world decided to death spiral, and I was still on the old heading. Things change. Maybe my plan should, too.

Then it happened. I felt my heart go redline, acking like a machine gun. Hard to believe Annie couldn't hear it, so loudnoise. Then it backed down, stopped a long second and went back to work. I swallowed. No pain. Tried to make like nothing happened. A little race is all, then back to idle. It's all good.

"You look funny, hon," Annie said. "You okay?"

"Yeah, no worries," I said, butching it best I could. I sucked down more brewski and swallowed. Waited. Nothing. The speedo read ninety and I set the cruise. The Linc had hot blue-white heads that pierced the blackness like lasers, so I could see jam-ups longway out. Brakes could shred the rubber off the rims, I wanted them to. I did gentle swerves to miss occasional wrecked or parked hoopties, but the road was clearer than I would have 'spected. Sometimes I had to use the breakdown lane to get around clumps of cars, but holding speed was easy-go.

We headlonged into the night. Annie never tired of searching for radio stations, a game to keep herself busy, I guess. Once she found Flamenco music. It was so sick. The world was meltdown, and some station was 'casting gypsy music, all clicky-click and guitar-gone-wild. Kurtz even clacked his claws a few times. Annie took the lid off the cooler and said, "You like this music, don't you, Kurtz?" Silence.

"See?" I said. "That overgrown June bug got no clue." The world was going cadaver and it felt good to turn bastard, just a little. In less than an hour the Flamenco hissed into static.

"Turn it off," I told her. She frownfaced, but did.

"Are you tired, Zac?" she wanted to know.

"Nah." I was telling the truth. If planet Earth was going down, I wanted to witness the fall, long as my beater kept humping. "I can hammer this sled all night," I told her.

"I'm really fading," she said. "It won't make you mad if I get some sleep?"

I reached over and touched her cheek. "You're all good, babe," I told her.

She lifted the console and laid across the seat, head on my nads, for god's sake. In the bluish dashlight I could see her lips, all moviestar-puffy. I tried to forget how close her mouth was, but my balls were on full ache. Oh, man. The plan had been to toss the lobby into some water to redboil, snack it down and dial up some porn for dessert. It had been way too long since I fired a load. And now a gorgeous glammer was dreamworld on my pecker while I guided the Linc-missile to the Atlantic. I fought against fantasy, but the movie kept running. Her cupping my balls, head-bobbing like an oilrig. I hoped my stiffy wouldn't waken her. Well, some of me did.

My beater did another round of froggy-hops. I held the wheel tight and waited to see if I'd croak. Shit, I thought. My luck, Annie would wake up, blow me and my ticker would explode.

Then it got stranger. We no more than crossed into 'Chusetts and four hu-noids held hands and jumped off an overpass, right in front of the

Linc. I think they timed it to get whapped, but they too-sooned and I only thumped one with the driver's side tires. Annie never stirred. Lucky. Last, I needed was her wailing over suicidals.

Next, light showed up in the rearview. I watched it split one for two and gain on us. Man, I was doing almost a ton and still the heads fast-moved like the Linc lost its juice. Was it trouble, or were they just in a hurry-more? I made sure the gat was cocked and ready to rock. When the car pulled longside, the pass window opened and a woman, naked much as I could tell, shot out to her bellybutton, waving her arms and yelling. The speedblast fanned her hair and in the Dreamsicle-color highway lights, it looked like her head was flaming. I buttoned the window to see what she was shouting, but it wasn't words. Just a yell. I closed the window, she ducked back in and they heavyfooted.

Another big shot of heart-thunking. This time, it felt electric-like. Coppery-acid taste in my mouth fright-freaked me. I couldn't dare it, anymore. Couldn't risk Annie with a high-speed if I vapor locked. I pulled the Linc into the breakdown and stopped.

I nudged her. "Annie, you're gonna have to drive a while," I said. Nothing.

I put my fingers against her forehead. Cold as clay.

I yelled all the volume I could push through my throat, til my cords felt like they ripped. Annie! I threw the door open, gentled her head onto the seat and pressed my ear to her chest. No heartbeat. I shrilled at the stars. Annie! The universe didn't care.

Now what? I never really knew her. All we talked was end of the world shit, not about the old belly-up one. Didn't know where her fam lived. Even if I did, her city could be burning, all I knew. Wasn't going to dump her, but keeping a dead glam in the car was too weird. I didn't even know where I was going, now. No place. That's where I wanted to go. My cardio did another floparound.

I sat down on the Linc's doorsill and packed it in. "It's over, Kurtz," I said. "Annie's dead. I'm on my way. Sorry it didn't work out."

Kurtz made a single click.

"Annie believed in that shit. I don't."

I didn't have the force, anymore. I couldn't go on. My heart was flipping. Any reason to move died with Annie. I would kick off right here, with her. And Kurtz.

Just then, big hu-noid came fast-stepping down from the trees to the x-way. "Gimme the car," he shouted.

Annie was in the car. So was Kurtz and our stuff. My circuits refired. I stood and faced him. I had less than twenty feet to change him up. "Wayback," I shouted.

"Fuck you," he raged, all sneerface.

I grabbed the gat off the dash and cranked one, sidelong of his feet. He paused, and that's all it took. I jumped in the Linc, buttoned the lockups and keyed the motor. I floored it and the SUV decorated the pavement with stripes of smoky rubber.

So, there I was. Headed east again. What the fuck? From plan, to no plan and back. I eased Annie's head onto my lap. "That bastard saved your bacon, Kurtz," I told him, talking over my shoulder. "'Lantic here we come, I live 'til then."

No clicks.

The trip computer said I had tane enough to make the coast. Ran the Linc to a ton-twenty since I didn't have to worry about hurting Annie. Hit Worcester in half a clock. Signs said I-495 routed to Plymouth, where America started. Seemed like a fit to free Kurtz there as it ended. Quarter a clock later, a sign said take M-44, so that's what I did.

Followed the signs to North Plymouth beach. Passed a couple hu-noids on the way. One of them, a graymane with a beard, waved and smiled like everything was normal-ways. I waved and smiled back, as though I didn't have a dead girl's head on my lap and a lobster on ice. Felt good, somehow. I wiped tears.

Trip was done, so damage didn't matter anymore. I drove over curbs and smashed through a couple fences. Stopped a few feet from the ocean. It was dark as the Devil's asshole, but the Linc's heads lit up the low breakers good.

I shut the motor down, got out and opened the rear p-door. I pulled Kurtz's cooler out and carried it to the water's edge.

I lifted him off the ice. "Bet you're one happy motherfucker," I said. No clicks. I had to laugh. He was going to have to make the last little bit on his own, I decided. I put him on the sand a few feet from the water. "I promised Annie we'd get you to the ocean, and there it is," I told him. "I do what I say."

I waited. Kurtz didn't make a move. I wondered if he died, too.

"Kurtz," I finally said, "you never understood a fucking word either Annie or I ever said, did you?"

His antennae whiplashed. Then, he raised his small claw and clicked once before he skittered into the sea.

I got back into the Linc, shut off the lights and lifted Annie's head onto my lap. I barely knew her, but in my way, I knew I loved her. So, quiet. So kindlike. Fuck. Wanted to save Kurtz. A little tilty and strange-girl, but she made the world better when she was in it. She made me better, too. Made me into somebody who did what they said. Took Kurtz to the ocean, even after I didn't have to.

The horizon was going red-sky, the sun on its way back from Europe. I cradled Annie's head and settled in to see if I would live 'til its arrival.

REFLECTION

So now what? Your move, Mr. Smartguy. Riding the subway from your minimal-wage job, bussing in a diner catering to the human equivalent of go-to-work clunkers. Sadly, you recognize you're no standout in that worn linoleum service station. The waitresses crack gum, continuously brush oily tendrils of bleached hair from their heavily-mascaraed eyes, and screw you out of your share of tips like it's an Olympic event. Your boss hollers, "Iraq", instead of Eric. Yes, you are dark with dark eyes, but not Middle-Eastern. You stay primarily because he lets you gobble table scraps. Your expenses dropped dramatically with the no smoking laws; customers no longer stub out on their leftovers. Helps to afford the closet-size apartment you share with leaky pipes and a cat that acts like she took *you* in. At least invading wolf spiders devoured the roaches.

So, Mr. Smartguy. The money rests on the floor near the seat of the only other passenger in the car. Dropped from her purse? She's not Playboy material, but her blouse is crisp and white, shoes un-scuffed. Additionally, she has serenity. Even in the raucous cacophony of the train, you sense a wrap of tranquility surrounding her. You're drawn to this girl, but reality slaps you wise. Maybe in a parallel universe somewhere a chick like this would be interested in you, but you've never found its entranceway. Odors of stale grease and dish detergent aren't seductive.

Your stop is next. Better make a decision. You can't see the denomination. Probably not huge, but it could be a ten. Twenty? Not enough to change your life, but even five would add comfort.

There's something about the way she sways with the bucking subway car; in rhythm, like women you saw riding horses on television.

The tilt of her head bespeaks a naive openness that endears and provokes your protective impulses. You cave. Step over and pick up the money. She startles, eyes wide and brimming with wonder. You unfold it. Not one. Two twenties. A breath stabs your lungs, but you offer the bills.

Her head wags. The most delicate little smile breaks the silky smooth of her cheeks. "It's not mine." Her lips part yet more. "Finders, keepers," she giggles, happy for you. Your heart slams at your ribs. Two twenties. Nearly a day's pay. The train slows and you brace. She gets up to leave. You follow her off, still wallowing in disbelief with a twenty clenched in each hand. She waves and starts down the platform.

"Wait." The word leaps like a frog. She turns, eyes wide. "Can I buy you some ice cream?"

Her fingers flutter to hide her grin. "I'm married." She takes her hand away and her mirth dissolves. "You have kind eyes," she adds, and walks away.

On the last leg home, you stop to look at your mirror image in shop windows. Was the girl right? You wonder. Or did she merely mistake your kindness for her own, reflected back?

ALTERING TERMS

When Roxanne Bayer was a little girl, her mother told her it was good luck if you caught a falling leaf before it hit the ground. The recollection brought a smile, but didn't raise her spirits. She sat on the chaise in her enclosed front porch petting Mofus, her fluffy little mutt, and watching orange-red leaves drift from the big front-yard maple through the jalousie windows. She wished she was a little girl again, or youthful enough to want to catch a leaf. She wished she believed she could change her luck, or was someone who still believed in luck at all. But Roxanne was resigned to believing in choices, and living with the ones you made.

Roxanne's husband, Tom, didn't want the furnace used until October, a week away. The nights had been cool and the house remained chilly. Even with the sun streaming in, the porch was cool. Mofus whined and lay his head on Roxanne's thigh. The pup's warmth felt good, but it was merely physical. What Roxanne longed for was emotional heat. What she wouldn't give for Tom to take her in his sinewy arms and kiss her. The 1960 Tom she married twenty-three summers ago, after they graduated from high school. She stroked Mofus' head. Outside, another leaf took its promise of luck to the ground.

Roxanne startled when she saw Tom's new Jeep rolling slowly down Bittersweet Drive. Their modest ranch home nestled between the turn-around at the end of the short cul-de-sac and a narrow stand of trees. She checked her watch. Tom's foursome teed off at nine, so she didn't expect him until close to dinner time. He couldn't have finished eighteen holes, not to mention the beer afterward. She gentled Mofus' head from her leg and stood, studying Tom as he parked on the driveway and got out. He didn't appear drunk, but his face was red and it looked like he'd been crying. Spiders danced on Roxanne's spine. Whatever was wrong, it was serious. She rushed to the door and shoved it open. "What?"

Tom stopped ten feet away. Tears ran down his cheeks. His mouth twisted in a way she hadn't seen since his brother was killed in a motorcycle accident. Tom straightened his lips, but that seemed to stiffen them, and his voice fluttered. He said something she couldn't understand.

She hurried out and grasped his upper arms, the way she might grab an enormous child. "What happened?"

He looked into her eyes, something he rarely did. "I think I killed a guy," he said, then began to bawl. Laid his head on her shoulder and wept.

"You what?" she shrieked. "How?"

He gathered himself, lifted his head and wiped his eyes with his thick fingers. "My tee shot on eight. Swung it bad and it sliced like crazy. I yelled. Heck, we all yelled. But this guy, he was putting on number four and he never flinched." Tom shook his head. "Dropped like a plugged duck."

Roxanne stepped back. "Where did you hit him?"

"On the head," he said, in a ragged child-like cry that became words. "I couldn't believe it. The minute I saw it going toward him, I knew. Like I saw him get hit before he did. Time we got there, he was out cold, but shaking. All spastic-like." He winced. "Horrible."

Roxanne felt like she'd been punched. She couldn't gather enough breath to make a sound.

"The ambulance came out on the course. Took him to Toledo Hospital."

Roxanne gasped some air. "You think he died?"

Tom crossed his arms, as though he was hugging himself. "I'm scared he might." He shuddered. "I mean, a direct shot to the head."

"Do you know his name? We could call and check."

Tom fished in his pockets. "The guy in the pro shop wrote it down for me." He produced a ragged scrap of scorecard. He moved it up and back to find the right focal length. "Vickery," he said. "Al Vickery."

Roxanne snatched it from him. "You're shitting me?" She looked at the printing and at Tom. "Our neighbor's name is Allan Vickery." She pointed two doors down. "The people who just moved into Jervis' old house. I haven't met them, but Lonnie, next door, did. He goes by Vic. Wife is an "A" name. Anne? Maybe Annette?"

Roxanne looked at the Vickery's house. Trying to focus on the thoughts whirling through her head was like reading the label of a record on a spinning turntable. Tom was a good player. Accidental bad shots happen. Even pros made them. It was too early even for Tom to be drunk, so it was an unpreventable errant shot. But, what were the chances of them being sued? A lot better than the odds of Tom's ball hitting a neighbor, for sure.

"Come on, Tom," Roxanne said, desperate to get into the house. Somehow, it felt like if she and Tom were inside, that would end it. They would be safe. But how? The house couldn't shield them from this. Regardless, her urge to get into the house was overpowering. She wanted more than anything to go indoors. Being outside made her feel vulnerable. "Come on," she said again, taking Tom's hand this time. "Let's call the hospital."

A leaf fluttered past and she thought about catching it, but it was out of reach before she could react. Even if luck existed, it couldn't be that easy to come by, anyway.

~ * ~

Toledo Hospital acknowledged Allan Vickery as a patient, but wouldn't release information on his condition. "Well, at least he's not dead," Roxanne said, hanging up as Tom opened his first beer of the day. The first at home, anyway.

Roxanne took her usual tack. Commenting on his drinking only made him surly. He never missed a day of work, so why ask for trouble? And though she could barely admit it, she kept secret thoughts she hoped weren't disguised wishes. Thoughts she pushed against. If he wanted to drink himself to death, wasn't it up to him? She couldn't stop him. She'd tried. And who knew? There just might be happiness out there for an attractive forty-three year old widow.

She lit a cigarette. That was her poison. Cigarettes helped her keep her figure. Hungry for a snack? Fire up a Marlboro and forget it. She figured, what the hell? If I die, there might be happiness in the afterlife, as well. There were days when death seemed preferable to life with an alcoholic husband.

The rest of that Sunday was unusual. It was odd for Tom to be home, but if he was, ordinarily he would watch golf or football on TV. Not this day. He sat on the couch and stared out the windows, drinking beer. He said he wasn't hungry, but when Roxanne warmed some soup and made a ham and cheese sandwich, he ate most of it. He asked her to phone the hospital again. She wondered why he thought it was her responsibility, but she made the call. No information. When she returned to the living room, Tom was asleep. Or passed out. Roxanne stubbed out her cigarette and poured a glass of wine. Tom would finish the night on the couch, as usual. She turned off the lights.

The bedroom was her clandestine refuge. Curled up on the loveseat with a novel, she'd sip chardonnay and let Rosemary Rogers transport her from her celibate marriage. When Tom wasn't too inebriated to perform, Roxanne was often too angry to have sex, even though she craved it. Rogers pushed romances into a new sphere, with unflinching explicit situations and descriptions. Vicarious romance and sex were better than nothing.

When she tired of reading, Roxanne made certain the curtains were gap-free and undressed, carefully hanging and folding her clothes. She stood in front of her full-length mirror and gave herself an unbiased appraisal. She wasn't movie star material, but she had a nice-looking face. High cheekbones, flawless skin and a narrow turned-up nose. Her eyes were a strong point—piercing blue-green, and she could make them flash. She wore her not-yet-graying hair in a conservative and easy to care for bob. Roxanne was the sweater queen in high school, but the years and a couple pregnancies ending in miscarriage caused her breasts to lose some volume. She turned sideways and straightened her spine. Regardless, her boobs were still impressive. She caught men looking all the time, their eyes drifting when they thought she wouldn't notice. She slapped her hip and winked at the image looking back at her. Yep, not too damned bad for an old gal. She laughed, probably for the first time that day.

Roxanne closed and locked the bathroom door. She was entombed, but in a good way. Tom, and neighbors with broken heads, were sealed outside. The shower massage was the best gift she'd given herself in a long time. It took days of asking, but Tom finally installed it. When the water was as hot as she liked, she stepped into the spray and pulled the glass door closed. The cascading water beat on her shoulders. Roxanne could feel knots of muscle begin to loosen and relax. She soaped up, rinsed and let the spray dance on her skin. With a fifty-gallon tank, the hot water seemed endless.

She lifted the showerhead from its cradle. The long hose allowed her to aim the intense spray anywhere she liked. She turned the dial to a slow rhythmic pulse, let the eddies of water caress her breasts and used her free hand to massage one nipple, then the other. Tom was the first and only boy to touch her breasts. He was the leading ground-gainer on the 1960 Championship Libbey High School football team, and she was so proud when he walked her to classes, her books tucked under his arm the way he carried the ball on Friday nights. The control she exerted over him with her boobs was almost mystical. The promise of an hour in his car with her bra unfastened got her anything she wanted, back then. In addition, the pleasure she experienced when he squeezed her breasts in his big hands, his warm mouth pressed to her nipples, doubled the thrill.

The wet heat and drumming spray transported Roxanne out of Tom's back seat and into the shower, again. She directed the soft needles of coursing water onto her stomach, lingered at her navel, then aimed it downward. The surge tickled her pubic hair. She spread her legs. Though life with Tom was wonderful before he began his affair with alcohol, there was one thing he would never do—Tom Bayer didn't give oral sex. Oh, he enjoyed a blowjob anytime he could get one, and Roxanne enjoyed giving head. But nope, *no way I'm going down on you*, he would say.

She rocked her hips forward and trained the water issuing from the massage head on her clitoris, beginning a rhythm that would take her to her destination. She thrust against the explosion of warm wet tendrils and felt her arousal build. An image of the young man who'd carried her groceries to the car in Jagles parking lot that morning took form. She clasped his shock of brown/blond hair in her hands and gently, but insistently, guided him. Urged him to do what she lusted for. He was eager and persistent. The feeling deep in her core built steadily. Oh, he was so easy to direct. Yes, there. Now faster, turning the knob on the shower massage head.

Roxanne erupted in orgasm, holding the gushing water against her clit until her nerve endings overloaded. The breath expelled from her lungs in a guttural rush of sound that echoed in the ceramic stall, and she went limp, fighting to keep her knees from buckling. She could feel a smile pull into her cheeks. She would sleep well.

~ * ~

Roxanne thought there should be a name for the several seconds of bliss when she first awakened, before life's current problems avalanched onto her consciousness. As soon as her mind cleared that Monday morning, the image of the neighbor in a hospital bed settled in and would not be discharged. Did he die overnight? Would he croak today? What if he was disabled and couldn't work? Would he sue? Did Tom have insurance to protect them? Christ, we could lose the house.

She called the hospital while Tom dressed for work. "Guarded condition," was all the woman would say. Tom had no clue about insurance when Roxanne asked. The idea of a lawsuit seemed like something that flew in at him from empty sky. He shrugged and trudged to his car, leaving Roxanne a helping of worry slathered with resentment for breakfast.

Tom wouldn't hear of Roxanne getting a job. He made a good living working the assembly line at the Jeep plant, and his patented response was, "I work so you don't have to." Of course, she was expected to keep the house tidy and cook, which felt like work. She voluntarily took over the yard. "I mow so you don't have to," she told him, in paraphrased parody.

Roxanne actually enjoyed it. Cleaning the house and maintaining the yard were her stress-relievers, and she kept the place spotless and manicured. After the accident, working outside gave her a good view of the Vickery's house so she could track Mrs. Vickery's comings and goings. When Roxanne was inside, the front porch was like a crow's nest and damned little happened on Bittersweet that she didn't witness. She was desperate to find out how Allan Vickery was recovering, to apologize and to assess the possibility of a lawsuit. But how do you approach the wife of the man your husband nearly killed? Over the years, being married to a man who drank and could get obnoxious deadened Roxanne's desire to socialize, and her former outgoing personality and glib conversational skills faded. Of course, the more Roxanne allowed hours to slip past, the harder it was for her to call Mrs. Vickery.

Tuesday was Tom's bowling night. He claimed he wouldn't be able to concentrate or enjoy himself, but Roxanne convinced him to go, so she was alone. Mrs. Vickery pulled in about six that evening, and after half an hour of her stomach doing flip-flops, Roxanne got the Vickerys' number from their neighbor, Lonnie, and phoned.

"Mrs. Vickery, this is Roxanne Bayer. From two doors down." She endured a pause that seemed interminable. "My husband, Tom … he's the one who hit the tee shot."

"Yes?" Mrs. Vickery said, sounding like she'd been called on while daydreaming in math class. Roxanne hoped it would be easier than this. And why in hell didn't I walk down there, instead of phoning?

"Well, both Tom and I are beside ourselves with worry. How is your husband doing?"

It was like something clicked. Mrs. Vickery's voice gained intensity. "You can just call me Angie, and everyone calls him Vic. May I call you Roxanne?"

"Oh, of course. I'm so sorry. I should have walked down, but I didn't want to intrude, you know, any more than a phone call would. This is no way to meet." She paused. "Even under the best of circumstances."

"Oh, no. Really, it's so nice of you to call." Angie's voice changed again, going up in timbre and beginning to waver as though she was fighting for control. "Vic's still unconscious." Roxanne heard Angie inhale. "The doctors are hopeful. His vitals are good, and he's what the doctor calls 'actively unconscious.' He moves a lot. You know, he isn't just laying there. That's a good sign."

"Well, I know talking about it must be hard, and I don't want to keep you," Roxanne said. She got a prickly feeling around the base of her nose and her eyes began to water. "But if there is anything at all I, or Tom, can do, please ask."

They said goodbye, and Roxanne felt a little hope and relief when she hung up. She wished Tom was home so she could tell him what Angie said. She looked at the mantel clock. Apparently, the beer washed away his reluctance to bowl. Shit, if it was another woman, I could compete. But I don't stand a chance against that whore, Budweiser.

Roxanne's mind was too stirred up for her to focus on her novel. She went into the kitchen and got to work on a casserole. Angie probably had little time or ambition to cook, and she might appreciate a homemade meal. She was taking the Pyrex dish out of the oven when Tom walked in.

"I talked to Angie Vickery tonight," she said. "Vic is still unconscious, but the doctors are hopeful." She watched him closely, waiting for her words to register. She knew it would take a moment. As much as he drank, he managed to function pretty well. The mere fact he made it home with no DUIs or accidents testified to that. Roxanne worried he'd hurt someone. Worried about lawsuits. She decided she would look at the insurance policies tomorrow and see what their coverage actually was. "Did you hear me?" she asked. Tom blinked and turned away. Why won't he look at me when we talk? "I made a casserole. We're taking it down there tomorrow when she gets home from the hospital."

Tom's mind seemed to engage and his head snapped in her direction. He was looking at her now. "What?"

"You heard me. You and I are delivering this casserole tomorrow. We have to get this woman on our side, or they could sue our asses from here to Uranus."

Tom bristled. "You know I don't like that kind of language, Rox."

"Well at least I got your attention," she said, throwing the oven mitt on the counter. Rage coursed through her. She wasn't angry he hit Allan Vickery with a golf ball—that was an accident. She was angry over being ignored, and deserted for alcohol. "And now that I have your attention, maybe a little *oral* sex will keep it." She stepped toward him, putting her face near his. "Fuck you, Tom," she spat. "Hope that was as good for you as it was for me."

She whirled and walked to the bedroom, feeling much better. A soothing rinse of calm eased all her tension, as if she'd just stepped from the shower. A shower was in the offing, after a few hours of reading, now that she could settle and enjoy Rogers' novel.

~ * ~

Tom didn't arrive home the next day until nearly six-thirty. Roxanne was antsy. Angie had rolled in at six, and Roxanne almost went alone, worried Angie might leave again. When Tom walked in, Roxanne wished she had gone earlier. He wasn't as drunk as he could have been, but it was obvious he'd had a few more than a few. His watery red eyes were a giveaway.

"I'm sorry, Rox," were the first words out of his mouth when he walked into the kitchen. "About last night and about everything. I want to go with you."

Roxanne was caught off guard. "I'm sorry, too," she said. She gave him a quick kiss, then opened the refrigerator. "I'm stressed out, big time. I'm so worried about getting sued," she said, lifting the casserole.

"I stopped at the union hall after work and talked to one of the U.A.W. lawyers. He said he thought our homeowner's insurance might cover it." Tom raised his eyebrows. "He also said we better hope they don't sue." He nodded toward the Vickerys' house. "I'm ready."

Oh, he's ready, all right, Roxanne thought. Medicated with a six-pack of sedation. She hoped he wouldn't make a fool of himself.

He didn't. Now and then, there were glimmers of the old Tom Bayer. Roxanne accepted them as she would have welcomed flowers or candy. Just when she thought her husband was lost forever in dark caverns of intoxication, he would step out into the light. It was dusky when they rang the bell at the Vickerys' front door, but the Tom whose memory she still loved surfaced, showing more brightly than Roxanne dared to hope.

Meeting Angie Vickery face to face wasn't as comforting as Roxanne wished, even though Angie was giddy over the fact her husband had regained consciousness. "He sleeps more than he's awake, but he's out of the coma. He even said a few words, and he squeezed my fingers." Angie was a fresh-faced woman with blond hair that tended to frizz where it wasn't controlled with hair clips. Roxanne sensed a cool formal side to Angie's personality her happiness couldn't mask. She accepted the casserole graciously, but didn't seem overly appreciative. Roxanne formed the opinion the dish would be returned quickly, clean, but with the food trash-canned.

Roxanne was doing much of the talking, but Tom surprised her when he gently cupped Angie's elbow, making the startled woman's blue eyes widen. "I'm so incredibly sorry, Mrs. Vickery," Tom said. "I can't get the image out of my mind. I don't think I'll ever be able to play golf again. I mean that." Angie seemed to recover, actually rested her fingers lightly on Tom's forearm and opened her mouth to speak, but Tom went on. "You always think about the possibility of hitting someone, or even getting hit yourself. But I'm telling you, the reality, when it happens ..." He pinched his words off in an obvious attempt to keep from crying, but it didn't work.

Angie seemed moved. She eased her arm from his grasp. "Vic loves golf, and he would hate it if you stopped playing," she said.

As they spoke their goodbyes, Roxanne mentioned she hoped Vic would recover quickly and be back at work soon. She made a reference to financial hardship and Angie brushed it aside. "He's a teacher and he has a load of sick days accumulated. And of course, we have my salary, too."

"And what do you do?" Roxanne asked.

"I'm a legal secretary for Jonathan Fairchild at Fairchild and Associates."

Roxanne felt like someone cut the cable of the elevator she was riding. She forced a smile, said goodnight and they started for their house. "We're fucked," she whispered on the Vickerys' driveway. Tom didn't even jump her about foul language.

~ * ~

Roxanne called Angie several times to check Vic's progress. Eight days after the accident, Angie told her he was being released from the hospital. She sounded upbeat. There were no obvious neurological problems. He was moving slowly, was experiencing vertigo, but the doctor expected that to subside.

As hard as Roxanne tried to befriend her, Angie remained cordial, but distant. Roxanne's fear of a lawsuit persisted. Since she couldn't break through Angie's chilly persona, she was anxious to try her husband. If she and Tom could get on Allan Vickery's good side, the threat of a lawsuit lessened, Roxanne figured. Angie said they could come for a visit the following Sunday. Roxanne tried to schedule it close to noon, so Tom wouldn't drink beforehand, but Angie said the earliest convenient time was two o'clock.

Roxanne rang the doorbell and fussed with her hair. "I'm so goddamn nervous, I can't stand it. We can't fuck this up."

Tom elbowed her gently. "Rox!"

Angie opened the door and greeted them with her makeup-model pretty, but aloof, smile. "It was so nice of you to come down," she said. "Vic's in the living room."

Roxanne took Tom's arm, in case he staggered. Like a hundred-fifteen pound woman can support a two hundred-plus pound man, she thought. She focused on making it look like they were in love.

Vic was sitting dead-center on the couch, wearing a robe. He wouldn't have stood out in a crowd. Sandy brown hair, square jaw and blue eyes; he was nondescript, but nice-looking. It was when he talked or smiled, a warmth Angie could never approach came glowing through. Roxanne knew she would like him the instant he smiled and began to speak. And she knew he blended with Angie the way oil mixed with water.

"Tom, Roxanne, nice to...well, meet you, I guess," Vic said, leaning to extend his hand. "I'm sorry we never got down to introduce ourselves, but at least Tom found a way for us to finally get together."

Tom stepped forward and began to shake Vic's hand like he was trying to wiggle it off. Angie took Roxanne's coat, and moved to Tom's side. "Can I hang up your coat?" she asked. Roxanne was certain it was a ploy, and it worked. Tom let go of Vic's hand and shucked his coat like it was on fire.

Roxanne stepped to Tom's side. "Nice to finally meet you, too. It's great to see you're doing so well. You're feeling okay?"

"Feeling pretty good, thank you." Vic smoothed his robe. Roxanne got the idea he was self-conscious about wearing it in front of strangers. "Still moving slowly. Dizziness now and then. A few headaches, but no seizures, so far."

"Seizures?" Roxanne took Tom's arm and guided him to the nearby loveseat.

"Yeah. According to the doctor, they're fairly common with head injuries, but the chances diminish with time. So far, so good."

"He's really doing terrific," Angie said, back from hanging up their coats. "The hospital would have arranged for a nurse to look in on him, but we decided to go without. He hasn't had any problems yet. He sleeps a lot, but that's just what the doctor ordered. Could I get either of you something to drink?"

Tom's arm shot up like he'd just heard last call. Roxanne pushed it down. "Thanks, but no. We don't want to stay too long and tire this guy out," she said, sensing her people skills were back, which made her smile as she nodded toward Vic. "How soon will it be before you can get back to work?"

"Not sure. The doctor said maybe not until after Thanksgiving, but nothing's written in stone. Have to play it by ear."

"Thanksgiving? My God, what will you do for money?" Even as she said it, she remembered Angie explaining about his accumulated sick time, but she figured it was good to seem concerned, regardless.

Vic smiled. Roxanne decided it looked genuine. "Oh, money's not really an issue. A lot of jobs pay better than teaching, but we have great benefits. I've got a lot of sick days accumulated." He winked. "The checks'll keep on coming."

Tom fell forward, catching Roxanne by surprise. His knees made dull thuds against the carpet. He dropped so quickly, he lost his balance and wound up on all fours. Stranger yet, he stayed in that ridiculously awkward position. "I'm...I'm so gosh-darn sorry," he blubbered. "Jesus! Forgive me!"

Tom's head dangled toward the floor and he sobbed, his chest heaving as though he'd just finished the Boston Marathon. Roxanne grasped one of Tom's arms and managed to get him back on the loveseat.

"Tom. TOM!" Vic said, raising his voice a notch. Tom looked at Vic, his mouth and chin quavering. "It's okay, honest," Vic said. "Look, you shouted. I *heard* you. Hell, your whole foursome was yelling." He grinned. "I just never figured I'd get hit. I mean, how often do you hear somebody howl 'fore' out on the course, and the ball doesn't even come close? Right? I chose to ignore your warning. You did what you were supposed to do. I didn't."

Vic sipped the ginger ale Angie handed him. He started to say something, but Roxanne was sure he changed his mind at the last second. She had a good sense for such things, and he appeared to do the conversational equivalent of shooting across two lanes to hit an expressway exit ramp.

"Ah, look, I'm doing just fine. The doctor says there's no permanent damage. None whatsoever. I know I look a little shaky, right now." He chuckled. "God's truth, I feel a little shaky. But, I have no doubt I'll recover fully and be able to do everything I used to do, the way I've always done it, in just a couple weeks." He turned up his palms like he was checking for rain. "Meanwhile, I'm home on paid vacation. I can paint, catch up on some reading and have dinner waiting for Angie when she comes home from work. What could be better?

"So, there's no blame. Ain't gonna be no lawsuits. You didn't intend to hit me. The only thing that bothers me is you feel so badly. Hey, check this out." He reached into the pocket of his robe, pulled out a golf ball and tossed it to Tom. "Look familiar?"

Tom rolled the ball in his fingers and began to look relaxed for the first time since they'd arrived. "This is the one, huh?"

"Yup. One of the guys I was playing with brought it to the hospital. If it's okay, I'd like to keep it. Kind of like a good luck charm."

"Good luck?" Tom asked.

"Well, yeah. The ball could have killed me, but it didn't. It might be like, ah, what's the word?"

"An amulet?" Angie offered.

"That's it. An amulet. Or talisman, kind of. Who knows? I'll carry this ball in my bag from now on, and it might even make me a better player." He smiled.

"Sure, you can keep it." Tom half-stood to hand the ball back. "The least I can do."

"We really should be going," Roxanne said, getting to her feet and grasping Tom's arm to keep him from sitting back down. She locked on Vic's eyes and smiled. "I, we enjoyed meeting you, Vic. I'm really happy you're doing so well."

Vic said something, but Roxanne didn't hear him. She was staring into his eyes, and his didn't waver. She felt a flicker. It was a moment in time when she felt a change, but had no idea what it was. The earth didn't tilt. Nothing was different. But suddenly, nothing was the same.

She and Tom walked down the Vickerys' driveway, arm in arm. For the first time in a long time, Roxanne wasn't worried about a lawsuit. She wasn't worried about anything. And she couldn't wait for whatever was next. Leaves were falling, and watching all that fluttering luck lifted her spirits.

~ * ~

Roxanne's hand shook when she dialed Vic's number the next morning. She barely managed to keep her voice from cracking because she was so nervous. "Hello, Vic? This is Roxanne Bayer."

There was a long pause. If he was trying to hide his surprise, it didn't work. "Oh, Roxanne. Hi...how're you?"

"Great! I didn't wake you or anything?"

"Oh, no. In fact, I was just sitting down to paint."

"That's right! You said you get to stay home and paint. What are you working on?"

"A landscape. Hard to describe. The central image is a pumpkin smashed on a country road."

"Sounds neat. I'd like to see it sometime." She paused. "I called because I've got a few errands to run. You're kind of a shut-in right now. Can I pick anything up for you? Anything at all?"

"Gee, it's nice of you to offer. I can't...no, I can't think of a thing."

"Do you get the morning paper?"

"No. We used to, but we cancelled. Never had time to read it before work."

"Well, if it's okay, I'll bring ours down. There's a story on Jack Nicklaus Tom thought you'd like." The truth was Roxanne pointed it out to Tom, but he never read it.

"Oh, gosh, I hate for you to go to the trouble."

"No trouble. I'm on my way out the door to pick up some things. Have to drive right past your house, anyway. See you in a few."

Roxanne adjusted her sweater and checked her makeup in the hall mirror. Yep, not too bad, she thought, smiling at her image. There just may be some happiness for a good-looking older gal, but the clock was ticking. She carried Mofus to her Catalina, eased him onto the seat and fired the engine. After backing down the driveway, she drove the short distance to the Vickerys'. Mofus curled up and settled. He loved to ride, but he went right to sleep anytime the car was parked.

She walked to the door and rang the bell. Almost a minute passed before Vic opened it.

"Hi, Roxanne," he said. He stepped out onto the front porch and turned his face to the morning sky. "Man, that sun feels great. I haven't been out much. Miss it."

"Well, hope you can get out more before winter hits. Not many days like this left."

The two of them stood, smiling at each other.

"Uh, so that's the paper?" Vic finally said, pointing with his chin.

Roxanne forgot the paper was why she stopped, and she tried to cover her embarrassment. "Oh, yeah," she said, handing it to him. "The article on Nicklaus. Tom really liked it. He used to be an Arnold Palmer fan."

"Who wasn't?" Vic said, folding the paper in half. "They didn't call it 'Arnie's Army' for nothing. Poor guy's over fifty now. Everybody's looking for a new young hero. Heck, Nicklaus is no spring chicken, forty or thereabouts."

Roxanne exploded in laughter. "Careful now, sonny," she said, trying for a playfully reproving tone. She was in full-tilt flirt, and it felt wonderful. She was good at it when she was in high school and it came back easily. "You're talking to a gal who's pushing forty-four. Hope I have a few good years left in this old bod."

Vic's face reddened. "I meant for an athlete, you know. He's getting older. You, you look terrific." He let his gaze drift the length of her body. When he looked into her eyes, she made certain he saw she'd noticed.

"Compliments like that will get you anywhere," she said, waited a beat, then gave him a gentle push on the shoulder, to defuse the obvious come-on. "So, your pumpkin painting is going well?"

"Yeah. I should have it finished later today."

"You paint upstairs, do you?" she asked.

"Yes, in that room," he said, leaning to point out the studio's window on the gable over the garage. Roxanne didn't step back and their faces were very close together.

"You'll have to show me sometime. I'd love to see some of your work." She raised an eyebrow. "And your studio."

"That's one of mine right there," Vic said, stepping back, holding the storm door open.

Roxanne leaned in next to him to look at the painting hanging above the first flight of stairs.

"Oh, God. That's beautiful. I noticed it yesterday when Tom and I came down. I love the way the sun shines on the old farmhouse with the dark purplish sky behind. I can just feel the storm coming, like that big one last August. The sky was like that then. Real dark clouds, but the sun still bright. The contrast..." She looked up at him. "You're very good. I used to do the paint-by-number kind when I was a kid. Craft Master, I think they were called."

Vic smiled and jerked his thumb in the painting's direction. "That one's a paint-by-number, but I make up the numbers."

Roxanne shook her head. "Will we know you're recovered if your jokes get funnier?"

"I'll get better, but my jokes won't." He laughed. "It was really nice of you to go to the trouble to stop with the paper."

"I will again tomorrow," she said, turning to walk to her car. She was wearing a pair of snug-fitting corduroys, and over her shoulder she saw Vic's eyes cruising her, hair to heels.

"Oh, that's okay," he said. "Maybe I'll call and have it delivered, since I'll be home for a while."

"Do that and I'll lose my only customer. Tom doesn't let me work. This paper route's the first job I've had in years."

Roxanne and Vic joined in laughter. She believed they would laugh together again. She was still laughing when she got to her car. She waved at Vic and opened the door.

A falling leaf landed on her shoulder and, without thinking, she brushed it off. What did I do? Then it occurred to her, she didn't catch the leaf. It caught her. And she didn't believe in luck, anyway. She believed in choices. She lived with her choice. But maybe, just maybe, she could alter its terms.

CLICKING

Jack Traggor was whipped when he pulled his Toyota onto the gravel parking spot next to his rented mobile home.

Two runs the night before. He'd just fallen asleep in the bedroom that the funeral home provided when he got the first call. A nineteen-year old kid lost control of his crotch rocket and hit a tree. Jack picked the body up at Patrick General. He could smell the alcohol even before he unzipped the bag. He had to check the ID number on the boy's ankle tag, but he would have looked anyway. Morbid curiosity. Humans are wired that way. The kid was virtually unmarked and looked like he was sleeping. The tech at Pat Gen said his neck snapped. He wore a full-face helmet, so it would be an easy prep for Preston, the mortician. No restoration.

The other pickup was a different story, a forty-three year old woman whose boyfriend shot her in the face. Jack had to pick her up at the scene, so unlike a hospital removal where there were staff members to assist, Jack had to call Fredo, the daytime removal guy, to meet him at the scene and assist. As often happens, someone called for pickup long before the site investigation concluded. Hell, the medical examiner wasn't even there yet, and Jack and Fredo wasted nearly two hours, standing around. Smoking. God, Jack wanted so badly to quit, but sometimes smoking was all he had. Cigarettes. Buddies of the bored.

When the M.E. finally arrived and declared, Jack and Fredo covered their suits and ties in HAZMAT coveralls, gloves and masks, and moved inside with the body bag and gurney. The woman was covered with a plastic sheet, and when they pulled it aside, Jack confronted another fascinatingly repulsive sight. Most of the left side of the woman's face was

92

a good five feet away, under the bed. She was naked except for panties, her pudgy body adorned with tattoos and piercings. She looked like a broken doll, smashed in a fit of rage. Jack tried to imagine, as he often did, what series of events propelled this human from a tiny newborn to her current state of wreckage in a little over four decades. He wondered if even she could have explained.

Jack and Fredo, using well-practiced moves and non-verbal communication, gentled her body into the open bag. Too much movement or pressure could cause purging. Fluids weren't of much concern because of their protective clothing, but if the torso purged gasses, it would take at least one cigarette to neutralize the memory of the smell. Before they zipped her in, Fredo caught Jack's eye and used the crown of his forehead to point out the piece of face. Since Jack was the first-caller on duty, he accepted it was his responsibility. He was surprised at how much the piece weighed. At first, it felt like it might be stuck to the floor, but it was just unexpected heft that made it difficult to lift. He quickly, but carefully, laid it in the bag near her head, attached her ankle tag and zipped the bag closed.

The morning sun heated the Toyota's cabin and Jack dropped out of his reverie. He climbed out of the aging car, shoved the door closed and walked up the rickety wooden steps. Cox barked before Jack could shove the key in the lock. Christ, he'd have to walk her right away, and all he wanted was to peel off his suit, shower again and fall into bed.

"Hey, Coxxy, how's it going?" Jack said, stooping to pet the small brown dachshund. He glanced around. "You behave yourself last night?"

The little dog rolled on her side and chuffed high-pitched squeals while Jack rubbed the pup's stomach. From what he could tell, there were no accidents—all the more reason he should get Cox outside right away. He took the leash and a poop-bag from a small closet by the door, hooked Cox up and let her lead him outside. The little pup pulled hard, but she wasn't interested in going far. Around the trailer to the tree line was plenty enough. Lots of steps with those short legs, Jack decided. With her stiff little tail sticking straight up, Cox looked almost like a radio-control toy. A squat to take a leak, another to poop and she was ready to head back into the air-conditioning. Jack kept a patter going, as though Cox understood or cared, while he picked up her warm issue with a plastic bag. Jack didn't want the responsibility of a dog, especially in such a small trailer. He only took her because his former wife threatened the pound. "She's yours or she's gone," Sarah said. Thing is, she was the one who pressed for a dog to begin with, and Jack tried to talk her out of it. He was fairly certain she was conning him and would have kept Cox if Jack didn't take her. Regardless, he'd learned early on never to call Sarah's bluff. Besides, Cox deserved better than life with Sarah.

Just as they rounded the corner of the trailer, a full-size Ford four-door pulling a U-Haul rolled up to the mobile home next door. Jack almost rented that one, but it was a bit nicer and they wanted twenty more a week for it. A woman who looked to be in her late twenties or early thirties got out, turned and stooped to look back into the passenger compartment and said, "You stay in the car, Scotty. You hear me? I'll be right back."

When she noticed Jack, she waved half-heartedly, as though she decided against it after she began, and smiled. She had an attractive face and hair that hung in a sweep of dark ringlets. She was built a lot like the woman Jack picked off the floor earlier, a little chubby, but pleasingly so. Built for comfort, not speed, Jack thought. Jeans and a flowered blouse. Sandals. She'd take a few steps toward the trailer, then look over her shoulder, apparently to make sure Scotty stayed in the car. Jack couldn't see who or what Scotty was.

The woman just reached the top of the steps when a full-grown man in jeans and a white tee-shirt somersaulted out of the driver's door opening and rolled to a sitting position, laughing so hard, he was hiccupping. He rolled again, this time onto his hands and knees and began to get up. Although he appeared to be about the woman's age, his movements, his voice and his demeanor reminded Jack of a very young child—maybe five or six years old.

The woman shrieked, charged down the steps and grabbed the man-child's arm. "Oh, Scotty," she said, "why won't you listen to me and behave?"

Jack stood immobile, watching. He didn't know what to do. Should he offer to help? Would his approach only upset the guy?

Cox apparently decided she didn't care, and started pulling in the direction of the air conditioning on the other side of the trailer door. Jack saw this as an opportunity to offer help without seeming pushy or threatening.

"Hi," he said, trying to make it appear as though Cox was pulling him away, which probably looked pretty silly, he decided. "Can I give you a hand?"

The woman wheeled in Jack's direction, waving her arms like she was stopping traffic. "Oh, no thank you. Really. Scotty and I can handle this. We've been driving a while and he's just a little wound up, but we'll be fine."

Her facial expression didn't match the confidence in her voice, but Jack was beat and wanted to sleep. He nodded, dropped the little bag of poop in the trash on his porch and followed Cox inside. The pup had water and kibble, so Jack showered, cranked up the air and hit the sheets. Sleeping in temperatures cool enough for a blanket in the dead of summer was one luxury he allowed himself in his otherwise downsized life.

~ * ~

Jack ordinarily got his night's sleep at the funeral home and, at most, caught a fast nap before his next shift began at 11:00 PM. When he rolled over and focused on his bedside clock, he saw it was late afternoon. Shit. Now I'll be out of sync for a couple days.

He pulled on some shorts and a tee-shirt, slipped into some flip-flops and grabbed a cigarette. He never smoked in the trailer, an attempt to cut down. Additionally, he'd seen numerous stories of people who couldn't escape trailer fires. He used to look down on trailer dwellers and never imagined at age forty-two, he'd be living in one. It helped for him to view his situation as temporary, and he wanted to make certain he survived this unfortunate phase.

It was cloudy, warm and humid, but without the direct sun, it was tolerable. Each rental trailer had a picnic table, and Jack's was positioned under a large tree out front. He sat on the table, put his feet on the seat facing the road and lit up, inhaling while he savored the quiet. Most of the residents in this park were elderly. Even the younger ones were nothing like what Jack saw on *Cops*; drunken scrappers and low-lifes. He felt badly about classifying everyone who lived in a trailer that way in the past, based on what he saw on TV.

Jack heard footsteps, and anxiety tightened his shoulder muscles like a jolt of electricity when the new woman neighbor and Scotty rounded the street corner. The man/boy was much more controlled now, and though Jack's tension eased, it was impossible for him to tear his eyes from the guy. Scotty was every bit of six feet tall and built like a fullback. But he walked like a very young child, sometimes skipping and hopping between steps. Now and then he would start to jog-run, until the woman called him back. He followed her commands, but not immediately, reminding Jack of the way Cox obeyed only after nosing around long enough to assert it was her choice.

When the woman noticed Jack sitting on the table, she took Scotty's arm and led him in Jack's direction. "Hello," she said. Her smile made her freckled nose wrinkle. "We never got a chance to talk, before. I'm Dustyanne Krolac, and this is my brother, Scotty." She offered a handshake and her grip was firm.

"I'm Jack Traggor," he said, looking into her magnetic green eyes. He noticed she wore no makeup, but she didn't need any. "It's nice to meet you both," he added, looking at Scotty.

"Scotty, are you going to shake Mr. Traggor's hand?" she said, placing her hand on Scotty's shoulder.

He twisted away, but held his hand out. When Jack took it, Scotty didn't grip Jack's hand and held his arm rigid, like a mannequin.

"Scotty was wounded in Afghanistan," she said to Jack, then turned to Scotty. "Weren't you, Scotty?"

"No not," he said, whining the words like a very young child. Then he walked a few steps, sat on the grass and began using a twig to dig some pebbles out of a patch of dry soil.

"He really doesn't remember," Dustyanne whispered. "An IED took out the Humvee he was driving." She pulled a pack of cigarettes from her hip pocket and Jack lit the one she held to her lips. "His physical injuries weren't serious, really, but he suffered a severe closed-head wound," she said, turning to watch Scotty play in the dirt.

"So, it's organic damage, or psychological? I mean, I hope I'm not prying," Jack added quickly, before Dustyanne could answer.

She batted away his concern with a graceful wave of her hand. "Not at all. Do you work in a hospital?"

Jack took a final drag, rolled his cigarette between his thumb and forefinger, then crushed out the hot ash when it hit the ground. "Not by a long shot," he said, walking to the trash can. "I sold high-end sports cars until the boss' daughter did me a favor and divorced me." He dropped the eviscerated butt in the can and started back. "So now I work the nightshift, picking up bodies for a funeral home." Dustyanne's expression made him chuckle. "A temporary gig, I hope, but the job taught me more about wounds and injuries than I ever hoped to know."

"Yeah, the way you asked, it made you sound like some kind of medical guy," Dustyanne said. "But to answer your question, they don't really know what it is. All they know is it's real, and he's on ninety percent disability from the military, plenty for us to live on. We moved here to be closer to the VA hospital. He goes every weekday. Rehab and therapy. It's almost like daycare. Our parents are dead, so I'm his full-time caregiver, when he's not at the hospital." She puffed some air through her lips. "*My* new gig."

"I hope it turns out to be temporary, too."

"That would be nice. I'd like to get a job, but I can't until we know more about how Scotty will do. No way to tell, right now." Her voice trailed off.

There was a long silence, protracted enough that Jack started fishing for another cigarette until he remembered his pack was in the trailer.

"I mean, sometimes he … he just all of a sudden is his old self," Dustyanne said. "I call it clicking. He just … clicks in, sort of. You can see it in his eyes. His voice goes back to normal. His … "

"Mannerisms?" Jack offered.

"I guess. The way he moves and even thinks. It all comes back, but only for a few seconds. Sometimes minutes." She shook her head and frowned. "It's just so strange. He was a hell of a Marine."

Jack looked at Scotty, still happily digging away with biceps the size of Jack's calves and a smile on his five o'clock-shadowed face. Then, without moving his head, Jack shifted his gaze to Dustyanne, who was also watching Scotty.

More than just pretty, she was desirable. He imagined how she would feel in his arms. How her hair would feel in his hands. The soft crush of her lips. And she was going to be alone all day because Scotty would be at the VA. Everything clicked, as Dustyanne just said. Jack was suddenly certain he would get something going with her, unless she had a boyfriend. Maybe even if she did. Sometimes he just knew something would happen before it did, and this was one of those times.

Jack was older. Probably smarter. He knew how to treat a woman. How to compliment. How to ask a question, then shut up and listen. Hold doors. He'd dated a few women since his divorce, but up-class women were put off by a guy living in a trailer, even if it was temporary. Might as well tell them you're living with your parents. But Dustyanne lived in a trailer herself, right next door. Jack was certain a trailer and a worn Toyota wouldn't put her off.

"Come on, sweetie," Dustyanne said, holding her hand out to Scotty. "By the time you get a shower and change clothes, it will be time to go to McDonald's for supper."

"Donald's," Scotty shouted, leaped to his feet and began to dance around. "Donald's Donald's," he riffed as Dustyanne grabbed his arm to still him while she brushed dirt from the knees of his jeans.

"Yes," she told him. "Tomorrow, I'll get to the store, but tonight, you eat like a king." She winked at Jack and laughed. "Let's go," she said, turning to walk to their trailer.

Jack watched Dustyanne begin her languid stroll, ample hips gently rolling as she crossed the stone drive. When Jack glanced at Scotty, he found himself locked in the kind of look he'd expect to see from eyes fixing on him through a gun sight. Scotty stood erect, his shoulders thrust back while his eyes burned into Jack's. Dustyanne was still walking, her hand held out behind her like a relay runner, no doubt expecting Scotty to take it. Just as she began to turn her head toward them, Scotty's eyes tore free of Jack's and his expression went happy child again. He charged toward Dustyanne and the two of them disappeared into their trailer.

Jack stood, replaying the baleful glare Scotty leveled at him. He spent several hours that evening nursing a bourbon and wondering if he witnessed the click Dustyanne mentioned. Was that it? Did Scotty click into a thirty-something Marine for a moment? He sure as hell seemed to morph from a child. And why such a sinister look? All Jack was doing was standing there, looking at Scotty and Dustyanne. Scotty knew who Jack was, or did all that go out the window when he clicked? Jack finally put on his suit and tie and went in to work, pondering unanswerable questions.

It was a great shift, that night. Not one call. Jack watched Action News at 11 and was heartened when there were no reported accidents or shootings. Preston, the embalmer, asked Jack to help dress the crotch-rocket kid, a job that definitely went better with two sets of hands and arms. The family wish was for the boy to be dressed in riding leathers, which turned out to be more challenging than a sport coat and tie. Jack helped Preston move the boy into a showing room once he was casketed. "G'night, Preston," Jack said, when the coffin was in position, and continued upstairs to his small, comfortable bedroom. The image of Scotty's malevolent glare crossed his mind, but it wasn't enough to delay Jack's tumble into dreamless slumber.

~ * ~

The next morning, Jack couldn't wait to get home. He usually hung out to make certain no one needed help moving flower arrangements or dressing a body, but he was eager to see if he could spend some time with Dustyanne. He pushed the little Toyota a bit more than usual and it smoked like a mosquito fogger on the beltway. Gotta get a better car, he thought as he pulled into his spot on the stones outside his trailer.

Dustyanne stepped out of her place just as Jack got out of his car. "Hey, neighbor," he called over.

"Well, good morning," she said, smiling and shaking a cigarette from its pack. "How's Jack the body snatcher today?" She lit her smoke, took a drag and leaned against the railing of the small deck that served as a front porch.

Man, I'd love to snatch her body, Jack thought. He pulled out one of his own cigarettes and walked across the stone drive. "No snatches last night. Just Jack the sleeper."

He sat on her steps and they talked. Her body language told him she was comfortable with him there. She'd already dropped Scotty off at the VA hospital for the day, so she had no plans, she said. Jack was on his game. Witty. It was easy to make her laugh, and it was fun to banter and joke with her. After an hour or so, Cox began to bark.

"I better get her outside," Jack said, groaning as he got to his feet. "I could use a walk myself. Want to come along?"

She did. They walked Cox around the trailer park and Jack filled her in on all the local gossip he knew. She didn't have to pick Scotty up until 4PM, so they ate lunch at McDonald's and Dustyanne went car shopping with him. Jack wasn't actually ready to buy. He was still a bit unsteady, financially, but it was a great excuse to be with her and to learn more about her. He revealed things about himself, too. "I used to drive a Dodge Viper, back in another life," he told her, as they walked up to his Corolla. "You wouldn't have liked the noise." He liked her giggle.

The week passed quickly. The next day, they picnicked in a park. The day after that, Jack rented a romantic comedy and they watched it on Dustyanne's flat screen. There were several times when Jack could have kissed her. Times when she seemed to expect him to. Jack played it cagey. Too slow was better than too fast. It started as lust, but Jack was growing to like Dustyanne. No missteps. He didn't want to screw this up.

As they stood at her door when Jack was leaving, she moved in close to him, her face hovering mere inches from his. "Tomorrow's Saturday and Scotty doesn't go to VA. I'd like to take him to the beach," she said. She looked into Jack's eyes and took a breath. "Would you want to come along? Would you have a problem being with Scotty in public?"

Scotty in public. It was hard not to watch a child piloting a full-grown man's body. But, for that matter, Dustyanne in a bathing suit would be an attention-getter, as well. Jack smiled. "I'm honored that you asked." He kissed Dustyanne on the forehead. "What time are we leaving?"

~ * ~

The day was close to perfect. A nice onshore breeze mitigated the heat. There was a good-sized crowd of beach-goers, but everyone was able to find ample space. Jack stopped on his way to work the night before and bought a Frisbee. It took a bit of training, but Scotty was soon flinging it with delighted authority. He also loved playing in the surf, diving into waves and shooting skyward like a happy dolphin before the next roller arrived. "He's fine alone," Dustyanne said to Jack, while they lay together on beach blankets as Scotty played in the whitewater. "Not like a real kid. We don't have to worry about him drowning or anything."

Still, Jack kept a close eye on Scotty, when he wasn't tossing the Frisbee, building sand castles or tussling in the sand with him. After a few hours, Jack felt a bond forming. Scotty seemed to like him and accept him as a friend. Jack careened between caretaker and sage, never quite certain about how much of either to offer. Regardless, the day at the beach was proving to be more fun than Jack dared to hope, and he knew it was cementing his relationship with Dustyanne, who seemed to glory in Jack's easy manner with her brother.

Jack noticed people watching Scotty, from time to time. He saw some of them trade smiles, or even occasional laughter, but always at long-range, and never anything that pissed Jack off. Scotty was, after all, a strange amalgam of man and child.

The closest thing to an incident occurred when a teenage boy, probably sixteen or seventeen years old, walked up to Jack while he was standing at the water's edge, watching Scotty play in the surge.

"What's his deal?" the kid asked.

Jack's first impulse was to bristle, but one look at the boy's inquisitive expression rerouted that urge.

"He was a Marine," Jack said. "Head wound in Afghanistan. IED got him."

"I hate that fuckin' war," the boy said after a pause. He patted Jack on the shoulder. "I'm sorry about your friend," he added, then walked back to where his family was gathered.

Later, Jack and Scotty sat together on the blankets. Dustyanne had gone for a walk, and Scotty was actually worn out, preferring to stay behind. He would lie for a while, then sit up and watch people pass by. It was the quietest time Jack ever spent with Scotty.

"When do we go, Jack-man?" Scotty asked. Jack-man was what

Scotty had been calling him for the last hour or so.

"Your sister will be back soon, and then we'll hit McDonald's," Jack said, looking down the beach where she disappeared earlier.

"Donald's Donald's Donald's," Scotty babbled happily.

Jack looked down the beach and spotted Dustyanne. He loved to watch her walk. She had a rhythmic gait that made all the parts of her body complement each other as they rolled and swayed. He felt a wonderful heat inside and savored it all the more because it wasn't just lust. He honestly liked this woman, and her brother, too.

Suddenly, it felt like Jack's wrist was caught in the jaws of a shark. He turned to look and, once again, was locked into the gun-sight eyes of an infantryman. The eyes burned like lasers, and the heat felt like it might sear the back of Jack's skull. "Dusty is my wife," Scotty growled. He clamped his hand even more tightly on Jack's wrist. His reflex was to pull away, but he truly feared it might snap, or Scotty might snap it, if he did. Then, Jack could see Scotty's eyes soften. The child was back. The little boy. He let go of Jack's arm and started to laugh.

Jack rubbed and flexed his wrist. The pain ebbed, and there didn't appear to be any damage. He looked at Scotty. The fucking irony. An IED turned him into the equivalent of an explosive device—Jack couldn't tell when Scotty would detonate. And then there was the marriage thing. Was Scotty merely delusional?

"Frisbee, Jack-man. Will you play Frisbee?" Scotty said, just as Dustyanne walked up.

"We're going to be leaving, honey," Dustyanne said. "You take one last dip before we go."

"Dip, Jack-man? Swim with me?" Scotty said, dancing like the sand was hot on his soles.

"Jack's suit is all dry, Scotty," Dustyanne said. "He doesn't want to get it wet again." She looked at her watch. "You have five minutes, then we're leaving."

"Donald's Donald's Donald's," Scotty chanted. He picked up the Frisbee and ran for the ocean.

Jack watched Scotty run into the water, then toss the Frisbee up into the air over the surf. The onshore breeze caught it and blew it back in his direction. He missed his catch, but tossed it up again and waited for its return.

"What's wrong?" Dustyanne asked Jack.

Jack turned and gave her a look. "Wrong?"

"Something's wrong. You look different. Your face." She wagged her head. "What?"

Jack huffed a breath. "Scotty clicked. Just before you walked up."

Dustyanne smiled. "You saw it? You saw him click?"

"He told me you're his wife."

Her face fell. She blinked her eyes, reached into her beach bag and got a cigarette. She lit it and exhaled, turned and leveled a stare that almost reminded Jack of the one Scotty shot at him. She licked her lips, then turned toward where Scotty played in the surf, throwing the Frisbee and trying to catch it. Missing every time.

"I told you he's my brother," she finally said, still looking away. "That's all."

Jack turned to watch Scotty. He threw the Frisbee up another time, missed the catch again and picked the saucer out of the surf. He started toward where Jack and Dustyanne sat.

Dustyanne got up, brushed sand from her bottom and began rooting through her beach bag. "We better head for McDonald's."

Jack sat motionlessly, his focus passing Scotty until it fell upon the horizon. The water was especially dark blue where it cut a sharp straight line against the bright sky. He thought about how nice it would be to just sit and watch the sky darken and eventually match the water's shade. Sit and listen to the waves roil against the beach. Sit and wonder.

"Did you hear me?" Dustyanne asked, pulling her slacks up over her bikini bottoms.

"I did," Jack murmured. "Donald's Donald's Donald's."

INTERVIEW

You lived in a breathtaking McMansion with your wife. You loved her so much. You both made great money. Everything was better than you realized at the time, which is often the way of things. She had early meetings that Saturday and couldn't interview the housecleaner, so she entrusted the job to you. Laughed about you blowing the assignment, a joke because you knew she believed in you and your judgment, which helped you to believe in yourself. Someone to dust and vacuum. Clean the bathrooms. The kitchen. Chores you both wanted to eliminate to free up time, which was more valuable than money, back then. If she's a good fit, show her where the supplies are and how the security system works.

The girl drove a little foreign piece. Needed a muffler. Her exhaust smoke arrived before she did, so it may have needed a valve job, too. She had a rhythmic roll to her hips. You were tuning your classic car and she walked up and said it was beautiful. You figured she was schmoozing, but when she caressed the fender, you sensed she savored the feel of the polished steel.

You liked her, right off. Neatly typed resume with three references. I'm in nursing school and need money for tuition and books. Looking for other clients, if you know anyone. At that moment, the rain clouds made good on their threat. You took her inside through the garage. I live here with my wife. She's away. Took the girl to where the brooms and mops were stored. She'd never seen a built-in vacuum and examined it as thoroughly as she did your muscle car. Just plug the hose into the ports on the wall. Oh, and I'll show you how the alarm works. When you handed her the key, you had to tilt your head up slightly to make eye contact. Irises containing almost too many golden flecks to remain so richly brown. She blinked in what seemed like slow motion.

What year were you born? For the security system you explained, laughing, and she joined in. You entered the sequence on the keypad. 1-9-7-0. You're three years younger than my Chevelle, you joked, prompting a look as though you'd guessed her weight. She pecked the digits on the keypad and followed you out the front door. Forty-five seconds until it'll be armed, then we'll go back in, the way you will when you arrive. While you waited, an October gust dislodged rainwater from the canopy of oak leaves above, showering you both. You ducked under the overhang and she followed your move. Suddenly, you and the nineteen-year-old were within inches of each other. Her skin glowed in the overcast. You watched a droplet run from the outer edge of her slender eyebrow and down her cheek. Her eyes widened for a reason you'll never know. You looked at her lips, the most delicate hue of lavender. Her upper-right front tooth was noticeably grayer than the others. You imagined tonguing it, mid-kiss. She seemed to move her face toward yours, but you weren't certain. Her lips appeared poised for a kiss. Was she waiting? Did she teeter on the same precipice you straddled? Your mind pin-wheeled.

The memory of the woman you loved ferociously ended the whirling. The slippery crush of lips didn't happen. But, that instant when your faces appeared to be on converging orbits and her eyes widened—that sliver of your life—haunts you, even outlasting the marriage that put an end to any possibility of events cascading, that day.

She was a diligent worker, but her employment concluded when she graduated from nursing school. All these years later, on nights like this one, your mind often lingers in that lost autumn day and you wonder, does hers? You strain to see the face of every nurse who passes your hospice room.

RED SKY

Kit stood in front of the sofa, bouncing a tennis ball on his racket. He caught the ball first on the strings, twisted the racket a quarter turn to bounce it off the frame, and another quarter turn to the strings again. It didn't take concentration. He did this all the time while he instructed students at the club or decided which serve would catch an opponent off-guard.

The winter light coming through the windows was gray-blue, and with sunrise still distant, there wasn't enough illumination to lift the ball, or anything else in the living room, out of the gray scale. The eye has two types of receptors, rods and cones, Kit remembered from college biology. Rods image in black and white, and work in any available light. Cones handle color, but require a certain level of illumination to function. Kit passed biology with a C. He earned an A from his lab partner, Jayne.

He looked through the front window, still bouncing the ball. His vision crossed the yard, past Celeste's snow-covered tricycle and the road, to the horizon bookending the fallow fields and empty trees. A blush of sunrise stained the clouds.

Kit began to drop the ball to the floor between bounces. Bounce. Drop on the right side of the gun between his feet. Catch. Bounce. Drop on the left side. Catch. Bounce. He tried to drop the ball as close to the small .38 revolver as he could. Catch. Bounce. Drop.

Kit wondered why he even pulled the gun from its hiding place, wedged between the mattress and the headboard. Oh, he played with the suicide thing. Held the gun to his head, imagining a bullet ripping through his brain. Pictured the cherry pie filling-like wall-splatter he saw in movies.

106

Opened his mouth and slid the short barrel past his teeth until the muzzle poked the roof of his mouth. Again, images of his head erupting in a Vesuvius of brain and bone and blood. His finger was never on the trigger. His mother's voice played in his head, sing-songing her favorite phrase. "Never cut your nose off to spite your face." Kit smiled. Never blow your brains out to spite your wife. Besides, he had his little girl, Celeste, to live for. He would no longer be a husband, but he would always be Celeste's daddy. He pulled the gun from his mouth and let the hand holding it plunge toward the floor, dangling. Kit couldn't imagine ever being happy again, but he'd managed to settle into a kind of "new okay" that was good enough.

Today, Jayne was coming for her stuff, including the gun. She bought it because of its light weight and stopping power. Easy for a woman to handle. "The best choice for protection," the salesman lectured, "is a shotgun. Fill the hallway with buckshot, and no worries about hitting someone next door." There was no "next door." Not for a quarter mile, one of the reasons Jayne wanted a gun. "Now with Celeste," she said, "it's important that I have protection at night when you're at the club." The recoil when she pulled the trigger of a twenty-gauge shotgun solidified her decision. She favored the Rossi .38.

Kit never believed there would be an intruder. But if there was, Kit would have bet his left lung Jayne would use the gun. She was spunky. A shade over sixty inches of high-output womanpower. Played tennis on a full scholarship. She was the sole woman Kit ever played against who tested him on the court. She was lean and strong. She raced to the ball no matter where he hit it, and she returned it as hard or harder. The two of them won the Toledo city championship their first time out. Kit remembered how his and Jayne's parents sat on either side of Celeste, cheering them on while Celeste slept through the courtside din, her cheeky little face banked awkwardly toward the sky, sporting red-framed sunglasses.

Ironically, an intruder did materialize, but Jayne didn't shoot. She welcomed him.

An unlikely December fly lumbered past Kit's head. He performed a half-hearted wave of his hand to shoo it away and watched as the fly landed above the shelves holding his tennis citations and trophies. He could place a shot, and the old farmhouse's ten-foot ceiling allowed an overhead forehand. The ball slammed the wall and shot back in his direction, bouncing once before he caught it. The fly was a dark smudge in the half-light. Kit looked out at the horizon. Sunlight seared the clouds to a crimson turn. Red sky at morning, sailor take warning, Kit remembered.

He looked back at the smashed fly, but his attention drifted to the shelves of trophies. He scrutinized the awards, but soon centered on the crystal trophy Jane and he were awarded for the Toledo Mixed Doubles Championship last August. Jayne had to have already met her online lover, back then, while pledged to stay-at-home-mom status. Were they still merely talking, or had they done the face to face? Pelvis to pelvis? Kit didn't want to know. He tossed the ball and slammed another overhead. The crystal chalice exploded against the wall. Kit smiled. No other trophy was damaged or destroyed.

What else? His Interclub Instructor of the Year award? He won honors while being away too many nights as Jayne surfed websites and chat rooms for the lonely. Kit provided for his family and Jayne sought companionship. The intruder entered and she banged him, but not with her Rossi. Kit tossed the ball once more, and rifled it at his target. The glass shattered and the framed citation crashed to the floor.

Three perfect serves. The fly. The mixed dubs trophy. The Interclub Instructor award. The score was forty/love, and Kit needed one more ace to win. He walked room to room, stalking a target for his victory. What would make the perfect opponent for his match point? He passed their bedroom. No, his bedroom. Weeks since she was there. Weeks since he came home to the note on the kitchen table. *Sorry to let you know like this. Celeste and I are at my parents'. Can't stand the loneliness.* No mention of the intruder, though. Kit didn't have to poke around much. Everyone knew before Kit found out, it seemed.

Kit prowled the house. The final victim had to be something Jayne would see as meaningful. She wouldn't notice the bug in her rush to claim the items on the list their lawyers negotiated. His instructor's award would catch her by surprise, he figured. She may or may not pick up on the significance of his smashing it. The crystal chalice would definitely piss her off. She loved the prize, even though it represented something they accomplished together. There was no together anymore, but she loved the delicate glasswork. He would hear about it. "The chalice was half mine, and you destroyed it," she'd yelp. His cheeks pinched into a smile as he solidified his rejoinder: "Our family was half mine, too."

He glowered at the flat-screen she bought him for his birthday. Probably chosen to keep the ruse of their loving relationship alive while she fucked her lover. Kit wondered if Jayne and her lover ever watched that TV while Kit was earning the money to pay for the satellite feed. He wanted to rocket an ace at the screen, but decided there had to be something more significant.

It occurred with the mental rush of a forgotten-then-remembered lock combination. Their wedding picture. Kit sprinted upstairs. The photo, its gold-finish frame adding artificial legitimacy, stood on the dresser between the his and her mirrors. The upstairs ceilings were eight-footers, so Kit would side-arm this shot. No problem. He used this serve to catch opponents off guard when they expected his usual overhead. Kit gave the ball a low toss and banged it. The Penn 1 rocketed toward the photo, missing by several inches. One of the mirrors exploded in shards of reflective glass. Kit couldn't believe it. A miss from such a short distance? And Christ, the bedroom suite was something he was allowed to keep.

Before he could take a second serve, a door slammed outside. He checked his watch. Jayne wasn't due yet. Kit hurried to the window and looked down at the driveway. A Haskins County Sheriff patrol cruiser, glowing an opalescent salmon color in the waxing sunrise, idled in his driveway. "What the fuck?" he whispered aloud, simultaneously remembering the gun laying on the floor. He jogged down the hall, vaulted down the steps and raced into the still dusky living room. He picked up the compact revolver and slid it into his hip pocket before he turned on a light next to the sofa. He heard the deputy's footsteps on the porch, a slip and a curse, but no thud on porch floor, probably slick from last night's storm. He wanted to get rid of the gun, but the deputy was right there, looking at him through the door's beveled glass window.

There was a loud knock. "Mr. LeBeau?" a woman's voice called out. "I'm sheriff's deputy Tarrah Bradmoor."

Kit walked over and opened the door, recoiling at the rush of cold air. "Can I help you?" he asked.

"Ms. LeBeau requested police presence while she removes her belongings. I've been assigned to be here."

Kit could feel the cool density of the gun through his warm-up's thin Gore-Tex material. He flexed his glutes and felt the pressure of the steel pressing the fabric. Shit. He should have left the gun in its hideaway.

"I can't believe she thought she needed police protection to get her stuff," he said. "Jesus, I'm a fucking tennis pro, not a, a … madman," he sputtered. "Besides, I still love the bitch," he added. "No way I'd hurt her."

"Mr. LeBeau," the deputy said, in a tone that admonished. "I need you to calm down. I'm not here for anyone's protection. I'm here to make certain everything goes smoothly."

"I'm sorry, Deputy," he paused to peer at her nametag, "Bradmoor. I'm calm, I'm just upset. This isn't easy." Kit shivered and was about to ask her to step in out of the chilly morning twilight, but remembered the shattered trophy and tennis award on the floor across the room. He didn't want to try to explain broken glass to a sheriff's deputy. "Hey," he said, smiling, "if you're here, I don't really need to be, do I?" Kit didn't want to get into it with Jayne over the trophy. There was the off-chance Jayne would bring Celeste along, but Kit doubted it. Better to be gone. He had a lesson to teach at nine-thirty, anyway. He could stop somewhere for breakfast, or just go to the club and kill time in the weight room.

"Yes, you do, Mr. LeBeau," Bradmoor said. "I'd definitely advise you to stay. I'm only here to keep the peace, not to do inventory. You need to watch what she takes, and make certain the house is secure before you leave." She turned as though she was going to go back to her car, but hesitated. "Oh, Mr. LeBeau, are there any weapons in the house?"

Kit was certain he looked like a kid caught stealing candy. He was in the process of swinging the door closed when she spoke, relieved he would have time to shove the gun between the mattress and the headboard before Jayne arrived. Now he had to decide what he was going to tell the deputy.

"Uh, just a small revolver. It's Jayne's. She's taking it with her. I don't hunt or anything. The one gun is all." Kit started to push the door closed again, but Bradmoor stiff-armed his attempt.

"Where is that weapon?" she asked. "I'd like to secure it, and any ammunition."

"Why?"

"Because I'm not a part of the situation," the deputy said. There was a wariness in her eyes that punctuated her statement. "I'll keep it in my cruiser while you two deal with each other. If Ms. LeBeau has title to the weapon, I'll give it to her just before she leaves."

"It's … ah, upstairs. Yeah, that'll be fine. I'll go get it for you."

Again, Kit tried to swing the door closed, but Bradmoor resisted.

"Unless you object, I'd like to retrieve it myself," she said, pushing against the door more firmly and putting her foot on the concrete doorstep.

Kit did reruns of Columbo, remembering the TV detective who never broke off cleanly when he interviewed a suspect. Always one more question, one more request. He could clearly see the deputy's eyes, trained on him now in the mounting red-orange sunrise. They were quite pretty, actually, and reminded him of Jayne's movie-starlet eyes. Although he was a step above Bradmoor, her eyes weren't much lower than his. She had to be over six feet tall, and this big deputy with mascara eyelashes wasn't going to let the gun thing go. Kit realized his hands were fluttering around like butterflies. He rubbed his forehead to give one of them something to do.

"Look," he started out, "the gun is actually in my pocket."

A powerful shift in Bradmoor's demeanor hit Kit like a forehand volley. The hair on the back of his neck stood in reaction to the nearly magnetic vortex of energy she radiated. The arch of Bradmoor's eyelids floated her dark irises in moats of eye white as her right hand snapped quickly onto the grip of her holstered gun.

"No. No, it's all good," Kit said, putting his hands out in front of his chest. "I'll give it to you."

"Don't move," Bradmoor ordered, her voice terse and cold. "Which pocket?"

"My back pants pocket."

"Is it loaded?"

Kit swallowed. "Probably."

"Put your hands behind your head. Now! Interlace your fingers."

Kit couldn't believe this. One of the endless re-runs he blurred through on sleepless nights was Cops. He could be on an episode this minute. His takeaway from watching the show, however, was to comply. To the letter. He slowly raised his arms, interlocking his fingers in a tight weave which he then pressed against the back of his head.

"Turn slowly, Mr. LeBeau," Bradmoor said. "Face away from me."

"No problem, officer," Kit said softly.

As soon as he completed his low-speed pirouette, Bradmoor's hand slid between his hands and his hair. She gripped his entangled fingers like a vice. "Are you suicidal this morning?" she asked, as she patted him down with her other hand, beginning at his chest and working her way south.

"It's in my back hip pocket," Kit said. "And no, I'm not suicidal," he continued, wondering how he would answer the question he knew would come next.

"And why would you have your wife's loaded weapon in your pocket?" she asked, continuing the pat down, working her way to the pocket holding the Rossi.

He felt her lift his warm up jacket and begin to slide the gun out, but the revolver seemed to catch on something. "I don't know," Kit said, his mind spinning. He had no plan when he pulled it out of its hiding place, and now he had to make one up—fast. "I uh, I—"

Kit heard Bradmoor hiss the word, "Shit," then he heard a metallic clatter and a blast. It felt like someone rammed a white-hot shaft into his lower back and out the right side of his chest. Kilowatts of pain seared through him and he felt his body go rigid. Kit never sensed he was no longer standing, but suddenly snow pressed against his cheek. He couldn't breathe. What made him gag? He tried to suck air, remembering a fall into a swimming pool when he was a child. Choking. Meteors of light cannonballed across blackness. But wasn't it dawn? The flares disappeared in the kaleidoscope of brilliant sunrise when he opened his eyes.

His ears still rang from the explosion, but a voice slid into an audible frequency, as though he was tuning a radio. "Ten thirty-three! Ten thirty-three! Man down. I need immediate ambulance transport!"

Kit caught a good breath and rolled his head toward the voice. Bradmoor. She pressed her face close to his. "Stay with me." Her eyes were wild. "You hear me, Mr. LeBeau? You stay with me. Help is coming."

He really wanted to stay. He wanted to cradle Celeste and tell her not to cry. Wanted to take off her little red sunglasses, smile into her eyes and tell her Daddy would be alright. Bradmoor pulled off her coat, which warmed Kit like a space heater when she tucked it around him. There was a furry collar that tickled his skin, but Kit didn't mind. The pain was gone now. He felt like he was teetering. Running out of balance. But there was no agony anymore. He spit out another mouthful of pool water. It seemed thicker than water, but he caught decent breath. "Whaaa?" he managed, unable to coordinate a bite on the final "t." His voice echoed strangely in his head.

"I dropped the fucking gun and it went off," Bradmoor said. "I'm so goddamn sorry."

Kit's next breath wasn't good. He choked and spat. He had to tell her it was okay. He shouldn't have had the gun. All his fault. He wanted her to know. She begged him to stay again, but her voice was far off now. She was drifting away.

He caught some air. "It's all good." He forced the words out, but wasn't sure he spoke loudly enough for Bradmoor to hear. He hoped she did. He couldn't see her, but he could see Celeste's tricycle, covered in snow, glowing scarlet in the sunrise. He remembered. Red sky at morning.

The colors faded. Kit slipped into another new okay.

GIRLFRIENDING

Archie Descamp eased his aging Jeep through the iron-gated main entrance to Toledo Memorial Park. He wasn't certain how many of his girlfriends resided there, but every time he came here to pay his respects to one, he tried to remember as many of the others as he could. Not by name usually, but by the images he recalled from their obituaries. Today, as their faces appeared, then faded in Archie's mind, Incubus played on the radio. The group sang so hauntingly Archie's eyes misted over. He joined in, but changed one very important word. *"Love hurts ... but sometimes it's a good hurt, and it feels like **she's** alive..."*

Archie felt most alive when he was on one of his near-daily jaunts. That morning he was alive to admire the heavy spackle of snow on the fat boughs of the pines and on the skeletal branches of the maples and sycamores. Alive to breathe in the cold January air and to experience the crunch of crusted snow beneath his tires. But, Archie also felt sadness because Sondra Dillsaver died this twenty-sixth day of the month, only four short years previous. Two years his senior at her death, but a comfortable two years younger than he was now. A good age difference for a couple, he believed.

He checked his note in the upper margin of the yellowing obit. Four graves north of the tallest pine near the Tarkington mausoleum. It was impossible to remember the exact locations of all his girlfriends from one yearly visit to the next. With the continual influx of new ones, the only way he could keep track was through notes he jotted.

Archie brought his Cherokee to a stop at the edge of the lane, extracted his fireplug-shaped body from the driver's seat and slid the obituary into the front of his puffy coat. He pushed his glasses tightly against the bridge of his nose with his other hand, walked past the Tarkington family crypt, under the tall pine, and counted graves. Sondra's polished granite stone still gleamed like new. Her name was written in feminine script. Archie wondered if it was a copy of her actual signature.

Sondra Louise Dillsaver.

June 12, 1966 ~ January 26, 2009

Archie scanned the notes he'd made in a small pad he pulled from his coat pocket. Each time he left a viewing, he took a few moments to write down pertinent facts regarding how the new girlfriend was dressed, how she looked relative to the photo in her obit, and any other noteworthy occurrences he might forget over time.

After scanning what he wrote upon leaving Sondra's visitation, he closed his eyes and allowed the newly-jogged memories to flicker across his mindscreen. It had been a typically gray winter day. He arrived an hour after the showing began, which was always the best time because the greatest number of mourners was usually present. It was easiest to blend in then, and not risk a conversation with family members. However, on the downside, it was more difficult to manage any privacy with people swirling in eddies around the casket. In Sondra's case, refreshments were offered in a room off the parlor lobby, and mourners tended to congregate there, around the table laden with her favorite treats: Twinkies, peanut M&Ms and Diet Pepsi. Archie managed to stand alone with her for a minute or two that day, gazing down on Sondra and lamenting the fact they'd never met.

Cold January reasserted itself as he pulled the obit from under his coat and looked at Sondra's picture. The opportunity to snap a shot with his cell phone never materialized, so the one from The Toledo Times was the only picture he had. Sondra had a beautiful smile in the obit photo. At rest in her coffin, she looked almost as pretty, although Archie considered mortuary science to be an imperfect art. The slight shrivel he often noticed in the fingers bothered him the most. Sondra was a solid woman, but pleasingly curvy and rounded. With the lower portion of her casket closed, he could only imagine the girth of her hips, but he was certain they matched the swell of her bosom. He wished he'd been lucky enough to know her when she was alive, when he could have wrapped her up in his arms and nuzzled her neck. Whispered to her while simultaneously savoring the smell of her skin. Her perfume. The tickle of her hair's tight ringlets against his nose. Instead, he recalled gently touching her wrist. She felt like a cold clay doll. She had a Marilyn Monroe-like mole near the corner of her mouth, and even in death, she had an impish curl to her lips. She'd looked like a gal who would enjoy a funny story, and one who could deliver a punch line, as well.

Archie braced against a chilly breeze and cleared his throat. "Hi, Sondy. That's what I would have called you, unless you didn't like it." He paused to decide what he would say next. He never rehearsed. "Anyway, I just wanted to stop by again this year so you know you aren't forgotten." He looked at the smooth, untracked snow. "I mean, no one else has been here, but I'm sure they are thinking of you, too. I wish we could have met. I think we could have had a wonderful time together. In fact, I know we could have." He looked at her obituary. "You loved animals and volunteered at Paws Are Us. That would have been one of our shared interests, you know. I love animals, too. I probably mentioned it before, but I have a cat named Gloria and I'm sure you two would have hit it off. And I'm not so big on Twinkies and Pepsi, but M&Ms are the best." He fumbled into his coat's big pocket and brought out a one pound package of peanut M&Ms. "Here you go, Sondy. These are for you." He laid the bright yellow package at the base of her dark charcoal-colored tombstone. He arranged and rearranged it several times until he liked the way it was positioned. "I'm a realist," Archie went on. "I know a squirrel will probably wind up eating these. But this afternoon, I'm going to get in bed and imagine you eating them while you think of me.

"We could have had a ball. Your obituary never mentioned a husband, or even a boyfriend." Archie tipped to put his hand on the cold granite stone. "I would have been proud to be either, Sondy." He backed away from her grave and his nasal cavity began to prickle, behind where his glasses rode his nose. He sniffed, but that didn't work. Tears came to his eyes. He put the notepad in his pocket, pulled out his cell and got a photo of Sondra's grave with the M&M package, bright against the dark stone. He'd print the photo and add it to her folder. "I'll be back next year,

Sondy, unless I join you first." He started for his car. "And I'll miss you in the meantime, sweetheart.

~ * ~

Back in his car, Archie took a few minutes to sink into the seat and close his eyes. He often pondered the afterlife. He believed it would be a lot like life on Earth, but so much better because all the girlfriends he never met would be with him when he joined them in death. He hoped they would all live together in a huge house, and everyone would get along. They would have wonderful meals, and in the evening, they would sit together and watch TV or maybe play cards and board games. Or go out. Maybe for dinner. There might even be movies. Archie loved movies, and if heaven was heavenly, there would be movies to take his ladies to see. Just a couple at a time. Whoever felt like going, but it would always just be five or six. Or maybe they would live in a big hotel-like dwelling, and there would be rooms for each of his girlfriends. There would be a swimming pool, and a huge dining room where they could all eat.

Archie opened his eyes. The afterlife was hard to pin down. It was like when he awakened and remembered a dream clearly at first, but when he got into the details, Archie would find he didn't recall it as well as he thought. It eventually became more of a feeling than actual images he could describe or explain. It would be him and his ladies, and that's all he needed to know. The particulars would work themselves out. Someone smarter than Archie was in charge, and he was delighted to leave the minutiae to Him. Faith in God. That was what was so wonderful about religion. Admit you aren't perfect, and let The Perfect One do the heavy lifting.

Archie started the motor and turned up the heater. He placed Sondra's obit in its folder and picked up another that held a new death notice, the one he cut from the Times yesterday. Lorraine Blair Heaton. He re-read the obit. February 11, 1974 ~ January 23, 2013. Died unexpectedly just short of her thirty-ninth birthday, at home. Archie believed that was often obit-speak for suicide.

He locked onto her image and even the crappy quality of a newspaper photo couldn't hide her beauty. The Times didn't print obits in color, but her hair had to be very light brown. A mane of ocean-like swells ending in peaks sculpted to make her look active and vibrant, like a model in a sportswear ad. Head turned to three-quarter view, displaying the gentle slope of her nose. Her thumb pressed against her chin with fingers curling against her lower cheek in a pensive pose. Archie would have loved to know what she was thinking when the shutter snapped. Did she know then she would eventually end her own life? Did she have an inkling? The line from a drug commercial played in Archie's head, something to the effect that if you had suicidal thoughts while taking the medicine, you should call your doctor. Archie smiled. Yeah, doc. There's a gun pointed at my head. What do you suggest? The smile quickly faded when he looked back at Lorraine's face. Would she have killed herself if we were together? Could I have talked her out of it? Given her more reason to live than to die? Would I have been smart enough to see the symptoms if we lived together? Or even just dated?

Archie scanned down through the rest of the obit. Preceded in death by her father and an older sister. Survived by her mother, one brother, the brother's wife and several nieces. No husband listed. No boyfriend. No children. Bestest buddy, Nicole. That jumped at Archie. Was Lorraine gay? He looked at her photo again. Nah.

Archie put his car in gear and began the drive to the funeral home, lamenting the fact he never knew Lorraine existed until she was dead. It was the same with Sondra, and Megan and Amy and Joanie and all the others. He had a file cabinet drawer full of girlfriends he never knew of until they died. It was heartbreaking. How many more were out there? He passed women on the street every day and he always wondered, are you longing for a friend? A lover? Someone to take you to the movies, or shopping, or out to eat? He could easily find out about dead women, but the living ones that surrounded him daily were a total mystery. He would have had to ask. To talk to them. Approach them. Scary stuff when you aren't good at it. The obituaries laid it all out for him.

He pulled into the parking lot of the Dunn-Schumaker Funeral Home and parked in a space at the back of the lot. He liked to leave spaces close to the building for people who had trouble walking. He gave Lorraine's obit one last perusal. Loved all the friends she made in her thirteen loyal years at Bar Louie. Yep, that would be the deal. If anyone asked, Archie knew her from Bar Louie. A steady customer. He wasn't certain where it was, but he'd heard people at work talk about it. Should he Google it on his phone? Nah.

Archie always bristled with excitement at viewings. Every neuron felt like it was firing white hot, the way his welder did when he repaired equipment on the night shift at the Jeep plant. Of course, he was eager to meet Lorraine, but the thrill of not knowing just how it would go was frightening and exciting. Things could go wrong. That never happened, but the notion it could was scary-good.

Archie walked confidently to the showing room that had Lorraine's name on the placard outside the door. As soon as he entered the room, he went cold-water stiff. There were only five or six people inside. The parking lot held twenty or thirty cars, but Archie hadn't taken into account there was another viewing, and the majority of the mourners were apparently across the hall. Oh, shit. Now what?

A very pretty woman, dark-haired with luminous pale skin, looked at Archie, smiled, and began walking over to him. She was lovely. Serene. She looked almost as though she moved in slow motion.

"Hello," she said warmly, as though Archie was an acquaintance she hadn't seen in a very long time. "I'm Nicole, Lorraine's friend." She took Archie's hand in both of hers. "And ... you're?"

Archie felt like the contents of his head were being pureed. "I'm Archie," was all he managed to choke out.

Nicole's smile wavered briefly, but she reconstructed it. "And you know ... uh, knew ... Lorraine how?"

Why didn't I just think to say I was in the wrong room? Took a wrong turn? I'm terribly sorry, but I'm here to see what's-his-name, across the hall. Instead, "I'm Archie Descamp. I knew Lorraine from the bar. The Louie Bar." He smiled. "I'm sort of a regular there."

Nicole's eyebrows looked like they might collide. "You mean, Bar Louie?"

Archie's head felt like a swollen blood blister. "Oh, yeah. I'm so upset by her passing, I've been up all night. Yes, Bar Louie," he said, praying he'd covered his slipup.

Nicole put her hand on his shoulder. "Oh, I so understand. We're all just devastated." She took her hand back and rocked her head side to side. "So sudden...unexpected."

Archie tipped his head forward. "Was it...did she...?"

Now Nicole rubbed her palms together, fingertips pointed at the carpet. "The coroner ruled it a suicide." Her hands swept up to squeegee her cheeks. "I have trouble with that, but she left a note. I haven't seen it yet." She looked away, the skin around her mouth pruning. In a few seconds, she shook her head and sniffed. It was like that eased her pain. "I just wish I'd have realized ... "

Archie reached out to touch her shoulder, but his hand never landed. Nichole, still looking across the room somewhere, didn't notice. Archie stole a moment to look around the room, and was shocked. There was no casket. Against the far wall there was a low table with a photo of Lorraine sitting in front of a box about the size of the lunchbox Archie carried to school as a kid. Cremated? That beautiful woman was cremated? Burned? Nothing left but ashes? Archie's mouth felt sandy. He worked his tongue around to find some moisture, but there was none to be had. Would being burned up affect her afterlife? If her body was burned, would they give her another one to use in heaven? In all the visitations Archie attended since he began girlfriending women a couple years ago, this never happened before. Sometimes the caskets were closed, but Lorraine was the first one to be burned.

"Come on," Nicole said, taking Archie's elbow. "You'll love this photo of her," she went on, as they drew within a few feet of the table. "She was really happy, back then." Nicole may have sighed. "It was before she met—"

A tall thin man burst through the door, and Nicole stopped mid-step. Archie could feel her hand tighten on his arm. Her rich, melodic voice became pinched and tiny. "You shouldn't be here, Avery," she wheezed.

The awkward scarecrow-like man spun in their direction, flailing his arms theatrically. Every one of the man's movements seemed studied and exaggerated.

"Oh, I think the restraining order pretty much went up in smoke with our dear Lorraine," he cried, his voice grinding like a boot heal on concrete. His lips drew into a near-perfect rectangle, framing his gleaming horsey teeth.

Mick Jagger. It hit Archie like two hundred decibels. The guy was a ringer for the lead Stone in every way.

Avery yanked off his leather cowboy hat and tossed it like a Frisbee toward the nearest armchair. "Besides, I'm merely here to pay my respects to my beloved wife." His hand shot upwards like a traffic cop's. "I'm not even going to mention that juicy little tidbit was left out of her obituary, as well as anything regarding my humble existence," he added, in full strut now, striding toward them while his shoulder-length auburn hair flailed like it was mad at the surrounding air. He brushed past Archie and Nicole, picked up the chest holding Lorraine's cremains, and waved it above his head. "That, and to take my lovely wife home with me at the end of this visitation."

Archie was transfixed. All he wanted was to girlfriend a poor unfortunate woman so they could be happily together in Eternity. From the moment he stepped into the room that day, the visit threatened to avalanche. Now it was thundering downhill because a madman husband entered the landscape and turned it into an unnatural disaster.

A wail resembling a police car siren began and Dopplered past Archie, who was still anchored to Nicole, via her vise-like grip on his now-throbbing elbow. The shriek emanated from the mouth of a woman who appeared to be a few years older than Archie, but who was still damned attractive. Her arms were outstretched and the numerous bracelets riding her forearms, as well as her blindingly blond hair, glistened in the weak January sun slanting through the windows as she charged Avery.

"You are not taking my daughter, you son-of-a-bitch," she shrilled. "Put Lorraine down, now!"

Avery began to dance from one foot to the other, with Lorraine's memory chest still held on high. There was a look of genuine glee on his face, just like Archie saw on Jake Wallace's face when he held third-grade Archie's lunch box high above his head in the school cafeteria, daring Archie to try and take it back. Avery bounced from one foot to the other, singing a song he obviously made up as he went:

"Oh, sweet Lorraine, you left us in such pain.

We're all bereaved to know, we'll not see you again."

He danced like an organ grinder's monkey and began another chorus of his song, bouncing to and fro on his athletic-shoed toes.

Lorraine's mother began to beat Avery with her fists, flailing like a lightweight boxer and shrieking, "Put Lorraine down!"

Without altering his toe dance, Avery flipped the latch on the box, flopped the lid open with a twitch of his long-fingered hand, and pulled out a clear plastic bag that had a ribbon matching the soft lavender color of the box, wrapped around the closure. Lorraine's mother stopped flogging, Avery stopped singing and dancing, and a collective gasp rushed to fill the silence.

"Hey, I have an idea," Avery enthused, his mouth forming a Jagger-esque leer. He stretched his arms and legs apart, forming a humanoid X. "How's about we divide her up. Yes, friends; each and every one of you can take a bit of Lorraine home for your very own." His head swiveled while he apparently gauged the number of mourners, and perhaps subtracted the onlookers who'd heard the commotion and spilled in from the visitation across the hall.

At that moment, Lorraine's mother reared back and performed a kick an NFL punter would have been proud to execute, directing her high-heeled patent leather boot squarely into the crotch of Avery's corduroy trousers. He pitched forward, doubling into a fetal ball while simultaneously slamming his face into Lorraine's mother's knee. A web of blood squirted from the point of impact, then Avery snapped back to his full height. As he did, the bag of Lorraine's ashes, intentionally or not, shot like the space shuttle for the ceiling of the room and exploded on contact.

The remnants of Lorraine hailed down on anyone within a ten-foot radius. Archie, Nicole, Lorraine's mother and Avery were engulfed in a light gray cloud of dust that remained after the granular particles grounded. An image of the debris cloud formed by the collapse of the twin towers flashed through Archie's mind. He ran his hand through his hair and could feel the granules of Lorraine against his scalp.

Avery made a strange gagging sound, brushed at his hair and shirt, and quick-stepped toward the chair holding his hat. Lorraine's mother hooked his ankle with her boot and he went down hard. Lorraine's mother vaulted onto his back, grabbed a hank of his hair and pulled hard enough to bring his head back into what looked like a painful whiplash.

"You aren't going anywhere, you bastard," she screeched.

Several others, maybe the brother and his wife, each grabbed an arm. Then more of the onlookers came over to make certain Avery stayed put. To Archie, the cluster of volunteers looked like zombies feasting on a writhing victim.

The funeral director entered the room, hands splayed as if to fend off questions.

"The police are on their way," he said, calmly as a waiter describing dinner specials. "My assistant is cleaning out the Filter Queen, and we'll have the cremains retrieved and back in the memory chest in no time. All those affected, please wait to be vacuumed off."

Archie made eye contact with Nicole, who at some point had released his arm. "I can't believe Avery showed up," she whimpered, stepping away from the zombie apocalypse and waving for Archie to follow.

He did. "Were they really married?" Archie asked, tasting ash as he spoke. He fought against a dry heave.

Nicole nodded as she brushed cinders from her shoulders. "Still are. They met at Bar Louie. Avery has a band called Carved in Stone—a Rolling Stones tribute band. Avery Tarkington is his name, but Lorraine kept hers."

Archie was incredulous. "The rich people? The ones with the huge family crypt in Toledo Memorial?"

Nicole rolled her eyes. "They were rich 'til Avery, his father and grandfather before him, pissed it all away after Avery's grandmother died." She shook her head, then locked on Archie's eyes. "And how did you say you knew Lorraine?" she asked, still slapping dust and granules from her clothing and skin.

"Uh, from Bar Louie," Archie said, delighted he'd gotten the name right, this time.

"You worked there?"

"No," Archie said. "Just a regular customer."

"But Lorraine was an assistant cook," Nicole said, still slapping at her sweater, dust beginning to cloud around her. "She didn't work the bar."

Archie could feel it. A sneeze was forming. The tickle in his nose was a dead giveaway. It could still dispel itself, but if he sniffed just right, he could nurture a good one. Archie didn't sneeze often, but when he did, he sneezed repeatedly. Ten. Twelve. Sometimes fifteen in rapid succession. Once, until his nose bled. He had to sneeze now, and he would not be denied. Just one more careful, perfectly timed sniff.

It worked. Archie let go with a hurricane-force sneeze, taking a step or two backwards for increased effect. Oh, he was on cruise now. He could feel another forming. He began to wave one hand, while pointing to the door with the other. Nicole nodded. Yes, she understood. She said something the next sneeze drowned out, and Archie hurled himself toward the hallway. Another sneeze typhooned just as the funeral director hurried over to him in the hall.

"Excuse me, sir. It's important that we vacuum you off," he said, still calm as a minister doing the liturgy. Archie began to rear back to let loose with another jet-stream burst, and pointed to the restroom, widening his eyes to add some panic to his appearance. The mortician nodded. "Yes, of course. Hurry back."

Archie let go just as he reached the door to the parking lot, and since both hands were employed in pushing the bar that released the latch, his sneeze spattered the cold glass with a pattern that approximated the spray Avery had unleashed, also with his nose. Archie turned to make certain no one noticed his departure, and saw everyone was occupied. He sneezed three more times before he reached his Jeep.

He was a mess. His coat was still dusted with Lorraine's ghostly presence. He hated the way the puffy rolls between the stitched tucks Michelin Manned him, anyway. He shucked it like it was on fire and tossed it on the slushy blacktop. His shoes weren't bad, and there was no way he was taking off his pants; but his hair still contained a harvest of BB-sized granules. Shit.

He got in and started the engine. He was maybe twenty minutes from home, and a long hot shower. He felt the beginnings of another sneeze, but feathered his breathing and avoided another mucus monsoon. Good. Maybe they were over. He slammed the shift lever in drive and passed the police on his way out of the driveway. He heaved a sigh, and froze when it felt like he may have precipitated another sneeze, but the tickle dispersed before the next traffic light.

~ * ~

Archie stood with his back to the showerhead, engulfed in the hot needles of spray coursing across his body and hair. Gloria was in her usual position, pacing back and forth on the top of the tub, between the shower curtain and the transparent liner. Ordinarily, Archie played with her, spraying water against the liner. But not today. Rivulets of Lorraine waterfalled down his chest and stomach, parting at his crotch to continue the plunge down his legs. Gray-stained water swirled at his feet. Lorraine, down the drain. He blinked against tears.

Over the three years since Archie started girlfriending, he attended almost a hundred visitations. Slip in and slip out, unnoticed. That was always his mission. Meet the woman, give appropriate funeral home near-smiles or nods to anyone with whom he happened to make eye contact, but get in and get out, anonymously. Don't be drawn into anyone else's involvement, and make damned sure your own interest remains private. Archie was expert at it.

Today, he got sloppy. He saw all the cars and assumed Lorraine's visitation was packed. After all, a beautiful woman who worked in a bar? She would crowd them in, he figured. So, why were just her immediate family and Nicole the only ones there? Well, and her asshole husband. Where were Lorraine's co-workers? Her other friends? Why didn't he look before he walked in? It saddened him to think a good hour after the visitation began, Archie was the only outsider to show up. And sadder still was the fact she'd been cremated. Smoke. Ashes, some of which were still in Archie's tub. He sloshed water around with his foot to catch the shorelines of ash bordering the flow.

He shut off the water, toweled and carefully pulled the curtain and liner back, so Gloria wouldn't lose her balance. She knew what was next, so she headed for the bedroom. Archie's shift at the Jeep plant began at 11:00 PM. He liked to be asleep by early afternoon so he could awaken at 9:00, have time to eat, and be at the factory half an hour or so early.

He drew the curtains, put on his sleep mask and tumbled naked into bed. Gloria settled into her spot on his pillow, near his head. With the mask blocking light, Archie was usually asleep in a few minutes, but not today. His mind wouldn't leave the outrageous visitation scene alone, replaying it like a movie trailer. A trailer for a very bad movie. Eventually, the soft drone of Gloria's purring faded as he slipped into sleep.

~ * ~

If there was one thing Archie was great at, it was welding. Stick weld. Mig. Tig. Didn't matter. He learned his skills from a crusty old sculpture professor at Cleveland Institute of Art, back when Archie wanted to be an artist. So many masters of a craft hold back some of their magic. I taught myself more than I was taught, you can do the same, sonny. Play with it. Invent. Burn a lot of welding rod and see what you learn. Not Archie's instructor. He saw Archie had a gift, and he nurtured it. Not only taught him technique, but helped Archie develop a feel for the metal. How hot you could get it without weakening its temper, or warping it. When Archie joined metal, he formed perfect puddles and fashioned ideal ripples of weld that looked like rows of lazy overlapping dimes when the red-hot glow died away.

Selling art was difficult, so Archie took a job at Jeep. Robot welders began their invasion about then, and Archie thought he was screwed. But robots are only useful for repetition—set them up to weld chassis together, and stand back. Just the same, equipment in a plant the size of Jeep broke all the time. Hell, even the robots broke, and Archie and his maintenance crew welded the broken parts. He loved it. He was all over the plant. Never the same work any two shifts in a row. Variety.

Most nights while Archie fused steel, he watched the sparks, flame and molten puddles of metal through the near-opaque window of his helmet and thought about how agonizing Hell would be for those who murdered and raped. Tortured and killed. Unless it was in war against an enemy of the United States, of course. That was different. But Archie never even pressed his luck being a soldier. No, Archie was a good guy, and his place in Heaven was pretty much cinched, he figured. Other poor souls were going to Hell, but not Archie. He wasn't perfect, by a far shot. He had lots of impure thoughts, but he fought to keep impurity in his head, not acting any of it out—well, except with his hand. And masturbation was for health purposes, anyway. Archie believed prostate cancer's origin was disuse. No, Archie made certain to keep that type of cancer at bay.

But tonight, after the botched Lorraine visitation, Archie's mind did an eight-hour shift of apparitions ranging from gut-retching to heart-rending. Incineration. That beautiful woman, reduced to Grape Nuts-sized gray granules and dust. The sparks and flame danced on red hot metal as Archie ran beads of searing weld, but he couldn't shake the nightmarish images of charring flesh peeling away from smoking bone.

After he clocked out, he steered his Jeep home with his mind in hyper-drive. Even before Lorraine's showing, he'd wondered if he should do any more visitations. His file drawer was almost full. And he was only one man. Sure, some of the girlfriends might decline his intentions, but even if half of them liked Archie and wanted to spend Eternity with him, he would have more than enough. He wouldn't want any girlfriends to feel neglected. He wanted to give each one his very best. But what was the best he could give to that many?

No, Archie was done with visitations. He would keep the girlfriends he already had, but he would go on Craigslist and look for a woman. He would register with eHarmony. Archie was determined to find a living woman to spend time with. To take to movies and dinner. To talk over the day with. She didn't have to be beautiful. He didn't care. Just so she was nice. And really, from his limited experience, the girls who weren't knockouts were nicer than the beauty queens, anyway. No more obits. After he died, Archie would have more women than he deserved. He wanted one while he was still alive. Someone he could make happy, while making himself happy with her.

Archie let himself in the side door and Gloria was at his feet, rubbing against his pant legs and yowling softly. Archie cooed and talked to her while he prepared her breakfast on the kitchen counter, telling Gloria what he'd decided. "No more visitations, honey. And I'm going to find a really nice lady, but don't worry. She's going to have to like kitties, or I'll keep looking." Gloria sat on the linoleum, licked her lips and watched him work. To him, it appeared she understood. He liked to think she did.

Archie wouldn't usually stand and watch Gloria eat, but this morning, he did. He'd seen The Times on the doorstep in his headlight beams as he pulled into the driveway. The Times, with the obits in the second section, next to last page. He wasn't certain he could trust himself. Reading them was such an obsession. The first page he read, every day. But, today would be different. Tidy up after Gloria when she finished and head into his rec-room and his computer. Craigs and eHarmony. No more girlfriending.

Archie turned on the small TV on the kitchen counter and switched on the morning news. There had been a stabbing overnight. What was Toledo coming to, anyhow? Next, the weather tease. Mixed precipitation moving in. Full forecast in ten minutes. Archie looked at the window and saw spatters. He could hear it hitting the panes. Sounded like it was freezing. Shit, the paper wasn't in a plastic bag.

Archie hurried to the front door and snatched the naked paper off the front step. Damned paper kid. What could one of those orange plastic bags cost, anyway? Archie separated the front section from the second one, and laid it over the back of the couch to dry. It was his normal move. Pull out the second section to check the obits. Not this morning. He was determined to change.

But the second section was already in his hand. There was no harm in just looking, after all. Archie walked into the kitchen, paper open, scanning the obits for women in their forties and early fifties. Gloria mewed, but Archie couldn't look at her. He knew she was disappointed in him.

CRAPSHOOT

The band is loud tonight. You're no music major, but you recognize three-chord riff repertoires—four, giving credit to speaker-shrieking feedback. You dislike vacant-of-talent groups who use volume to supersede vapid lyrics and meager musicianship.

The woman you've mined for the last hour, a striking jeans-and-blouse tall redhead, began sipping the second watermelon martini you bought just as her "friend" Jeremy set up on her right, at the bar. You dropped to an idle on the left. Stay cool. Rise above this interruption in the flow you nurtured. Sure Red, go on and do a memory lane. You feign interest in the brocade of rosy spotlights intended to inject warm excitement into another evening at Howlers, the current A-list place for singles looking to double-down.

Red and Jeremy free-stream about someone they know. She keeps feeding you small asides she hopes will tug you along their storyline, but due to what you miss because of the ambient cacophony and your general disinterest in any scenario that doesn't physically entangle you and Red, you begin to detach. You're over your self-prescribed limit of a drink per wheel because you rode your Kawasaki tonight. You look at the remainder of your fourth Jack and Coke and wait to see how the balance beam drops, valiantly trying to keep your mental thumb off the scale. It finally tips with the clatter of ice against your teeth. Smooth burn going down. The season on redheads just closed. You ease away from your auburn-haired quarry like a sweaty hunter with buck fever. Apparently sensing the absence of your crosshairs, she calls after you. "Hey, babe, where you going?" she says.

Outside, the flashing red Howlers sign makes your gleaming bike glow like an ember. You're a bit unsteady on your Nikes, which rolls a wave of worry. Four drinks in—was it three hours? Maybe two. Who can remember? Regardless, the instant you swing your leg over the saddle and feel the gas tank take its familiar position against your abs, confidence coats your synapses like frosting. As at home on this ride as you are on your sofa. You know every nuance of its balance and power. Could ride in your sleep. You don't even steer anymore—you just think about where you want to go and the Ninja goes there. If you forget to think, it just knows.

As you depress the starter, Red walks up, her rolling gait sexy/rangy. "Hey, don't leave, baby," she whines.

You wave her off. "Goodnight," you say, "and tell Jer-e-my the same." She begins to protest, to reach for your arm. You twist the throttle, dump the clutch and answer with a wheelie that withstands the shift from first to second, the front wheel barely bobbing. Some clown in a Ford is in your way, and you perform the perfect swerve. The traffic light ahead goes red. What are the odds? You're into the throttle and up for the gamble.

A red Kia rolls craps.

FINAL CHOICE

Dan was in no hurry. The hearing was scheduled for 1PM and it wasn't even 11:30 yet, but he couldn't make himself stay in the house. For that matter, the only thing keeping him in his car were the sheets of rain drumming on the roof like a heavy metal percussion solo. Waterfalls of rain pounded Terrasburg. He slammed his palm against the steering wheel. There was no peace for Dan anywhere.

Perched at the end of his driveway, he awaited the passing of several cars, head-lighted against the storm-induced late morning dusk. Those cars cleared his intended path, but another's lights appeared from around the corner and he decided to wait that one out, too. Dan lifted his foot and let the Buick roll into the wake left by the passing car after it splashed past. He glanced at the window of the upstairs bedroom he shared once with Bobbi as he shifted into drive. The curtains were pulled on every window of the house, unopened for weeks. Dan's twenty-nine-year-old world slammed closed on him. He shut down in response, surrounding himself in soothing darkness. Today, the storm was complicit in assuring the gloom outside the car matched that on the inside.

He forced his eyes from the house and began to brake for the speed bump half way down the block. It may have slowed traffic, but Dan still hated the thing. It nearly launched him off his motorcycle one night, a week or so before the speed bump Bobbi took him over, last spring.

Dan decided to stop for coffee. He usually didn't drink it this late in the morning, but he had time to kill and he wasn't hungry. Besides, a jolt of caffeine might be just what he needed to get through the next few hours of legalese. He pulled into Starbucks and yanked the key from the ignition, but his arm dropped and when his wrist hit the seat, the keys slipped from his fingers, jingling onto the carpet. The rain all but stopped, perfect for a dash to the door, but Dan was immobile. A robot out of juice. A marionette with cut strings. He rocked back against the head rest and closed his eyes. Darkness again. He let himself sink into the inky lightlessness.

Tapping. Short persistent bursts. Increasing in tempo. Dan opened his eyes and rolled his head toward his driver's-side window. Melody Lutz, smiling and pecking the glass with her fingernail.

"My God, Mel," Dan said, grabbing his keys as he opened the door slowly so she could step out of the way. He hugged her hungrily, tears cascading down his cheeks. He lost the battle and dragged in a ragged sob.

"Hey, big guy," Melody said, pushing herself out of his hold. "What's up with all this?"

Dan could read surprise in her eyes. He would have to tell her the last thing he ever wanted to tell anyone, much less Bobbi's maid of honor. A woman both he and Bobbi loved like a sister. Dan swiped a hand across his wet cheeks. "You're going to hate that you ran into me today," he said.

"What?" she said, her eyes wide enough to show white all around her chestnut irises. "Is it Bobbi?" Melody reached up and grasped his shoulders like a stern teacher. "Is she all right?"

"She's fine." He glanced at his watch. He was only minutes from the courthouse and still had well over an hour before the proceedings would begin. "Our marriage isn't." Melody started to say something, but he waved her off. "You got a little time?" he asked. "I was headed for 'Bucks. I'll buy." He sniffed. "I think I'm under control."

They walked hand in hand, Melody quickly catching him up. She was in town visiting her parents while her husband, whom Dan met at Melody's own wedding several years previous, was on a business trip. She was unchanged, skin aglow and still willowy-thin. She looked like the women in commercials for health foods or running shoes. Bouncy, but with effortless grace. Her breathy contralto lilted like a sweet clarinet. Melody's eyes always spoke more succinctly than her words, and they were intense and questioning. Dan bought coffee while she staked out two chairs in a remote alcove.

"Thanks, sweetie," she said, taking the tall mug in both hands.

"Now, what's going on?"

Dan suddenly had pangs of guilt. Bobbi should be present to give her side. He felt like a jailhouse snitch.

"You know I can only give you my truth, which may not match Bobbi's."

She shot him a so-what's-new look, rolling her eyes toward the acoustic tile. "I *do* know, goof boy." She touched his knee gently. "Who's leaving who?"

This would work. Just facts. No editorializing. "She's leaving."

"Because of drunken cruelty, or is there another man?"

"I probably drink too much, but I'm not cruel. And it's another woman."

Now Melody's eyes flashed disbelief. "She's leaving because you're seeing someone?"

Dan took his first sip of coffee and decided it was his last. "Bobbi's leaving me for a woman," he said, putting the mug down.

Dan dropped back into darkness. He didn't see Melody anymore, or the coffee shop or the light coming in through the window next to their chairs. He rambled through the last half-year in a stream-of-consciousness narration, edited down from the slideshow Power-Pointing in his mind.

"It was all good. I was never happier in my life, and I was pretty sure Bobbi felt the same," was what Dan said. What he left out was a curious increase in Bobbi's sex drive. They usually made love once or twice a week, but shortly after the New Year, Bobbi initiated sex three, four, occasionally five times a week. Dan was certain he was in heaven, and yet the change made him wary. He wondered what caused it, but he didn't ask.

"Then, right about February, Bobbi told me about a new friend at work. Her name is Rue Bailey, and Bobbi said she was married, but she and her husband were having problems." What he didn't mention was sirens went off in his head the very first time the three of them met at a sports bar. Rue was short and built like a gymnast. Bobbi said Rue worked out six days a week, and she looked it; compact and powerful, both physically and in her social demeanor. But fun. Great sense of humor. She made Dan laugh all evening. Yet way down deep, he got the feeling there was more going on than he was aware of; that Rue was different than she seemed. After Bobbi brought her around the house a few times, however, Dan decided he liked Rue. He could talk and joke with her like a buddy, and he wondered why he ever felt uneasy about her.

"Late February or early March, Bobbi asked me if Rue could stay in our spare room. Things with her husband were impossible, and she needed a place to crash until she got settled somewhere. I had no problem with that." What he decided not to include was he actually liked the idea. Living with two pretty ladies. And sure, he entertained fantasies springing from old *Three's Company* reruns. "I have a hoop on the garage, and most evenings Rue and I shot baskets or played one on one while Bobbi made dinner. Rue's hell on a tennis court too, and Bobbi doesn't play." He came back into his eyes and gave Melody a wan smile. "Bobbi sometimes joked around as we were leaving to play a set, 'Don't you be stealing my husband, bitch.'" He turned his head, looked out the window and contemplated hindsight.

"You never had any inkling?" Melody asked, perhaps after doing some contemplation of her own.

"Oh, there were a couple odd moments. I walked in once and they were hugging, maybe embracing, but Bobbi said something like, 'We'll get you through this divorce,' and gave me a look I took to mean Rue was feeling down." What he left out was a night when they all got high on Toll House cookies Rue made with some really strong weed. None of them smoked, so Rue made baked goods every week or so that knocked them on their asses. Dan was really zoned, that particular night. The walls of the living room were pulsing with his every heartbeat, bending and distorting like images in a mental funhouse.

Hands grasped his arms and gently tugged. He floated free of his chair and grounded onto the soft carpet. Lips kissed him, and he kissed back. A kaleidoscopic blur of eyes and hair and body parts formed, and Dan conjoined with them languidly, savoring each for its beauty, or its flavor or feel or aroma before moving to the next. The wet sticky pleasure rolled slowly, but wonderfully. Dan never completely lost the sensation of floating, even with the carpet constantly pressing against some part of him. Surf—maybe that was it. Tumbling semi-weightlessly amidst warm soft breakers of skin.

He awakened the next morning, alone in a tidal pool of clothing. He got to his feet, pulled on his jeans and walked unsteadily to the bedroom. Bobbi wasn't there and the bed was an undisturbed cascade of smooth linen and frilly pillows. Where the hell was she? He looked into the bedroom they'd converted to an office. Nothing. As he passed the room where Rue slept, the door was half open. Bobbi and Rue were both asleep in Rue's bed.

"Anyway, about then I started to get the feeling there was a definite shift in polarities. All of a sudden, it felt like I was the guest. I admit, I never confronted it with Bobbi, or Rue. I mean, we all got along great. Laughed and joked. Had fun. Went to movies and out to dinner together, Bobbi on one arm and Rue on the other. We called it the Dan sandwich, and I could tell the men we passed all wanted a bite. Rue and I still played tennis a couple times a week." He didn't tell Melody there were times he felt more heat for Rue than for Bobbi, and tried desperately to remember any coupling with Rue on the Toll House night, and hoped for another. Yet, at the same time, he was desperate to keep Bobbi from slipping away, but felt he was battling a storm surf for shore sand.

"So, when did this all come to a head? What did Bobbi finally say?" Melody asked.

"It was sometime in April. All I remember is I surprised them with my world-famous spaghetti, which included pounds of ground chuck and a bit of molasses in the sauce. Italian garlic bread. Candlelight." Dan sat back and tossed his clasped hands over the seatback of his chair. "Bobbi finished her wine at the end of the meal and cleared her throat. It had to be a signal because Rue stood up, kissed me on the forehead and left the dining room." Dan's eyes went watery again, and he used his napkin to wipe at them. "Bobbi reached across the table, took both my hands in hers and said she was in love with Rue. Said they were moving out." He heaved his shoulders and eyebrows upwards in unison. "Said she'd sign a quit-claim and the house was mine. Said she'd take her clothes and nothing more." He left out the part about feeling disposed of. About being on the receiving end of the old "make 'em a deal they can't refuse" thing. She was willing to erase a lot to make Dan disappear.

"I said, 'no way,' at first. Begged her, please stay. Any bargain was okay. Said she and Rue could have the master bedroom. Said, 'I love you. I think I even love Rue. Just stay. I won't cause trouble. Honest. I can't lose you. Please. Please.'" He took time to gather himself. "We both got blubbery. Stood up and we embraced." His arms became anacondas that wouldn't let go until she submitted. Dan hoped his death grip and his pleadings would work. But, no. How could Bobbi establish a new relationship with Rue amidst the remnants of her liaison with Dan? "We are moving out. I'm sorry." Dan believed she was remorseful. And at some level, he couldn't blame her for leaving him. He had to admit he thought more of Rue than he did himself, at that moment, anyway.

Melody looked at her watch. "The hearing is at one?"

"Yeah, I better get over there," Dan said. He really wanted to close his eyes and retreat back into darkness.

"I wish I could go with you for moral support, but ..."

"Nah. It's all right. And, Bobbi may need some support, too. Call her later." He gave Melody a long hug, then stepped back and pressed the end of her nose gently with his forefinger. "I'm okay."

He believed that when he said it, but as he walked Melody to her car, he began to wonder. They promised a get-together before she left for home the following week, and he closed her door and walked to his car, stepping on the dried areas between puddles. He checked the sky. It looked like the storms were over, everywhere but inside his head.

~ * ~

The referee could have been a medical doctor, Dan decided. With surgical precision, she was prepared to separate two Siamesed lives in a matter of five or six quick minutes. She asked first Bobbi, then Dan, did they fully understand the terms of their dissolution agreement? Did they both understand the terms of the agreement could not later be contested? There were other questions, as well, but Dan only heard parts of them. He knew to answer in the affirmative.

His marriage was dying, and true to the lore, random events of the last eight years flashed before his eyes. The day he and Bobbi met, standing in line for The Raptor at Cedar Point. She chickened out at the last second, but she was waiting for her friends at the exit, and Dan managed to talk her into letting him buy her an ice cream cone. The day they married at Terrasbug's Arborarium, Bobbi out-blossoming the flowers. The day she told him she was pregnant, and the morning she told him she lost the baby. The Sunday afternoon when they were grilling, horsing around with friends and Bobbi's hair caught fire. Dan wrapped her head in his Hawaiian shirt before he realized he'd ripped it off. The night they stood at the rail of a Carnival cruise ship until dawn, sipping Manhattans and watching the luminous ropes of froth churned by the propellers on their way to Cancun, kissing and talking about a future that seemed limitless. Sometimes entire episodes played, other times mere snippets, like movie trailers.

Dan came out of his reverie and side-glanced Bobbi, who looked straight at the referee as she wiped her nose with a tissue. She sniffled. That simple act angered Dan. She decided to leave him, gave back everything that supposedly meant anything to her so he would slink quietly away and not cause trouble. He felt used and discarded and insignificant, like her tissue. It was important for a moment, but after she used it to wipe her nose, she'd throw it away. Dan wasn't certain if he felt more like the Kleenex or her snot.

Bobbi looked down at her fidgeting fingers, rolled her head toward Dan and mouthed the words, "I'm sorry."

Dan was not getting divorced. He got to his feet and broke for the door. An official-looking court employee reached out, as if to slow him. "Wait! You can't leave yet," she said.

"Like hell!" he shouted over his shoulder. He needed to be outside. His house, his car and now the marble walls of the courthouse made him feel imprisoned. Dan had to get out. He'd never been claustrophobic in his life, but knew he needed sky overhead. Fresh air. Wind. Yes, even daylight.

He did the stairs to the first floor as quickly as his legs could hammer his feet down the steps. To his right, a burst of light. A door. Dan was in a full-tilt run. Voices called out. Who were they yelling at? A chorus of shouts. No matter, Dan was nearly there. The sun played on leftover puddles from the early rain. He looked toward the sky, visible now as he closed on the ornate brass and beveled glass door. He put his hand out to push it open and free himself of the marble mausoleum of legalities.

Something was wrong. The door didn't budge. Dan's arm collapsed against the force of his dead run verses the immoveable barrier. Pain shot up through his shoulder, but the blaze of heat flared, then extinguished. So did the light. Dan had a feeling of weightlessness, then something hit him hard. It felt like the time a player from Jeffries High blindsided him just as he was rounding left tackle and plotted his path to the end zone. His head and shoulders sledge hammered.

Dan felt an incredible calming freedom. He couldn't feel his body, and he really didn't want to. Not certain of its condition and reluctant to pursue an audit, assuming that was possible, he retreated deep into his mind.

Memories, thin and wispy as cobwebs played—sometimes in Technicolor and sometimes in flickering black and white. The tree fort he built with the twins who lived down the block. They were in fourth grade, a year ahead of Dan. That year meant so much in the schoolyard, but next to nothing when the last bell rang and they headed home to continue construction. John and Jim, until John lost his footing and fell thirty feet, changing Jim from a twin to an only child in a scream and a thud. Dan endured swells of sadness over other lost friends and unfinished plans and roads unexplored.

But there was happiness, too. The first time a girl, Annie Eastmark, slipped her hand into his during the school play he took her to in his freshman year. He actually got a stiffy because of the insistent touch of her small, cool fingers! And a few weeks later when he kissed her impossibly soft lips, a god in heaven suddenly seemed like a possibility. The first time he got up on water skis on Devil's Lake. The heartfelt smile and wink he got from the President of Hawthorn State when he handed Dan his diploma. The call Dan made to his father to tell him he'd landed a job with Jacobs & Trell. Forty-seven grand to start, Dad, Dan said. He savored his father's chuckle, tickling his ear. Dan basked in film clips and snapshots. It was as though he was in a huge library of images and he could shop, picking and choosing as he wished.

But suddenly, he got an awareness the multi-media show was coming to an end. It was like that moment in a movie when you realize the end is coming, and no matter how much you love the film, you can't stop it from going dark. The camera pans out away from the main character and you realize just how small and insignificant the protagonist is against the backdrop of the universe. There is no stopping the inevitable. Put the last handful of popcorn in your mouth and slide the empty box under your seat. The lights will come up and the credits will roll.

Dan became aware of the fact he had a final choice, and the clip he decided on was of his mom and him riding in her new Camaro convertible. She was taking him to spend the weekend with his father. Dan had a Tupperware container of Toll House cookies on his lap and was trying to talk his mom into letting him have one.

"Those are for later," she said. "And remember, you have to share with your dad."

"How many are there?" Dan asked.

"A dozen for each of you," she replied.

Dan held his hand outside the passenger compartment, letting it become a wing that rose and fell as he changed the pitch of it against the wind. "Nah," he said. "Dad's getting chubby. I better eat eighteen and leave six for him."

He and his mother laughed. It was a bright day, and the air felt so good as the car sliced through it. Dan felt so loved. So secure. He had a mother he lived with most of the time and they had so much fun together. His father loved him too, and the weekends with him were always action-packed and exciting. Dan never felt like his parents were in competition. They both loved him and knew he loved them in return. It was perfect, except they didn't all live together, anymore.

"I'll tell you one thing, Mom," Dan said. "I'll never get divorced."

She smiled and reached over to rub the back of his neck, something she did often. "I hope you never do, honey."

"No. I mean it. I never, never will," Dan said, as the camera shot panned out and the Camaro with Dan and his mom in it became a very small red dot on the interstate. Then it disappeared.

THE CEREMONY

The big motorcycle sliced through the humid night air. Audra cuddled in the lee of the blast, her arms tight around Lexie's solid torso, a product of daily workouts at the gym where the two women met.

From the instant they moved in together, Lexie's abilities and intelligence inspired Audra's trust. Still, motorcycles scared her. "Never-evers," she called them. Lexie surprised her with a leather jacket and a helmet, but Audra couldn't make herself get on. Even a short ride was too frightening to contemplate, especially for a woman with only one flesh and blood leg. That night, however, on her way to face the ocean and its creatures once again, something told Audra that riding to the beach with Lexie made perfect sense. Stare down the motorcycle, as well, Audra decided.

To her relief, Lexie handled her Harley as assuredly as she struck a yoga pose. She cut smooth, stable lines through the curves and on the straights. The exhaust pipes fired like machineguns with a twist of her wrist. The rhythmic thrum caused Audra's prosthetic right leg, perched on the peg above one of the barking pipes, to resonate with the roar of the engine. She pictured her hair sailing like a contrail from under the back of her half-helmet when she rested her chin on Lexie's shoulder; and Lexie's chestnut mane flailed against Audra's cheek, at a blip or two above what would register as a tickle. It was just another of the sensations she assimilated as the moonlight glowed through the thick tropical atmosphere.

The public beach access loomed ahead, a hazy bubble of illumination in the sea of darkness engulfing the coastal road. Several fixtures perched on tall poles poured small yellowish pools of light onto the concrete parking lot. "That's it," Audra said into Lexie's ear. Lexie nodded, began shifting down to slow the cycle, and pulled in. She weaved through the maze of concrete curbing, many of its angular edges softened with wind-sculpted drifts of sand, and brought the big cruiser to a stop in one of the lemony light spots. She let the bike idle for a few seconds before cutting the loping motor to silence.

"Is it midnight yet?" Audra asked.

Lexie pulled up the sleeve of her crash jacket and looked at her watch. "Just past," she replied. "Careful when you get off. Those pipes are hot."

Audra bounced on her good leg as she swung the right one over the passenger seat and stood waiting for Lexie to dismount. The pungent smell of exhaust and fuel gave way to the pervasive smell of salt water riding the onshore breeze. Audra tried to pin it down, and decided the sea's aroma wasn't far from freshly-cut oats. For a moment, her awareness drifted and she walked with her grandfather in one of his fields.

"I don't like this whole damned thing, and I'm not going in the water," Lexie said, setting the kickstand and letting the cycle list onto it. She faced Audra and unfastened her helmet's strap. "So, you do this every year?"

"The last two. On July 23rd, the night it happened," Audra replied, starting for the beach. "I have to. I have to confront it. It's kind of become my very own little ceremony."

Lexie peeled off her jacket, tossed it across the bike's seat, and jogged a few steps to catch up. "And this David, the guy you were engaged to, he talked you into swimming that night?" she asked, as they walked toward the roar the rolling waves created when they disintegrated into foam against the sand.

Audra shook her head. "Not really. I was afraid to swim in the ocean, even in the daytime. The hotel had a great pool, but the night before we were supposed to head for home, David said, 'No way I'm leaving Florida without going in.' We were on our way back from dinner and dancing, and he stopped here. 'I'm only going to wade,' he said. Might have been the margaritas, but next thing I knew, I was in waist-deep with him."

"Well, just so I'm on record, no way I'm setting foot in that water, even if the worst happens," Lexie said. She was smiling, but Audra sensed an undercurrent of fear in her voice, which caught Audra by surprise. In the time they'd been together, nothing seemed to unsettle Lexie. "Just keep that in mind, sister," she added.

"I wouldn't want you to," Audra said, putting her hand on Lexie's shoulder. "If 'the worst' happens, then that's the way it's supposed to be, and you better not interfere." She shrugged. "Besides, if anything happens, that would be my answer."

Lexie looked puzzled. "Answer? But what's the damned question?"

Audra stood very still and her eyes wandered out across the sea, as though she'd lost focus. "I'm not sure," she said, still looking into the distance.

"Then let's just go," Lexie said, rubbing her hands up and down her upper arms. "It's creepy out here."

"I guess I didn't say it right," Audra said, locking onto Lexie's eyes. Looking into them often smoothed any turbulence in Audra's mind, allowing insights to surface in the calm. "Not an answer," she offered. "Maybe more like a sign."

Lexie shook her head. "So, if the shark, or one of his buddies, comes back to finish you off, that's supposed to be some kind of sign?"

"I don't see it that way, Lex. When *nothing* happens, that's the sign." She handed Lexie her jacket, then began to unfasten her jeans. "Plus, I need to prove neither of them beat me. Not the shark, not David." She let her jeans drop to the sand and stepped out of them. "You understand that. Like that time you dropped your bike. You started riding again as soon as you could, right?"

"Yeah, but I've never considered myself a paragon of sanity," Lexie cackled before a serious expression starved her grin. "The salt water, it's not gonna gum up the works?" she asked, using her chin to point at Audra's prosthesis.

"No way. These sports models are all carbon fiber and titanium. An atomic bomb wouldn't faze this thing. That shark comes back for another midnight snack and picks the wrong one, it'll break some teeth," Audra said, adding a chuckle. "Now, sit tight," she said, her eyes lingering on

Lexie.

"I goddamn wish you hadn't talked me into this," Lexie sighed, looking worried. "Being here makes me feel, I don't know … somehow responsible?"

Audra gave Lexie a soft kiss. "This is between me and the ocean," Audra said, not pulling back, breathing the words against Lexie's lips. "You supplied the transportation, but I'd have gotten myself here, one way or the other." She turned and walked toward the water. "Did the last two years. You're not responsible for a thing," she called, over her shoulder.

Audra strode into the sea, stopping when she was waist deep, probably twenty-five or thirty yards out. The water was warm and didn't offer much relief from the relentless heat.

"How long do you stay in?" Lexie called.

"Twenty minutes," Audra shouted. "That's how long I was out here with David that night. Are you timing it?"

"Shit!" Lexie yelled back, pressing a button to light the readout on her watch. "I am now."

Audra stood, head raised toward the starry heavens, bucking against the waves trying to bully her from her position in the surge. She would not be moved. She bit her lip and made herself return to the night that deflected the arc her life traced until that point. She remembered David laughing, yelling, "See, isn't this great?" in a baritone slurred by Jack Daniels and Coke. She remembered how white his teeth looked in the meager light emanating from the parking lot. Audra pressed her memory forward, to the instant something rubbed against her calf—something rubbery, but with a surface like sandpaper. Before she could formulate any concept of what it might be, unimaginable pain shot through her synapses with light-speed. She realized she was under water when she emptied her lungs in a scream that came out encased in bubbles. When her femur snapped and her poor knee finally ripped free of her thigh, Audra bobbled to the surface, yards from where she'd been standing. She had to give him credit, David was there in an instant. He swam her to the shallows and carried her onto the beach. "You'll be okay," he said, over and over. She joined in, although she never knew if the words actually cleared her lips. "I'll be okay," became her mantra, in time with David's low growling chant. She remembered him tying his shirt tight around her thigh, then she slipped off into a numbing darkness.

Something poked Audra's foot. She didn't scream. It was more a shout without words.

"What?" Lexie yelled.

Audra spun in her direction and was shocked to see Lexie was already knee deep in the roiling waves, apparently coming to the rescue. Audra held out her hands to stop Lexie's approach, and whirled through the possibilities. Intuitively, she knew what she'd stepped on. She disappeared into the surf, and then in seconds, popped to the surface again, holding it in her hand. "Look! My God, Lexie!" she shouted, bounding through the breaking rollers.

"What? What the hell is it?" Lexie asked.

"A shark's tooth, I think. Yes. It is. I stepped on it."

The two women made their way out of the waves and collapsed on the sand, clutching one another while Lexie wiped strands of damp hair from Audra's cheeks and forehead. Neither of them spoke at first.

"I can't believe how brave you were tonight," Lexie finally said, putting her hand on Audra's. Audra took that as a great compliment, but vacant of anything to say, met her statement with a self-effacing shrug. "No really," Lexie went on. "I'm so honored you asked me to be with you. I almost wasn't brave enough to come along, and I guess that's why I was so bitchy."

"You weren't," Audra protested.

Lexie shook her head. "Yes I was, but only because I was scared of what might happen. Thing is, the minute you said I could bring you out on the cycle," she added, tilting her head to where the bike glittered like tinsel, "I knew I was coming." She slid her fingers along Audra's prosthetic leg. "Do you hate him?" Lexie asked.

"How do you hate a shark for being a shark?"

"No. David, I mean."

"How do you hate a man for being a man?" Audra said, smirking. Then she shook her head. "I can't blame David because I lost my leg. Going in the ocean was my choice. But later, sure, he turned out to be a jerk. I overlooked so much to be his fiancée. His bald spot," she said, laughing, "the one on the back of his head he refused to acknowledge. His love handles. And, of course, all the suspicions about who I really am. The dagger in my heart was in the end, though, he couldn't overlook my stump," Audra said, turning the shark's tooth over in her fingers. "He tried to deny it. Desertion by misdirection. He came up with other reasons, but I know that's what it was." She gave Lexie a wink. "Guess it all worked out for the best, huh?"

Lexie smiled and nodded. "So, this means it's over?" she asked, sliding her index finger along the serrated edge of the tooth. "Is this your sign? You won't have to come out here again next year?"

"I don't know, right now. Maybe," Audra said, raising her eyebrows at the prospect. "I have to think. Let's just go home."

They got up and brushed at the sand sugaring their damp bodies and clothing. After Audra slipped back into her jeans, Lexie pointed at the shark's tooth. "One thing I'm sure of," she said, handing Audra her jacket. "Put that sucker under your pillow, the tooth fairy will leave you a bright shiny quarter."

Audra laughed and gave Lexie a gentle shove. Then, hand in hand, they started for the lot where the Harley sat cooling.

SLEEPING ALONE

Lemony light projects raindrops' abstract window spatters on your bedroom wall. You crave her soft warmth. You pray she'll have an epiphany and return. Meanwhile, insurgent-like, you slip across the demarcation between rigid reality and the pliable world of dreams. The slam of a car door lures you back across that foggy boundary, but drunken male laughter crushes your hope.

Earlier, your writing was effortless, but you fought to stay awake. Letters interlocked, forming words that flowed like wine and transubstantiated into your characters' lifeblood. The hum of the computer's fan composed a hymn celebrating literary sacrament. Without warning, the scrim of slumber fell. You slipped away, left pinky resting on the z key. Forty-two pages of zipper tracks when you awakened. No one to share the laugh with.

Drowsy, you switched on the TV for company. Leno was doing his headlines routine; "A lady charged with thirteen counts of failure to appear was released on personal recognizance." Comedic pause. "Hello!" he bellowed, awash in his own sarcasm. "Goodnight," you mumbled. Shucked your clothes on the way to your bedroom. Burrowed under the covers alone because she also failed to appear.

Consciousness deserted for an hour or so, but you're wide awake again. Watching the digital clock and remembering engines. 3:02. 3:18. 3:27. Never had a car with a three hundred twenty-seven cubic inch motor, but the Chevelle that lasted you through college had a three-fifty. You'll be awake when 3:50 arrives. And 4:09, too. You drown in seas of drowsiness when you're desperate to write, but your bed finds you resuscitated on the shores of sleeplessness, and the beach stretches all the way to sunrise. You'd gladly barter a tightly-written scene for slumber.

4:27. Now, there was an engine. Both Chevrolet and Ford had their own versions. She was driving a Ford when you met at the coin laundry. You helped carry her clothes to the old Taurus, and flakes of rust dislodged when she opened its door. Later, you made love and sensed a faintly metallic aftertaste. Like rust? Could have been blood, not that you cared. You lusted for all of her.

Everyone has a plan. Yours is to write scripts. Hers was to script you into what pleased her. Slept with you every night. Enmeshed with you in every conceivable way. Finally, confident you would follow her staging, she started in. "All you want to do is write plays. Can't we go out more than two nights a week?" Soon, she delivered it—the pivotal line of dialogue. "Keyboard, or me. Choose."

You made your choice, and as fast as it began, the affair blew like an over-revved engine, scattering emotions like shattered iron. She went off to cast a more directable lover, leaving you with memories of the way her hair eddied across your face in the night. Its fragrance made you dream of moonlit streams meandering through meadows of wildflowers, and deepened your slumber.

Now you pound out powerful scenes, but she no longer sleeps with you. The hell of it is, on nights like this, you don't sleep with yourself.

SHRINE

Back in late August, a young gal in a pickup augered into our ditch. Went off the far side of the road, overcorrected and hit our culvert like a battering ram. Troopers said she had to be flying. Happened about three in the morning, so she may have had a snoot-full. Anyway, damned if I wasn't in Canada hauling cars for a movie they were shooting up that way. My wife, Myrna, heard the crash, threw on her robe and ran outside. The little girl was pinned in, yelling for help. The truck was smoking, but there wasn't any fire. Myrn told the girl she'd get her out, but that's when flames started from under the hood. Myrna pulled on both doors with all her might, but the force of the wreck wedged them shut. Flames got worse and the girl was screaming bloody murder, so Myrn ran to get an extinguisher from the barn. Time she got back, she couldn't even cross the culvert, the heat was so bad. She ran into the house and called 911. Said it was the closest to Hell she's ever been.

Myrn was a basket case by the time I got home. Wouldn't go near that side of our property. Luckily, our driveway comes in on one road and goes out on another, because she wouldn't use the culvert where the girl crashed. Wouldn't sit on our deck because it faced that way. Day after Labor Day, a guy drove up, got out and opened the trunk of his car. I thought it might be an insurance investigator or something. I'm naturally nosey, so I moseyed on out. Seemed as though he made himself smile, like he wasn't all that happy to see me, but wanted to be friendly, anyway.

"I'm Bill Markham," he said. His lip quivered. "Megan, my daughter, my only child, she was the girl…" He took a framed picture out of his trunk and held it up. He was starting to lose it, tears hanging on his

148

eye lashes, then flicking off when he blinked. I looked, but I didn't really see her face. Too worried about what I was going to say. I mean, what could I say? My brain set up like concrete. I finally wrangled a couple words together. "Pretty girl," was the best I could muster.

"And a good girl," Markham exploded. Almost a sneeze. Started to cry, but it was with words. "Four-point-oh in high school," he kind of groaned. "Worked at Wal-Mart's." He sucked in a breath. "Saving for college," he slobbered. All the while, he's shoving a wrought iron stake into the ground between the road and the ditch. Shaking bad, the way I remember my father doing when my brother Nick was killed. About then, I spotted a little piece of plastic from his daughter's pickup. I slid my boot over to hide it. He got the stake planted the way he wanted and hung the picture on it. Stuck a little American flag in the ground and stood back to look it over. That seemed to settle him down. "I hope you don't mind," he said. "I just don't want people to forget her...how beautiful a child she was." I put my hands up like he'd just pulled a gun, but couldn't think of anything to say. I shrugged, as though that made it okay to lower my arms. He reached into the trunk, got a vase of flowers he'd wedged in against the spare and set them next to the little flag. He stood back again, liked what he saw I guess, and turned to shake my hand. "Thanks so much for understanding," he said, looking kind of like you do when you find out your fly is down. "I didn't get your name."

"Joe Mikita. Just Joe is good."

"Thank you, Mr. ... Joe," he said. Then he got in his car and drove off.

"Oh, Christ," I said out loud, walking real slow to the house. Myrna met me at the door.

"Who was that?" she asked, but I could tell she'd already figured it out. Before I could say anything, she stopped wringing her hands, grabbed my shoulders and piped a glare into my eyes, the way my mother used to. "He can't do that, Joe. He can't leave that...that...*shrine* out there." She spun around and walked to the sink. Started washing her hands. "You're going to have to tell him."

"But Myrn," I said, with no idea where I was headed. "The guy...it was his only kid." That sounded paltry even to me, but my blood wasn't cold enough to tell him to take the picture away. "It isn't what we would do, but it's his way of grieving. He doesn't want people to forget her."

Myrna spun so fast, water flew off her wet hands. "And what about me? I *need* to forget her. I don't want to remember that night. The fire. Her screaming. And me, not able to do a goddamned thing." She walked over and landed both her fists on my chest, like she was stabbing me. Knives would have hurt less. She saw it in my eyes, I guess. "God, I'm sorry," she kind of whined. "I can't believe I did that."

I shook my head. "It's okay. I was just thinking about Dad, is all. You know, when Nicky died."

I made a move to put my arms around her, but she stepped back. "Did your father put up a shrine?"

"Not exactly. But he used to drive over and sit in the parking lot at the grain elevator. Not every day, but most." I didn't want to go on, but I'd already opened the damned can. "I'd see him there, just sitting in his car. Staring at the silos. I never mentioned it, but we weren't talking much by then, anyway." I'd never told anyone about this, but I kept talking and hoped it would help her understand. "One day, the elevator people called. The manager. He was trying to be nice, but he said it had to stop. Said it was bothering the employees. That, and Dad was tossing bottles into the hedge out there." I opened the door to go, turned and looked back at Myrna. "I guess forty or fifty rum bottles were his shrine for Nicky. I drove over and picked them up, but I didn't have to ask Dad to stay away from the elevator." I rattled the knob back and forth a few times. "He had his heart attack that night." I made a move to go, but she took my arm.

"I'm sorry," she said. "You never told me."

"Not the kind of thing you broadcast." I kissed her cheek and walked outside.

After the shrine went up, Myrn was nearly a shut-in. Hardly ever went outside. Only time she drove was if she damned near had to. Kept her car parked on the side of the house away from where the little gal crashed. It was as though something came out of her; part of her spirit, maybe. I'd look at her, and it was like looking at her husk. Put me in mind of one of those full-size wax museum figures. Looked like Myrna, but her insides weren't there anymore. Or they were, but changed all around. Any rate, she sat and stared for hours. Not even seeing. I'd walk past and it was like I was a ghost. Sometimes it sounded as though she was humming, but if I listened close, she sounded more like a rabbit I found out by the road once, got hit by a car. Wasn't dead yet. Just laying there, kind of squeaking real soft. Myrna was one of the strongest people I ever knew, until that crash. Then, just like with Dad, after the silo people called to say Nick got buried in the grain, it was like part of Myrna died with the girl.

I called my boss at the movie car company. He was great. Told me, "No problem, Joe. Stay right there in Kentucky and take all the time you need. Just let us know when you're good to roll." So, I stayed home, chomping at the bit more than I let on.

See, being a trucker isn't just my work, it's what I am. A man gets used to roaming. Watching the rain or snow come slant-ways out of the clouds, the days turn to night and the plains change to mountains. Made me rich way beyond what money could. Back when my father kicked, five thousand dollars was all was left, time the debts was cleared. With Mom and Nicky both dead, I was the only one left, so I put the money down on a truck. Did good. Most part of a million miles with no accidents, and the ledger always showed black ink. Traded up to a used Peterbilt and it didn't take long to pay her down. Got hooked up with the movie car outfit, and they only used me three or four days a week. Not even every week, for that matter. I like doing mechanic work out of my barn when I'm home, but I'm always anxious to get back out roving. For her part, Myrna always said she enjoyed her time alone, long as she knew I'd be back inside of a week. In my mind, we had a nice kind of rhythm going, almost like one of them old romantic songs. The time we spent apart was the quiet between notes.

"I'll be staying home with you for a while," I told Myrna. We were in the kitchen, at the little oak table she got from her grandmother. Only sits two. Myrna loves lace, and she found a pretty piece that fit just right. I always thought Myrn was sort of like lace: real delicate and pretty, but stronger than you'd figure. I fingered that lace while we talked, hoping she'd get back to where she used to be, soon. "No more trucking until you're mended," I promised. Her hands were flat on the tabletop as though she was holding herself up.

"I don't know when that will be," she said, barely loud enough for me to hear.

I patted her hand and smiled. "Just take your time with all this." I stood to head for my shop. "Scoot Mathews, the damned fool, managed to crack the frame on his motorcycle. I'm going out to weld it up, then maybe we'll go to the Villa Fiesta over in Covington." I waited for her to say something, or even just look up. "Or someplace else, if you'd rather," I added, thinking she might have her own ideas about where to eat. Her fingers wiggled a little on the lace, but she didn't say anything. "We got time to decide," I said, rubbing her shoulder. "I love you." One of her hands landed on the back of mine, light as a bird. Her skin felt cool like a wet washcloth. She didn't say anything.

Out in the barn, I was welding on Scoot's cycle. Got careless, and some of the fumes found their way under my helmet. Like hot ammonia vapors. Started me to choking, so I dropped the welding tip, tossed the helmet and walked outside to get a lungful of good air. That's when Nick dying crossed my mind again. Him falling into the silo. Drowning in them oats. Grain raining down like dusty hail. Aspiration of a foreign agent, the coroner called it. I was watching TV the day it happened. My father took the call. He always said "hello" like he was asking a question, as if he wasn't sure he was saying the right thing. He listened for a long time, then tried to put the receiver down, but his hand was shaking so he couldn't hit the hook. That's when I knew it was serious, but I wasn't sure who, or what. Mom had already passed, so that narrowed the possibilities. He turned toward me, eyes all red. Blinking real fast. Tears rolling down his cheeks like little pearls. That wasn't what got to me the most. Back then, he cried if a kitten got run over. No, it wasn't the tears. It was his hands. They weren't just shaking. It was more from way down inside him than just a shiver, or a shake. Palsy-like, from right down in his soul, is more the way I'd describe it. Couldn't control his hands. Like one of them puppets on strings. Only God knows who was pulling them. "Nicky," he said, final enough I didn't have to ask how bad it was.

I shut off the memory machine then, and came back into that September day, standing outside my barn with one more cough left to go before I could walk back in and start welding again. That's another thing I like about driving. Out on the highway, shaking sixty tons of metal keeps my mind occupied. When I'm puttering around on my own, things I don't want to think boss their way into my head.

A week passed, and Myrn wasn't much better. I wasn't sleeping, lying there thinking about the shrine. Wondering how I could get across to that Markham fella the damned thing was tearing Myrna apart. One morning, I asked her if she might want to talk to someone, a counselor, maybe. "You know, someone to help you sort all this out," I said. That was the first she showed any spark since I got back from Canada. Daggers. She fired off a look like I'd said we ought to blow up the Statue of Liberty or something. Never spoke a word. Just cut holes in me with her eyes. "Look, I love you, Myrn," I said. "I want to help, but I'm lost without a GPS on this one."

She gave me a look. "You can tell him to take it down." It came out almost like a growl. Then she got up and walked into the living room. It was dark in there. She kept the shades pulled because it was on the side of the house where the shrine was. I had the feeling she could see it anyway.

I was on my cell pretty regular, worried about losing the movie car contract. "It was my lawn, I think I'd yank the goddamned picture out of the ground and toss it in the ditch," the dispatcher told me. "Of course, that's easy for me to say, not being in the situation."

"Yeah, it sits different on this side of the table. The father's all torn up, and the shrine tears Myrna up. The truth of it is I feel like I'm out of duct tape." I almost told him about my father when Nick got killed, but even though he seemed like a man who'd care, he was my immediate boss, after all. "I promise I'll get it handled. I know what I have to do, and I'll call you soon as I get it done." I no more than hung up, walked outside and Markham rolled up, out by the culvert. I didn't want to tell him to take it down, but I knew I was going to have to.

He hit me with a big smile soon as he saw me. "Hi, Joe," he said, grinning. I made myself smile, and shook his hand. We passed pleasantries, how nice a run of weather we'd had and such. Then I noticed his eyes turning red and blinking faster. "I've been mulling things over, Joe," he started out. "I think it's really unfair to keep Megan's memorial on your lawn here," he said, waving his hand towards the shrine. Talk about blindsided. Snapped my head around so quick, nearly put a crick in my neck. He patted my shoulder, smiled and said, "You and your wife have been so very kind." He had to stop and sniff a little. "So, I decided I'd move it," he said, getting a fresh pot of flowers out of his trunk and motioning with a twitch of his head, "to that side of the road." He crossed over and sat the flowerpot in the long grass. "I think it'll be better over here." He kind of wiggled it around to make sure it was sitting solid. He came back and got the picture and the stake it hung on, carried it over and stuck it in the ground. He stepped back and looked it over. "Now it won't be any burden on you, and people will still remember my baby when they see her picture, here." He wiped his eyes, put the old pot of flowers in his trunk and slammed the lid. He scuffed his foot over the grass where the shrine had been. "Sorry about your lawn, but it'll come back." He looked over at the shrine, took my hand in both of his and shook it hard. "You take care now, Joe, and thanks again for all your understanding."

I didn't move a muscle while I watched his car go down the road. Then, I looked at the shrine, cursed and walked into the house.

"So, you didn't tell him to just get it out of here?" Myrn asked later on, while she picked at her dogs and beans. I'm not much of a cook.

"Didn't get the chance." I spread my hands like I was turning a bird loose. "He said he didn't feel right about it being on the lawn, and moved it across the road before I could say anything."

Myrn put her fork down. I knew she was looking at me, but it took me a while to look her back. I finally did. My throat felt the way it did when the dentist had to work on a tooth and hit it hard with Novocain. I could barely swallow.

"And now it's not even on our property," she said. "We don't have any right to tell him to take it away." Then she lobbed one from way out in left field. "When are you going back out on the road?"

"I told you, hon. When you don't need me here, anymore."

"Why don't you call dispatch, then." It came out more an order than a question. I was going to ask if she was sure, but before I could get a word out, she raised both her hands and shook her head. Then she got up from the table and walked outside. I went to the window, saw her cross the culvert, like she was on a mission, and walk over to the shrine. She stood staring at it for a long while, not moving. She looked rigid, as though all her muscles were tensed tight. Her hair fluttered a little in the evening breeze, but no other part of her stirred. I don't know how long it was, but all of a sudden it was like something broke the strain, and she kind of relaxed. Shifted her weight over to one leg and brushed her hair back over her shoulders. It had been cloudy all day, but the setting sun dropped beneath the deck of clouds and the orange light made her glow like one of the glass figurines she collects. She started looking around, like she just realized the rest of the world was still there, and then she started back for the house. I hurried and sat at the table as though I'd never left. "Call them," she said, when she walked in.

They didn't need me right away, which was good. Gave me time to make sure I felt okay about going. Myrna seemed to be doing pretty well, best she had in a long while. The night before I was going to head off, I fell asleep praying Markham would get tired of the shrine and stop tending it so I'd know I could take it down. Or maybe he'd come and take it away himself. That next morning, I kept a close gauge on Myrna, and though she seemed a bit distant and not so quick to talk or smile, as far as I could tell she'd managed to find some peace.

I went ahead and took the load. Had to haul some late-thirties and early-forties cars down to Abilene for a picture they was shooting. I was on my way back, on a stretch of I-40 between Memphis and Nashville, when it hit me. I needed to take control of the situation. I mean, everybody has their reasons in this life. Markham didn't want people to forget his poor daughter, so he wanted the shrine. He shook like my father when Nicky died, and that was my reason for leaving it stay put. Myrna, she had to listen to that poor girl burn to death, and that was her reason for wanting it gone. I'd put more stock in Markham's and my reasons than I did Myrna's. She never took the shrine down on her own, which made me think she put more weight on my reason too, which flat tore me up. I decided I'd been an asshole, in plain terms, and I took my cell down from its cubby and touched the little phone picture.

When the ringing started, I pictured it on the counter in the kitchen, where we spend most of our time. The machine picked up, so I figured she was out shopping. "It's Joe, Myrn," I said, soon as I heard the beep. I let myself feel what the truck was doing. Checked the mirrors. It was all good, so I went on. "Sweetie, the shrine is coming down, soon as I get home. Tonight. Should be in about eleven or so. I'm sorry as hell. I never should have let this thing drag out like I did. I'm going to make everything right. I was dead wrong all along. I can't give you your September back, but I'm going to straighten this out. I love you. As soon as I hit the driveway, the shrine is history."

The road usually tore past, but after I left the message for Myrn, the miles peeled off slow, even though I had my foot in the injectors more than I normally would. Just like I promised, I was home at close to 11:00. I noticed right off the shrine was gone. Did Myrn get my message and take it down herself? I figured it was a good sign. I couldn't wait to see her smile dig those deep dimples in her cheeks.

I set the brakes, shut the engine down and climbed out. When I walked inside, all the smells, the creak of the floor and the sound of the mantel clock swept over me. I was home. Then, I noticed the light on the phone machine blinking. It felt like an electric jolt hit me when I flipped on the light and saw Myrna's crystal dishes and nick-knacks cleared off the shelves. I pushed the button on the machine. "It's Joe, Myrn," I heard my voice start in.

In the living room, her glass figurines were gone. I ran upstairs to our bedroom and Myrna's closet door was open, the hangers stripped clean. The shrine was propped against the bed's footboard with our wedding picture taped over the one of the girl. Across our smiling faces, in black marker Myrna wrote, "Leave this here long as you like."

The house was quiet, except for my message, still playing on the machine downstairs. It ended and I realized what I told her was true. The shrine was history. Myrna's and mine.

CONNECTION

Brenda opened Tyler's closet, sat on the soft carpet and inhaled. Smelled him. She sipped Shiraz. She lit a candle, though this was no séance. No, this was very much rooted in the tangible sense of smell. She remembered how her high school biology teacher explained it. Objects shed molecules. Molecules float in the air. When a human inhales these molecules, they come in direct contact with a postage stamp-sized area in the sinus cavity and register as odor. "Think about *that* the next time your doggie leaves a present on the carpet," Mr. Whooten cackled. Brenda could feel the smile that decade-old memory fostered.

As time passes, fewer molecules are apparently shed. When she first began, a few days after Tye's accident, all she had to do was walk into their bedroom and his olfactory presence was a soft, persistent, invisible fog. As time passed, the fog became mist. Soon, the mist lessened to vapor.

She did what she could. Both closets in the master bedroom had louvered doors. When she noticed a reduced potency in Tye's aroma, she covered the louvers on his closet door with black bulletin board paper from the supply room at the elementary school where she taught. It seemed to slow the dilution, but ultimately, fewer and fewer molecules migrate. That was the word Mr. Whooten used. Migrate. It made Brenda think of birds. What a sad twist. Birds flew. And landed softly.

The black paper wasn't horrible against the dark chocolate woodwork, and black was the perfect background for the photo of Tyler Brenda taped to it, the last one she took. His thumb thrust upward, bisecting his thousand-kilowatt smile.

She butt-scooted toward the open closet, her left arm propelling while she balanced the Shiraz as though it was liquid gold. She exhaled until her lungs would yield no more air, then took in as much as she could make them contain. Yes, a trace of Tyler registered.

Her eyes closed and the dark screen of her eyelids' insides were perfect for her to envision his image. Smiling, of course. The man smiled more than anyone Brenda ever met before. It wrinkled his broad face into impressively handsome furrows running from his prominent cheekbones to the soft curve of his jaw line. His dark brown eyes radiated warmth and interest, and their color matched his mahogany hair, which he wore long enough to ponytail. She held the image still for as long as she could, but as she began to exhale, praying more molecules would find that postal spot in her nasal passage on their way out, his image began to move. Tye was always in motion.

Full bore Tye. One hundred percent at work, where he handled his backhoe bucket like it was a fork. Said it was close to religious, pawing through the earth God created, vigilant for any buried artifacts. How he could spot a flint point from inside the cab was beyond Brenda's understanding, but he had an impressive collection. He dug holes with perfectly square corners, a smooth level floor, and walls as true as if they'd been laid up in brick. The night they met and Brenda told him she taught, his expression at first matched that of a student learning his answer was incorrect. In a heartbeat, he reenergized and flashed that high beam smile. I just dig basements, but nobody does it better. It proved to be true. Throughout their cohabitation-turned marriage, contractors called constantly. Two basements a day was his max, five days a week. No weekends.

Weekends were reserved for Brenda and full out play-a-polluza. That's what Tye called the things they did together. Scuba, waterskiing, and bicycling in the warm months; cross country skiing, downhill, and snowmobiles during the cold end of the calendar.

Brenda savored what little of Tye she got that night. So far, every piece of clothing in his closet and in his dresser drawers was just as he placed it. She would soon resort to what she considered last ditch—picking up his clothing and pressing her nose into the material. Tonight wasn't wonderful, but it would do. She thought of how connoisseurs described the bouquet of various wines. Smoky, but not overbearing. Subtle, but perky. She was damned happy she didn't have to describe Tye's scent to anyone. She loved it. That was all she knew or cared.

She sipped her wine. "Tomorrow," she whispered. She slowly closed his closet doors, chiding herself for telling Tye something he already knew. Brenda believed the dead were privy to all the secrets of life and of death. The door clicked shut with a gentle whoosh, and Brenda inhaled once more.

~ * ~

Brenda pulled up to the on-its-way-to-tumbledown building, a former restaurant-turned-tire store, with an apartment on the second floor. She drove past it every morning and afternoon on her way to and from Tamarack Elementary. She first noticed the neon sign in an upstairs window only a few weeks ago. MISS RONA. LIFE READER * ADVISOR * MEDIUM, it proclaimed, in a strange orangey neon. She would never have ventured here if Fran Guthries, an older teacher at Brenda's school, hadn't praised her own sessions. "I honestly believe she helps me communicate with my Gus," Fran whispered, across the lunch table in the faculty room. It was just the two of them, but the whisper somehow gave more credence to what she said. Fran blinked at tears. "It's been such a comfort."

Brenda got out of her Honda and walked up the steps to the second floor. The screen door was pinned open. Brenda tugged gently on the bill of Tye's hat. Her ponytail flowed through the hole above the size adjustment strap, the way his would have. She smelled her fingers, but in the open air, nothing registered. She knocked.

A woman who could have passed for a librarian opened the door, dressed in a pink sweater and a blue, pleated knee-length skirt. Her graying hair was pulled up and back, pinned into a loose sort of bun. Reading glasses hung around her neck on a beaded chain.

"You are Brenda," she said with a heavy accent, stating it as a fact, and without smiling or offering her hand. Her eyes tightened until Brenda could practically feel their intensity.

Brenda's reply caught in her throat, and she only nodded.

The woman turned and walked down a short hallway. "I am Miss Rona," she said without turning her head.

Brenda closed the door and followed, down the hallway and into a large room with two plastic-laced outdoor aluminum chairs facing each other near the middle of the room. The space was bare of anything else, except for the neon sign, buzzing softly in the window facing the road. The linoleum tile floor was dark and cracked, or missing chunks, in places. The aging wood paneled walls had several holes where speakers, or possibly lights, used to hang. The wires that once energized them stuck out like denuded twigs. The thing that registered as most strange to Brenda was the nearly overpowering smell of black licorice. She would have expected musk, or damp mold, but the room held a sweet odor that Brenda found calming.

"Please sit," Miss Rona said, gesturing toward one of the chairs.

That this chilly woman used the word please was a surprise. Brenda complied, and crisscrossed her arms on her lap. She expected Miss Rona to sit in the opposing chair, but she instead circled slowly, her Reebok running shoes sometimes squeaking against the linoleum.

"And, your issue?" Miss Rona asked.

Brenda was guarded. She'd decided she would not feed the woman information she could later use. "I want you to tell me everything you can."

Miss Rona stopped mid-step, her shoe squawking. Her face pulled into a mirthless smile. "I see," she said. She faced Brenda and her hands rose to perch on her hips. "You are here to test me, not to learn."

Brenda felt a rush of heat fountain through her neck and across her face. "No, no," she faltered. "I ... I just don't want to take you down the wrong path. The less I tell you—"

"The less you learn," Rona said. "You go to doctor and make him guess your symptoms?" She began to circle, again. "This is cooperative process. Work with me or I can't help."

Brenda took a breath. "I was hoping you could help me contact someone," she nearly whispered.

"Someone close to you?"

"Well ... of course."

Rona seemed to warm a few degrees. "Once, artist comes in. He wants to contact Picasso." Now her smile seemed genuine.

"I bet Picasso gets a lot of that," Brenda offered, hoping to smooth out their rough beginning.

Rona chuckled, then returned to her businesslike personae. "Is recent, this person's passing?"

Brenda could only nod.

Rona made several more circles. "I get a few things," she said. "This is like sculpture. I get a hazy lump and pare away layers." She shot Brenda a sharp look. "Sometimes very good. Sometimes, not so. If I can peel enough, I offer you a lot."

Brenda thought this made some sense, but she couldn't get a clear picture of what Miss Rona peeled. How could you carve anything as ethereal as a spirit? What kind of concealing essence could there be? Still, Brenda liked the idea of stripping something away to reveal an entity. She decided words must be the limiting factor when explaining something so otherworldly.

Rona's eyes slammed shut. She held her arms out straight, canted toward the floor, her fingers splayed stiffly as knitting needles. "Is a man," she seemed to growl, her voice deep and gurgley. Now her hands came up to make incomplete orbits of her head, like swarming bees. "Is older man, I can see."

Brenda was bewildered. Tye died on his twenty-third birthday, and Brenda was twenty-seven.

"This man, he very ill. Bent and staggered." The swarm landed, thumbs on Rona's temples and fingers sliding back and forth across her forehead. "I feel labored breathing. Very hard to get breath." Rona's hands flew from her forehead, drew into fists, and her arms slammed against her sides, as though she was at attention. Her eyes opened wider than Brenda would have predicted they could. "Who is this person to you?"

Brenda shook her head slowly, then shrugged. "I don't know," she said softly. "The person I was hoping—"

"Not hoping," Rona rumbled, her voice still several octaves lower than her normal speaking voice. "I only see who comes. This man, he is the only one here. He limps. Do you know him?"

Brenda's mind whirred like a blender. An old man. An old man who limped and couldn't breathe? That wasn't Tyler. Brenda's thoughts went to her father, but she hadn't seen him in over twenty years. The last time, she recalled, he was young, handsome and strong. Brenda was only six when her father got a job working on a pipeline in Alaska. All that ever came back was a monthly check. According to her mother, after a few years, the checks deserted the family as well.

Just as Brenda began to respond, Rona's eyes closed again, her hands opened and flew up to slap together only inches from the end of her nose. "Wait," she barked. She began another hoarse guttural snarl that morphed into words. "He is saying 'shell.' Something about a shell." Her eyes reopened, but not as before. Her lids barely parted. "Hard to understand, this man."

Brenda's teeth began to chatter. She felt like she was in a freezer; as though the temperature dropped fifty degrees. The smell of licorice was gone. "My mother's name was Rochelle," she said. Even to Brenda, the words came out in what sounded like a hiss. She cleared her throat and tried for a normal tone. "Everyone called her Shelly."

Now Miss Rona tilted her head back, and her hands went to her throat, sliding slowly up and down its considerable length. "Sorry, I'm getting ..." Rona said to the ceiling, her voice back in its customary range. Her hands swooped down and cupped her breasts. Her head lowered and began to wag. "... I'm getting terrible sadness from this man. He is not speaking now, but I can feel waves of misery." Rona began to sob. Tears waterfalled down her cheeks, and she continued to heave, almost uncontrollably. She looked like she might fall, and Brenda began to rise, thinking she may have to catch her.

Rona seemed to sense Brenda's movement. "No," she screeched. "Stay. Is just overpowering, this man's despair."

Brenda lowered herself onto the chair, her elbows on her knees, now, her hands clasped in front of her, a tight ball of fingers. She felt like someone poised on the seat of a dunk tank.

Rona fell back into her grizzled scratchy voice and began to yowl. At the same time, she dropped to a squat, then jack-in-the-boxed into the air, literally coming off the ground. When her athletic shoes hit the linoleum, she shouted, "I should have come home!" Then, she slumped to the floor, her right arm supporting her torso and her head coming to rest on that shoulder. Her mouth and eyes opened, but she said nothing and her eyes appeared unfocused.

Brenda was transfixed. She became aware of her own hot tears, cascading down her cheeks, and she almost allowed herself to slide down onto the floor with Miss Rona. She felt spent and wasted. It was hard to grab one thought and stay with it. Her father. Her awareness ricocheted through everything she just saw and heard. At the age of twenty-seven, everything she knew and believed had to be rearranged to accommodate what she just witnessed.

Brenda realized Miss Rona was on her feet. "Is all," she said, her voice back to its initial cool professional timbre. "No more. Fifty dollars." Her arm extended like a turnpike toll gate.

Brenda reanimated and she dug in her purse. She knew the cost and had two twenties and a ten folded where she could find them quickly. "When can I make another appointment?" she asked, placing the bills on Miss Rona's hand.

Rona shook her head. "No more. As you see," she said, waving her arm in a dramatic flourish, "I am leaving. No more work here."

"No," Brenda yelped. Without even thinking, she grasped Miss Rona's arm. Realizing what she did, she released it. "You can't. You need to help me. I need to reach Tyler. My husband." She began to sniffle. "He died. I bought him a skydive for his twenty-third birthday and the chute tangled. I killed him. I have to apologize. I have to make sure he's not angry and he still loves me. He's the one I have to talk to, not my father." Now Brenda was in a full-out bawl. "Now I believe. I know you can do it. But Tye didn't show up. I don't know why, but maybe he will the next time." She took Miss Rona's arm again. She didn't care anymore. She squeezed the soft flesh. "My God, you can't leave and take away my only chance to find out if he's angry."

Rona deftly and efficiently peeled Brenda's fingers from her arm, then gently patted Brenda's hand. "I am sorry your Tyler stayed away. No one can explain how this works. Is like I ride wild horse. The horse is real, but I cannot control which horse I ride, or where that horse takes me. I only ride.

"I cannot stay. An illness in family takes me away. But I will give you something. You are good girl and you deserve. I wish I could say it is gift, but I cannot. Gifts are good. What I give you can be good, but can be horrible. And a gift is something you can use. What I give you, you may, or may not. You must find the horse and ride. I can only give the key to the stable."

Miss Rona put her hands on either side of Brenda's head. Earlier, she felt chills. Now she felt heat. Heat seared through her head, and her ears began to ring. A bad taste, like charred meat, almost made her gag. She wanted to free her head of Miss Rona's firm grasp, but a weakness that nearly made her slump was overpowering.

Rona pulled her hands away from Brenda's head, and held them high like a ref signaling a good field goal. "Go now," was all she said.

"Thank you," Brenda managed, then she stumbled numbly along the hallway and down the steps to her car. The sun, the fresh air, and the sound of traffic all felt very foreign. When she opened the door and dropped into the seat, the Honda smelled like licorice baking in the sun coming through the windshield.

~ * ~

There are times when a person should not drive. One is if they are sleepy. Another is if they drank too much. Brenda wasn't sleepy or tipsy, but she definitely had too much to think.

Her father. Her father came to … apologize? Not really. What was it he said? I should have come home. Not exactly an apology. Miss Rona said he was suffering, wherever he was. Someone honked and Brenda steered back into the center of her lane. So, you take the infirmities from this life into eternity? That didn't make Brenda feel better. The anguish she and her mother suffered when her father left them ended long ago. Brenda wasn't vindictive, and she always hoped death was an escape from pain and suffering.

Her mother died two years ago, last March. Brenda was surprised *she* didn't take the opportunity to make a connection. The two of them loved each other and were extremely close. Brenda became her mother's confidant and friend, especially in the last ten years of her mother's life. Brenda missed a turn, and began to circle back. But, as Miss Rona said, she couldn't control who came and who didn't. How did she phrase it? Something about riding a horse. Yes, that was it. A strange analogy for Miss Rona to use, someone who seemed the antithesis of a horsewoman.

And, of course, why didn't Tyler show up? Was he angry? Brenda bought the skydive that killed him. Oh sure, he said it was the best birthday gift he ever got, but that was before the chute tangled. Brenda even wore his hat to seed his presence. To chum the water, so to speak. She wagged her head. Yes, that from a woman who never baited a hook. But Miss Rona told Brenda she gave her something she could use to ride, as well. The key to the stable, she called it. Brenda's job was to find the horse and ride it. Then she could tell him how sorry she was. But he knew that. He was dead, and knew everything. So, why didn't Tye come?

She drove past her garage, hit the brakes, and reversed to the correct door, which looked like every other in the condo complex. She pressed the button on the remote and the door began its slow yawn, revealing first the oversize mudder tires, then the shiny chrome front bumper, and finally the masculine angular body of Tyler's tall Ford F-350 pickup. It sat where Koo Koo Haines, Tye's closest friend, backed it in next to her Honda the night of his accident. Brenda's attention lingered on the license plate, EXCAV8R. Tye loved that truck so much. He used it to pull his backhoe for work, and he drove it wherever the two of them went for play-a-polluza.

Brenda pulled in next to Tye's truck and as she got out of her car, it hit her like the smell of licorice did, earlier. Miss Rona talked about riding a horse. She gave Brenda the key to the stable so she could find the horse and ride it. Now she stood next to Tye's horse. The badge on the fender told her she would ride a 6.7 Turbo Diesel with four hundred horses. She hoped they would take her where she longed to go.

~ * ~

Brenda walked into the garage that Saturday evening, at sunset. She wanted to see if being in Tyler's truck and driving it to places meaningful to him, and to the two of them, might connect her with him in some way. She didn't really believe Miss Rona could infuse the ability to unite with someone's spirit, but Brenda knew she had to try. And she couldn't explain away the surge of heat she felt when Rona grasped her head. As Brenda pressed the code for the overhead door into the keypad, she felt the same kind of trembling nervousness she felt the day she and Tye entered the justice of the peace office to get married. Brenda had no family, now that her mother was dead. Tye's father was his only surviving family, and they were estranged. It was just the two of them, along with Koo Koo and his girlfriend, Angelanne, their witnesses/celebrants. Brenda had no idea how the marriage would work out, and now she had no idea how her attempt at riding Tye's horses would go. If tonight went half as well as her short happy marriage, she would be delighted.

Brenda reached to open the truck's door, stepped up onto the running board, and hoisted herself into the driver's seat. Compared to her Honda, it felt like she sat two stories high. When she pulled the heavy door closed, she was overwhelmed with Tyler's scent. "My God," she said, shaking her head. Of course, his truck smelled like Tye. He was in it constantly. She laughed about sniffing desperately at his closet, when this virtual vault of his scent sat in the garage, unopened.

Brenda trembled as she slid the seat forward. She grasped the ignition key. Would it start? The truck sat since Tye's birthday, weeks ago. And if it did start, could she handle this beast? There was only one way to answer those questions. She rubbed the steering column, the way she might have rubbed the neck of a thoroughbred, took a breath and twisted the key.

The big diesel engine shuddered to life, growled loudly, then fell into its pok-a-ta pok-a-ta loping idle. Brenda latched the seatbelt, put her foot on the brake pedal and shifted into drive. The truck lurched, the engine straining to overpower the brakes. Brenda eased it out of the garage into the gathering darkness, switched on the headlights and pressed the remote to close the garage behind her.

Brenda was surprised at how easy the truck was to drive on city streets. It was three times the size of her Civic, but it was also tall, which gave her confidence. She was so totally focused on driving the truck, she never once thought about where she was going until she realized she pulled into the driveway of Tyler's building. T. Sommerfield Excavation, the sign above the overhead door proclaimed. She switched off the engine and sat back, immersed in dusky silence.

When they met, Tyler lived in an apartment he built upstairs. The building itself was quite old, but typical of Tyler, it was freshly painted, and he even planted some evergreens and flowers near the office door. The apartment was a beautiful man-cave kind of place, with a huge flat screen TV opposite a leather sofa. The kitchen was small, but well-equipped. They actually discussed the idea of the two of them living there, but her condo was closer to where she taught.

She planned to call a realtor and list the building and the business for sale. Of course, before she did that, she had to go through the office and apartment to remove Tyler's belongings. This was the first time she'd even been here since Tyler's accident. The thought of sorting through Tyler's possessions, deciding what should be kept and what to do with the rest was emotionally overwhelming. Brenda never so much as touched anything that belonged exclusively to Tyler since his death, except for his truck, tonight. Dealing with his things was for someday, not for now.

She started the engine. Driving his truck was breaking down the barrier she'd placed between herself and Tyler's stuff. She wanted to ride his horses, even though doing so hadn't put her in touch with Tyler, so far. She started to reach for the shift lever, but shut the engine off, instead.

Brenda didn't remember deciding to come to the building, but something brought her. Maybe there was a reason. If nothing else, she should look inside to see how much work was required to remove his possessions from the office and apartment. The apartment was mostly empty, she knew, but the office was the way he left it. Brenda wanted to know what lay ahead.

She opened the door and slid down onto the gravel driveway. It was cool, now that the moon hung in a cloudless sky. Brenda tried to talk herself back into Tyler's truck as she walked to the door, but she couldn't. She paused to take a deep breath. The thought that perhaps the office would smell of Tyler reinforced her choice, but she still wavered.

She slid the key into the lock and turned it. Before she could flip on the light when she opened the door, she kicked something. She caught the light switch, and saw mail was accumulated on the floor, where it fell through the mail slot. She got the door closed and stooped to gather it up. There wasn't a lot. There were some catalogues, typical junk mail, some envelopes that looked like they contained checks, and a few bills.

One envelope stood out. It was obviously a card. Probably a birthday card, Brenda decided. But who would send a card to his business? There was no name on the return address, just 2339 Whitehall Road, in Princeton, West Virginia. Brenda wanted to open it, but she hesitated. What if there was something inside she would regret seeing? She dropped into Tyler's chair at his desk and looked at the envelope. She smelled it. No particular odor. Finally, she shoved her fingernail under the flap and tore it open.

For My Son, the card said on its cover, in swirly script. Brenda opened it. On the inside cover, in script that approximated that on the front, was a handwritten message:

Dear Tye. I think of you every day, boy. I love you so much and want so much
to patch things up between us. Please call me. Please. I can't drive anymore, but
if you'll come down, we'll have a beer and sort things out. I love you so. Dad.

Brenda was stunned. Tyler rarely talked about his family, and only said his father and he weren't speaking. When she asked why, Tyler stiffened and shook his head. As kind and easy-going as he was, it was hard for Brenda to understand what could have made him so angry with his father. She hoped to find out eventually, but she never brought it up again.

Brenda stared at the card. There was a phone number at the bottom. Tye would know the number for his phone at home. The only thing she could figure was his father must have moved recently.

She pulled out her phone, but not to call his father. Her father-in-law. Meeting someone that important was not something you did over the phone, especially considering what she would have to tell him after her introduction. She opened the Waze app on her phone and spoke the address. Waze said it would take two hours and fifty-six minutes to make the hundred and seventy-six mile trip. She looked at her watch. It was 9:48. She needed to get to bed. She would be on the road early.

Brenda pulled open the desk drawer and was startled to see a package of Twizzlers black licorice. Both her car and Miss Rona's room smelled of licorice when Brenda went to the reading. She picked up the package and pressed it to her chest, but it was unopened and yielded no aroma. She tried to make a connection, but decided without the smell, there really wasn't any. Still, the coincidence gave her a chill.

She stood, and looked around the office before she turned off the light. It was no longer just the way Tyler left it. Now, the mail sat in a neat pile on the desk calendar. The licorice was in her hand. She would be back next weekend to begin sorting things out. The time had come.

Brenda was almost back to her condo when she decided she would drive Tyler's truck to Princeton the next day. She wanted his father to see it. It *was* Tyler. The truck would tell his father a lot about the son he hadn't seen in years. Brenda would tell him the rest, everything she knew about her father-in-law's successful, fun-loving and wonderful son. Maybe if they hit it off, his father might want to come back with her to help sort through Tyler's things. He might want some of them. He could stay in the guest room. He might enjoy learning about Tyler by seeing the things that were meaningful to him.

She drove Tyler's truck into its space beside her little car and shut the diesel off. She decided she would print some of the photographs of Tyler she still had on her phone for … Mr. Sommerville. She didn't even know his first name. He could look at them all, but she would print some to leave with him. Especially the last one. The one of Tyler in his parachute gear, smiling behind his thumbs-up.

Brenda reached for the door handle, but a thought made her eyes brim with tears. Miss Rona was right, after all. The message from Brenda's own father was unclear, but Rona did give Brenda the ability to ride the horse. She now had the power to connect the living with the dead, even if it wasn't in the way she hoped.

MOONLIGHTING

"Know anybody who'd like a good dog?" Brett asks.

Nora looks across the table, over the top of her glasses. She's bored. That's what she says. Bored with bologna on white, and bored with the end tables she packs into boxes on the production line. Bored with her life. Brett figures a pup could spice up her dreary existence.

"I don't need a dog." A smile curls the corners of her lips, painted a shade of ripe plum. "I told you what I'd like." She lifts an eyebrow, takes a bite of her sandwich, and returns her attention to the movie-fan magazine collecting crumbs on her lap.

Brett watches her jaw muscles working under the taut, smooth skin of her cheeks. He wonders if she's actually reading, or merely waiting for a response. She's been coming on to him since he began working second shift at Longworth Furniture, to supplement his teacher's salary. Years back, he was gluttonous as a little boy in a candy store, sampling every available flavor. Sometimes, it was a woman's physical attributes that piqued his hunger. Often it was a personality quirk, an attitude, or some combination of those. He always found the mixtures most appetizing. Nora is an intriguing alloy. He'd be on her like a kid on M&Ms if he wasn't married to Lou Ann.

She continues to scan the pages, but Brett's pretty certain she knows he's watching her. He likes the way she pulls her mane of woolly dark hair through the opening in the back of her blue ball cap. "Deluxe" is stitched in white letters across the front. He thinks it's a fitting description and wonders if she chose it for herself, or if it was a gift. She reminds him of Colleen, the small town cop with cerulean irises and acres of breast. She

170

liked to be handcuffed. That was a turn-on, but when she wanted Brett to caress her naked body with her city-issue Glock he walked, which precipitated three traffic stops in the next week. Never a ticket. Never a reason. Just a license check and a "Have a nice day…" from several of Colleen's ominously professional co-workers. The episode was so weird, thinking back, it almost seems like a dream.

Brett glances at Nora. She's locked her arresting eyes on him. "Why are they getting rid of it?" she asks, just as Junior Goings bursts through the door and struts into the break room.

Her question, accompanied by Junior's sudden appearance, catches Brett off guard. "Uh, I'm not sure."

"Is it a problem? Does it bite? Crap in the house?"

"You talkin' 'bout my kid?" Junior bellows, sitting down to flip open the lid of his lunch box. He pulls out half a turkey breast sealed in a ziplock bag.

"A dog, Junior," Brett deadpans, hoping to discourage further interruptions. "No, I don't think it's any problem," he says to Nora. "Don't know why they want to give it away. Just do."

"'Cause I'll give my kid away, but he bites *and* shits," Junior injects, laughing. "Free to a good home." He removes the plastic and gnaws off a huge hunk of the turkey. His mouth is too full to talk, but that doesn't dissuade him. "How big this dog?"

Brett shakes his head and tries to look disgusted. "A little bigger than average. Not huge."

Brett's verbal brush-off doesn't work, and Junior won't be ignored. He still hasn't swallowed. "'Cause I got a buddy with pit bulls. He always lookin' for bait dogs." His words are accompanied by a mist of turkey bits. He finally clears his mouth with an audible gulp and smiles widely enough to display the gold jackets encasing most of his teeth.

Brett fires the huge man a large caliber look of contempt. "Maybe I'll go have a cigarette." He stands, turns and tosses a half-eaten meal into the trash barrel on his way to the door.

Nora drops her magazine on the table. "I didn't know you smoke."

"I've been meaning to start," Brett says over his shoulder as he clears the door and begins his walk through the factory, which is eerily quiet because it's break time. Only the sound of compressed air, escaping from a fitting somewhere in the labyrinth of pipes twenty feet above, pierces the silence. He pulls the ear buds from his shirt pocket, puts them in and spools up his MP3. There's only one song on the player. It repeats endlessly, adding soundtrack to his shifts at Longworth. The haunting wail of the harmonica that follows the first base piano chords never ceases to give him chills. If he's obsessed with the song "The Long Way Home" by Supertramp, it's a fine fixation as far as he's concerned.

The vocal begins as Brett walks to his work station. He checks his supplies and waits for the horn to signal the end of lunch break. He glances at his watch and wonders why a meal consumed at eight in the evening is referred to as "lunch" by his co-workers. There are still a few minutes of break left, so he kills some time loading the air gun with nails.

Nora passes by, smiles and winks. "Enjoy your smoke?"

Brett pulls the ear buds. "I'd take lung cancer over a conversation with Goings anytime."

She stops. "You should have stuck around. I started joking that his pit buller buddy might want to use Junior's kid for bait." She laughs. "He actually got pissed."

"Good work."

"Where could I see this dog?" Nora asks. "I might like one after all. A little protection at the trailer wouldn't be a bad thing." She lets her eyelids close to slits and allows the corners of her lips to do their upward curl. "A woman alone … you know."

Brett tries not to sound overly enthusiastic. "I'll talk to the people who have it, find out when we can set it up."

"You just do that," she says, starting down the line to her station. Brett watches her ponytail sway in opposition to her hips, her firm round bottom fighting the confines of her jeans. He inadvertently squeezes the trigger on the nail gun, shooting a two-inch finishing nail into the floor between his feet. Nora turns before he can hide his embarrassed surprise. "Careful," she says, smiling lasciviously. "You don't want it to go off too soon."

As each hour at Longworth drags by, twelve or so trips through Supertramp's song at a time, Brett relies on a complex network of mental defenses he's built to fight the boredom. Moves with the nailer are so automatic now, his mind is free to pursue any avenue he chooses and he's charted a rich map of divergent routes. Sometimes he makes lesson plans, or reviews plans already made. Tomorrow's are done: give a test on Chaucer and show a video about Medieval England. Test days are a breeze, but he scrambles to get the papers graded in time for the next day's class meeting, something he demands of himself. He'll do that during his conference period and actual lunch, the one halfway through the school day.

With Senior English handled, Brett begins the back half of the shift in a fantasy dust-up with Junior while Supertramp idles in the background. Maybe your pit buller friend would like to use your kid for bait, he imagines himself saying. Junior leaps from his seat, six feet-plus of rage towering over a medium-build teacher moonlighting to keep his wife's standard of living where she likes it. You better take that back, motherfucker! Goings yells. See if you can keep more turkey in your mouth when you're shouting at me, Brett says casually, staring unrepentantly into the watery brown eyes of the giant looming over him like a tropical storm. Junior's mighty hands, still greasy from his turkey feast, grab Brett's shirt to lift him to a standing position. I'm gonna kick your sorry ass! he hisses. Before he can make good on his threat, Brett envisions himself drawing his head back from the hurricane of turkey halitosis only to snap it forward, busting the monster square on the nose with the crown of his forehead, a move borrowed from a vintage Bruce Lee movie. Junior's vise-like grip releases and he stumbles back, crashing into the break room wall and sliding slowly to the floor like a big glob of giblet gravy. Brett gives Nora a Lee-like smirk and a "whatcha-gonna-do" shrug before sitting down to finish his peanut butter sandwich.

Of course, that reverie initiates thoughts of Nora. Brett peers down the line as she hefts a finished end table into a box. She lays a sheet of plastic over the Formica top, fits Styrofoam packing into the corners and seals the carton before sending it on down the line to be palletized for shipment. All the while, she laughs and talks with the other packers, holding her own with them while performing her industrial ballet. Her hair swings across her shoulders in ropey twines, and Brett imagines dividing it into two thick wavy strands, one for each hand. She's naked, on her hands and knees. He reins her gently from behind and she bucks against him with more and more fury as their passions intensify. Her fanny slaps his lower abdomen, sounding like appreciative applause. Pulling harder now, Brett rows his arms like a jockey closing on the finish in home stretch. She tips her head back. "Don't go off too soon," she moans.

When the horn sounds, interrupting Brett's fantasy and signaling the end of second shift, he stows the MP3 in his lunch pail and gathers his coat. He trades quips with a few of his coworkers as they make their way to the time clock, and Nora punches out just as Brett arrives. She pulls his card from the rack and hands it to him.

"Thanks," he says. "Good shift tonight. We made flat rate by about 9:30. Got an hour and a half of premium pay."

Nora looks sleepy, but she manages a smile. "Great. I'll need some extra money if that dog comes to stay. You gonna call those people?"

By this time, they're outside, dodging cars in the parking lot. The moonlight dances on the plumes of condensation intermingling between them in the January night's air. "I'll get with them. Let you know what the deal is."

She presses a slip of paper into his hand. "Here's my number."

Brett glances at the digits penned in swoopy feminine script, stops walking and turns toward her. Something in her eyes suggests every nerve ending in her body is ramped up and pulsing information to a receptive processor. Makes him wonder if Lou Ann experiences anything close to that, other than when she's shopping. The last of the others pass and Brett waits until they're out of earshot. "You understand this is just about the dog, Nora. Right? I'm not going to cheat on my wife."

"She makes you happy, your wife? Nothing you wish for?"

"Nothing." He fears he's half a beat slow with his answer. "I'll find out about the dog and let you know. You could take it right away?"

"Yes." Nora's eyes have cooled somehow, signaling her resignation from the temptress gig. Brett reminds himself she's done this before. She never stays unemployed for long.

"Okay, then. See you tomorrow." Brett rewards his good behavior with another imaginary fling on the way to his car. Nora is in his arms and he splays his fingers like tines to comb through the loopy curls exploding from her hat. I could move in with you. It would be deluxe. Hell, what I make at school will easily cover the lot rental and monthly on the trailer. I'll quit Longworth and just teach. You could quit, too. Take classes at the community college. Nora honks on her way out of the lot, and his mind spins back to the reality of the heavy alimony a divorce decree would levy. He heaves himself into his Buick and keys the ignition. "Take the Long Way Home," the seventh cut on the CD that lives in his player, is cued and begins immediately. The harmonica yowls like a lost lover's ghost.

~*~

The dog has been prowling Brett's consciousness for months. It's chained to a large redwood doghouse in the side yard of a rural McMansion, three plays of Long Way from where he and Lou Ann live. They must really love that pup, he thought when he first noticed it. But the dog, a sand-colored husky or chow, is perpetually on the roof of its house, facing the owner's home as though it's waiting for someone. The absence of bikes or swings indicates there are no children. The residents, a thirty-something couple, are often in the yard, but no matter what time of day Brett drives by, he never sees anyone near the dog. The doghouse looks homey enough, but the animal's lonely vigil, waiting endlessly for a companion or just a pat on the head, grows Brett's concern like a tumor.

He considered offering to buy it. "Are you serious?" Lou Ann shrieked when Brett proffered the idea of getting a dog. "Some animal's toenails scratching my polished oak floors? Yeah, *that'll* happen. Besides, you're never home. I'd be stuck taking care of the damned thing." She had him there, working two jobs to pay for her polished oak.

The idea of stealing the dog evolved slowly. At first, it was just one of the fantasies Brett kept in the rotation to while away shifts at Longworth. But like many ideas which seem outlandish at first, it gained credibility the more he thought about it—the major reason he tries to keep notions of Nora in check. If I do steal it, what then? became the question. To his surprise, Nora may well be the answer. His mother is wintering in Florida, and the plan is to temporarily house the dog in her heated garage. Nora could pick it up there.

He stops at the Seven Eleven and buys a package of lunch meat. Back in the car, he reviews his plan as he heads out of town, amazed by the fact he's going through with it. The whole thing is totally outside the box that once contained an admired high school English teacher. Brett cackles out loud, imagining what the students and faculty at Bloomfield High would think if they could witness their 2008 Teacher of the Year on this mission.

The song ends and Brett hits the repeat button. His mind glides across the melody yet again. The lyric that first grabbed him was the line about a wife considering her husband furniture—a part of the living room landscape. One late night driving home from Longworth, the rest of the song flowed by unnoticed on the classic FM station, but that lyric jumped out and focused his thoughts on Lou Ann. There was a time when she would have come along on this foray. Brett loves the memory of her trigger-quick wit and the deep-dimple smile that accompanied it. He wonders what happened to that sweet and passionate young woman; the one he lavished with excess she once appreciated and now expects. Demands. He wonders if there is any chance the situation will ever change, and if he can hang in with Lou Ann if it doesn't.

~*~

Brett takes his foot off the gas when the house where the dog lives is in sight. In the light of the moon, the animal's coat glows against the dark background of the woods. As usual, it's lying on its house, facing its owner's home. The idea is to turn onto the crossroad and park on the other side of the woods. Brett's attention is on the dog and he's at the corner before he realizes it. He gets on the brakes hard and the heavy Buick skids on some gravel, wallows, but manages a clumsy do-si-do around the turn. The package of lunchmeat slides off the seat. He gropes, finds it and slips it into one of his big coat pockets.

When the tree line hides the house, he cuts the headlights, slips the car into neutral and lets the sedan coast to a stop on the berm. He flips the switch on the dome light to exit the car in darkness. Pushing the door open, he steps into the moonlit silence, pulls out a note, and slides it under the driver's side windshield wiper: CAR STALLED. WENT FOR HELP. He can't resist enjoying a rush of pride in his attention to detail, hashed and rehashed endlessly on boring Longworth second shifts. "I think of everything, man," he mumbles, gently closing the car door. He pulls out his cell, keys it off and walks toward the woods.

The narrow area of forest is less formidable to negotiate than he'd feared. There are areas of heavy brush, but they are easy to avoid. With the foliage down, the moonlight makes it almost daytime-bright, but with the absence of snow, he figures his dark coat and Levis should camouflage his presence.

Brett slows his pace as he approaches the rear of the yard and begins to pick his way carefully, trying to make as little noise as possible. The memory of long-ago snipe hunts at Boy Scout camp surface and nearly makes him giggle. His main concern is the dog may bark, a possibility he's pondered repeatedly. The animal appears docile, waiting day in and day out for companionship, but Brett worries it might startle and bark out of fear. If that happens, his only option will be to scotch tonight's operation, slip back into the woods and devote more shifts at Longworth to hatching a new plan.

The dog appears to be sleeping. Brett takes a breath, then clicks his tongue against the roof of his mouth. The dog snaps to attention, its big head oscillating slowly in Brett's general direction. When he repeats the click, the dog zeros in, stands and looks directly at Brett. It's larger than it appeared to be from the road. Shit, I hope Nora won't care.

"Hey, buddy, how you doin'?" Brett whispers. The dog doesn't bark. Instead, cocking its head, it whimpers softly. The hair between its shoulders is standing, a dull patch against the rest of its glossy coat. "It's okay, I'm your friend." The animal doesn't appear to be threatening, so Brett holds out his hands and takes several deliberate steps. "I'm gonna get you out of here. I know a sweet gal who'll take good care of you."

He continues to gentle forward and the dog lowers its head, a move Brett takes to be submissive. Again, the dog makes soft sounds deep in its throat; not quite whining, but nearly. Brett's within twenty feet now, and looking at the loops of chain, he's convinced the dog could reach him if it chose to. It shows no obvious signs of aggression or fear, but Brett senses a tingle of confusion in the way the big canine cocks his head. The moon reflects in the animal's eyes, making them unreadable, but its body language continues to register as non-threatening.

Then the dog begins to flick its tongue, almost snake-like, from the front of its mouth. Does it smell the ham, Brett wonders? "Yeah, bet you'd like a little snack before we go, right, buddy?" he whispers, sliding his hand slowly into his pocket. He pulls out the package of meat and tears it open. The dog thrusts its nose toward the sky. "See? I brought this for you," Brett tells it, pulling several slices free and tossing them onto the roof of the doghouse. The animal drops its head again and, tail between its legs, sniffs at the meat. "It's okay, boy. That's all yours." The dog looks at Brett, tentatively licks the ham a couple times, then laps it into his mouth, wolfing it down greedily. Brett pulls the rest of the meat from the package, takes several slow steps to reach the dog and hand-feeds the rest to the big husky, rubbing it behind the ears as it chews, then swallows.

Suddenly, uncertainty washes through Brett like a wave of nausea. The dog is much larger than he thought. Maybe too big for a trailer. What if Nora balks? Or what if she's okay with the dog, but the manager at the trailer park won't let her keep it? Then what? The dog begins to jump and lick Brett's face as he pets it. Shit, once I take you, the deal is done. He will be stuck with the dog if problems turn up on Nora's end. And yet, he doesn't want to back out. The dog won't leave Brett alone. It's down off the doghouse now, leaning to maintain contact with Brett's legs and tonguing his hands at every opportunity.

Brett swallows down his uncertainty. "Let's get you out of here." He walks over to the doghouse with the dog nearly tripping him in its eagerness for closeness. Brett unscrews the eyebolt securing the chain, and when it's only a thread or two from being free, he yanks it, splintering the wood. "Looks pretty convincing to me, big guy," Brett says, smiling. "You just broke loose. Now, let's hit the road."

With the chain coiled like a rope in one hand, and holding the remaining three feet of chain as a leash in the other, Brett walks the dog across the yard and into the woods. To his surprise, the big animal never looks back toward the house. On the contrary, there is no slack in the chain as the dog pulls, as though it knows where they are going. Bret wishes he was certain.

When they emerge from the trees on the far side of the woods, he fishes out his cell and swipes it on. It lights up and he's delighted to see there are no messages. He notices the time, 12:29. Good. Lou Ann must be sound asleep.

He and the dog make only another fifty yards before the phone ringtones. He doesn't have to look to know who it is. "Hi," he whispers.

"Hi?" she squawks. "Where the heck *are* you?"

Brett's mind is spinning. "I'm sorry. I found a dog."

"A what?"

He waits for more story to download. "Uh, a dog ran across the road in front of me on my way home. I almost hit it. Anyway, I can't just leave it here. And it's a little skittish, so it took me a while to catch it."

"A while? You got off work over an hour ago. And I told you, no dogs."

No dogs. Brett's anger surges like voltage. I'm not your fucking child, goddamn it. He chokes that down. "I think somebody at work might take it."

"One of the teachers?"

"No. Someone at Longworth. A woman I work with. Just tonight, she said she'd like a dog."

"What if she doesn't? And what are you going to do with it in the meantime if she does?"

Jesus, Lou Ann, get off my fucking case. "I'll keep it in the garage—"

"I'm not moving my car outside so you can turn our garage into a kennel," Lou Ann cuts in. "No way."

Strong emotions always bleed out of Brett as tears. He hates that about himself, but he's never been able to control it. Even as a teen, he came out of a schoolyard scuffle or two as the clear winner, but with tears washing his cheeks. He wipes his eyes with his coat sleeve. They are at the car now and he opens the door and coaxes the dog inside, tossing the chain on the floor.

"Brett. Did you hear me?"

He closes the door and leans against his car, the back of his head flat against the roof. The winter sky is crystalline, with stars, planets and the buttery moon hanging above him. The firmament is in fuzzy focus, and when he blinks to clear the tears refracting his vision, they tickle as they run down toward his ears. The expanse of the universe makes him feel very small, but at the same time, it gives him a sense of incredible freedom and possibility. He thinks about explorers who looked up in the same way, centuries before. Those adventurers knew little about where they were and where they were going, yet they pressed on.

"Brett? Are you still there? What did you say?"

"You didn't let me finish. I never said anything about *our* garage. I'm taking the dog to my mother's house."

"But she's in Florida. You can't just leave it there. It'll poop all over and tear the place up. She'll—"

"No." The word cuts her to silence, a hush Brett savors for a moment. Calm washes away his anger, and he finger-squeegees his cheeks dry. "I'm staying there with it." He bends to look into his car. The dog is sitting on the seat like an eager passenger. "The dog and I will be at my mother's."

Brett hangs up and slips the phone into his pocket as he gets into the Buick. The dog stands, but sits back down when Brett strokes its head. He keys the ignition, and when the engine starts, the Supertramp CD begins again. He shuts off the player and looks at the dog. "Tramp. That's a good name for you, big guy." He puts the car in gear and releases the brake. "We're both just a couple tramps. Free to a good home."

As Brett pulls away, his cell ringtones again. He looks at the display and when he sees it's Lou Ann calling, he turns it off and tosses it into the backseat.

EXPLANATION

You drop out of sleep. It feels like the last few feet of an elevator ride. The doors open and the dim image of the broken plastic light fixture above the bed glows in the morning's light, filtered through a grimy window. How the hell does an over-bed light fixture get broken? And why are most light fixtures breast-shaped? Repressed designers, chained too long at drafting tables in windowless production studios? Regardless, this booby took a hit. No pink ribbon for the perp.

You stumble out of bed, nearly falling when the grainy sheet wraps itself around your ankle as though it likes you. Tugging doesn't work, so you flail. Shake your foot like a surfer fighting off an attacking shark. You read they have sand-textured skin, the extent of your knowledge. Damn, the sheet won't let go and so you lift your knee toward the tit-fixture and pull the twisted fabric from your foot. Actually laugh as you imagine the video: a forty-three-year-old naked man, hopping on one leg while freeing the other in a tiny, rented gray room.

You recap on your way to the bathroom. Worked too late. Couldn't face another meal of Manwich and beer. Stopped at a watering hole where no one goes autobio on your shoulder. Caught her looking a few times, so you shot her a smile. Thin. Asian. A hooker, you figured. Another bourbon to assess caution vs. need. Finally decided, what the hell? You hate condoms, but self-sex wears thin. Finished your burger, picked up your drink and sauntered over. Your studied ramble.

She smiled and said yes to a martini. Told you she was in college. You bet against it, but played along. Slender as a mannequin. Pretty, angular face. Punctuating eyes that widened at the end of each sentence.

Curious to watch. Slender neck begging consideration. Out of nowhere, you imagined licking it, clavicle to chin.

"We could go somewhere," you whispered, at the finish of her second drink.

Never take them home. Help keep the Blue Gables Motel in the black. Bug heaven. Strip your clothes in the garage when you get home, then straight into the washer.

Some nights the momentum falls away. Your time with her passed too quickly. She was passionate. Bubbly. Made you giggle. She smelled fresh, like a windblown ocean beach in June. And at some point before you came, you ran your tongue from the notch between her collar bones to her chin, and savored her look of amused surprise.

Oh, shit! Sometimes they steal you blind. You panic and hurtle out of the bathroom to eviscerate your wallet like a shark. But, everything is there. Credit cards. Cash. You rush to find your keys in your pants pocket. Everything present and accounted for, except for Lian. Suddenly, the tiny room seems cavernous.

Next to where your wallet lay there is a fortune cookie. You tear the cellophane and crack it open. The little strip of paper reads, "Your happiness intertwines with your outlook."

Well, that explains a lot.

AFRICAN ASHES

Clay watched Robin lift the little plastic sword from her empty martini glass and pluck the olive from its end with her straight teeth. Her richly wrinkled lips closed, she chewed several times and the corners of her mouth drew into the faintest inkling of a smile as she swallowed. He couldn't pull his eyes away from what seemed at once so sensual, yet somehow innocent. He noticed she'd applied her lipstick so it slightly overran the boundaries of her lips, an illusion that fooled him, until then.

So many variables had to fall as they did for them even to be there together. If Ron and Stacy had picked another bar for the meet up. If their babysitter's grandmother hadn't had the stroke that called Ron and Stacy home before they could pick up Stacy's friend, Maureen. If Robin would have left with her friend instead of finishing a phone call at their table. If Clay didn't help her retrieve the innards of her purse when she dropped it, and happen to notice they both had passkeys to the same twenty-four hour access gym.

"You live in Brooklyn, you said?" she asked.

Clay nodded. "Gravesend. East 5th."

"You really aren't responsible for seeing me home, you know. My friend, Laura, wouldn't have. Besides, Chelsea's way north, and Gravesend's way south from here."

"Well, it's almost three hours since your friend left." He chuckled. "I've had regular dates that didn't last that long, and I always made certain they got home okay." He finished the last of his beer. "The shop's closed for the week, so I can sleep in. If we can flag a cab before we get to the station, we'll do that. Otherwise, we'll take the train." He sat forward and wagged his finger. "Not something you should do alone at this hour."

She made a face like a kid with the wrong answer in a spelling bee. Clay helped her into her coat and they went outside. The air was New York cold. No wind, but he couldn't imagine it would have made any difference. After a few blocks, his exposed skin reached a temperature at which it no longer felt it belonged to him. No cabs passed, and by the time they'd walked down to catch the train, the East Village already owned his forehead and nose, and was closing the deal on the rest of his face.

The platform was empty, except for an older executive-type engaged in a heated discussion with someone on the receiving end of his cell. Clay took a moment to study Robin in the overflow of fluorescent subway light. She had a spare delicate quality. Her short-cropped, reddish-blond hair was spiked, giving it an almost feathery look. She was so easy on the eye, he couldn't help but wonder why she felt her lips needed an extra bit of face. She gazed at some graffiti, so he relaxed and trained his full attention on her. She turned and caught him in mid-gape.

She smiled. "Sorry about the woman who had the stroke, but I'm happy your friends couldn't make it. I know that's selfish, but sometimes that's what I am."

Clay laughed. "It was a set-up. Some friend of my business partner's wife."

"A blind date?"

Clay nodded.

"Well, at least I'm one you can see." She moved a step closer and rested her head against his shoulder.

When they arrived at Chelsea station, Clay thought it colder even than The Village. They walked along 22nd Street, with only the muted noise of the traffic supplying the background for the cadence of her shoes clicking against the concrete. He liked the sound. They walked hand in hand, apart, and arm in arm, by turns. As the Chelsea Hotel came into view, she let go of his arm and began to skip.

"Leonard Cohen wrote a great song about that place," Clay said, tipping his head in its direction.

She swooped his way, turned, and danced backwards, facing him as he continued to walk. "The Chelsea?" She smiled, and sang, "Oh, I remember it well," her voice rumbling almost as low a timbre as Cohen's as she paraphrased. She spun and took his arm again. "I had to stop listening to him."

"And why was that?"

"His albums left me feeling flattened, I guess, like I'd been trampled by elephants or something," she said, guiding Clay into the empty street. "I like artists who push my buttons, but Cohen pushes all of them at the same time." She dropped his arm and pointed at a big brick box of a building ahead. "I live on the third floor."

Clay followed her up the steel staircase, watching dizzying flashes of the pale soles of her boots in the dim light. When they arrived at her door, a huge metal slider large enough to drive a bus through, she opened a padlock that could have been filched from an English castle.

"It came with the place," she said, anticipating the question Clay's lips were already positioned to ask. "Isn't it wonderful?" she chirped.

The huge door was suspended on rollers, and she effortlessly moved it with one arm, opening a slot wide enough to step through together. When they were inside, she used the same lock to secure it from the inside and flipped several switches, causing the room to explode in light.

Cavernous, the room was the size of a regulation basketball court and just as high. White walls ran to the girders supporting the roof, stopping short to allow five or six feet of window to show on three of the four walls.

"Sit anywhere," she said with a giggle as she took off her coat. "I'll get us some wine."

Clay handed her his jacket, looked around, and noticed there was no furniture. There were islands of pillows and heavy quilts scattered about on the polished wood floor. A wood-burning stove, a huge black beast perched on orange terra cotta tiles with a stack soaring to the ceiling, loomed in the center of the room. In the corner nearest where Clay stood, there was a kitchen area with a refrigerator and stove, a sink, and a large butcher's block.

"Where do you get firewood in New York City?" Clay asked, walking into the center of the room, noticing the walls were covered with a geometric mosaic of unframed canvases. A few of them were painted, but most were blank.

"You wouldn't believe it," Robin said, handing him a glass of wine. "Turns out the guy downstairs builds custom furniture." She laughed. "There's an endless supply. He has one of his guys bring me a box of scrap pieces every day in the cold months."

"And these paintings are yours?" Clay asked.

"Well, yes, some of them. I mean, they're all mine, in that I stretched the canvases. But, as you can see, I've only painted a few so far. The rest are still just oversized acoustical tiles." She blushed. "It must be a product of my working in a gallery."

"A minimalist gallery, you said?"

"Yes, down in The Village. In fact, it's called The Myn. Spelled M-Y-N." She sipped her Merlot. "Anyway, the point is, my older sister is a surgical nurse ... has been for ten years." She shook her head. "Now Lissa honestly believes she could do a heart transplant. I mean, she assists with them all the time, and she got to where she believes she could do one on her own. Maybe it's genetic, or something. After three years at The Myn, I believed I could paint."

"That one's really nice," Clay said, pointing. "What I like is the secondary colors are so subdued, you don't notice them at first. The browns and beiges jump right out, but the purples, oranges and greens filter in." He moved closer. "Oh, and the yellows," he added. Her brushwork was pleasing, with delicate small strokes floating atop bold broad ones. He turned and winked at her. "I think you're very good."

She looked at the painting a long while without speaking. Just as she didn't feel she had to cover every inch of canvas with paint, she didn't feel she had to fill every moment with words. A little smile crept across her face. "Thank you," she whispered.

She handed Clay her wine glass and walked to the wood-burner, opened its doors, and tossed a few pieces of wood inside.

"Chester, the furniture builder, imports this wood from Africa. I don't know what kind it is, but I love the smell when it burns. Isn't it good?"

Clay nodded. The aroma held a vague wisp of licorice.

They fashioned a nest from the pillows and quilts, got more wine, and continued to talk. Clay decided this woman was much like her paintings; unexpected nuances surfaced, the closer he looked.

She tapped the crystal of his watch. "It's two o'clock, and I work in a few hours," she said, laughing.

"Well like I said, today's Saturday, and I don't," he replied.

"Lucky guy," she said, standing. "So, why don't you just crash here tonight? It will be way late by the time you get all the way down to Brooklyn." She raised an eyebrow. "You said you live alone," releasing her lips into a "gotcha" smile.

"You saw through me, I guess," Clay said. "Mona's waiting back at my apartment, and she's going to be pissed."

"Why is it every time I meet a man worth more than a few hours' time, there's always another female involved?" She shook her head and let her round lower lip shoulder its way over the upper one. Her pout didn't appear contrived.

"You got it right," he said. "Female. Had you said woman, I'd have had to correct you." He leaned toward her conspiratorially. "Mona's my cat ... kitten, actually."

"Going from bad to worse," she groaned.

Clay's facial expression apparently asked the question before he could get it out.

"Not only are you so committed to ecology," she continued, "that you quit Wall Street to build bicycles and help save the environment, but now I find out you're one of those sensitive guys with a kitty." She fired a wink.

"It's not for the environment. Ron and I build carbon fiber racing bikes. They cost thousands. I'm half-owner, and I couldn't afford one."

"Well, that's better. Does little Mona have enough water and food to last her the night? I mean, you'll have to sleep on the floor." She chuckled. "I don't just work at a minimalist gallery, I also live a minimalist life." She flourished like a Price is Right model. "As you can see."

Clay got to his feet and Robin caught him by surprise with a soft kiss. A quick peck, but it left him with a feeling of promise. "I think I can get out of here without waking you," she said, "so take your time when you get up. Coffee's in the cupboard. The wood-burner heats up fast. Just lock up when you go. Oh, and the bathroom's through the door over there," she added, pointing across the room.

She walked over to what Clay assumed was a wall-hanging near one corner of the room, unhooked an end and attached it to another hook on the adjacent wall, making it into a hammock. While he arranged some blankets and pillows on the floor, she used the bathroom.

"It's all yours," she said, when she reappeared. Kicking off her shoes, she slipped into her hammock. "Last one in turns out the lights," she added with a giggle, swaddling herself in a quilt.

~ * ~

Clay fell asleep almost instantly. When he awakened, he experienced one of those panicky moments when he couldn't remember where he was. Sunlight slanted through the windows, slashing across the paintings and paintings-to-be. The hammock returned to wall-hanging status, and the room was silent.

Clay dreamed in strong visuals, and once he had himself placed, he cuddled under the quilts and recalled dreams of elephants dancing and kicking up clouds of red-brown dust on an African plain. His watch said nine o'clock, and his exposed skin said the stove needed a fire. He found a note lying on the wood box.

Clay—

Running late, so I had to fly. Hope Mona isn't too upset with you. I have your number. I'll call.

—Robin

Clay stirred the ashes, discovered some glowing coals, and used her note to kindle a flame. As the coffee heated, he savored its aroma mingled with the smoky good fragrance of African wood.

KNOCKING

Ryndell Klegg felt sucker-punched. He was certain the DNA forensics collected would take down the Alonzo brothers and their protégé, Pooch Clayburn. Nada. Not a nodding acquaintance between their slimy genes and the semen harvested from the woman's body. Now Ryndell would have to bust them loose. Pitbulls on the playground. Tarantulas in the sheets. Those monsters would be sharking around by sunset, sniffing out fresh prey. Plying the streets in their four-door Impala with their Neanderthal heads on auto-swivel. Twenty-inch wheels with fan-blade spinners whirling like meat grinders, even as the car sat motionless at traffic lights. Testing the vulnerability of every passerby—lingering on the soft pretty ones. Ryndell surveilled them once, from an unmarked car until they finally made him. Wily as snakes. Three middle fingers through the windows of the sedan. Three gap-toothed leers. Ryndell would make certain he was not there to witness their release, so he wouldn't have to endure those snarky sneers again when they cleared the smudged-to-translucence sliding glass at Metro. But Ryndell would still see, even if he wasn't there.

He stopped. No one in the corridor. He fisted his hand, stretched his arm nearly straight and slammed the tight ball of fingers into the side of his head. Just in front of his right ear, where his jaw hinged. Welder's sparks flamed inside his closed eyelids. Pain exploded from his jaw like an M-80. Tendons in his thick neck fought the concussion, aiming rounds of pain southbound into his trapezius muscles. Knuckles burned. Coppery-tasting blood tell-tailed cheek into teeth. He widened his size-twelve stance until he stopped reeling.

Phil Slater, Ryndell's great friend and partner, stepped into the hallway from the break room. His forehead avalanched, half-covering his eyes with bushy graying eyebrows. "You okay, big guy?"

"Working on a headache," Ryndell said, rubbing his acne-scarred cheek. "Labs are back. The dickwads go free."

Phil blew a column of air toward the ceiling. "I'd have bet my left lung." He shook his head. "Now we gotta start again, clean sheet."

Ryndell drew his mouth up as though he would lip-fart, facial shorthand. He and Phil didn't talk a lot. They'd worked together for ten years and knew each other's expressions like their own. Phil had no clue about Ryndell's personal life, however. Ryndell made certain.

"Connie called Jayne. We're coming over for steaks." Phil laughed heartily. "You never mentioned it, so you weren't in on the invitation?"

"Oh, yeah," he lied. "Constance and I talked. It slipped my mind to say anything, is all."

"Bring a DVD, she said. Any requests?"

Ryndell clapped Phil on the shoulder. "Anything funny." Ryndell returned Phil's goodbye, wondering if humor even existed, anymore.

~ * ~

Ryndell felt every one of his fifty-eight years. He'd blown it. When Marge, his first wife, died, between her family money and the insurance, he could have hung it up. Could have found someplace warm where he could become a clueless citizen. Take up fishing. Or golf. But coincidentally, in addition to being his job, law enforcement was his hobby. Like others who pursue dangerous pastimes, skydivers or free-climbers, he would pursue his sideline until he was too old, or until it smashed him into the ground.

He changed his life-style, however. Ryndell was the only detective who drove expensive sports cars. Who moved into a country club community and joined. He played tennis and golf. He ate at the club to use the monthly minimum. He rubbed elbows with executives and businessmen, who treated him like a celebrity. They were impressed with a six foot five, two hundred thirty-five pound police detective, even though they considered him nouveau riche. He played cards in the men's grille and they loved his stories. At a club dance, he met Constance. For quite a while, it seemed his life was headed for the better. Wrong turns often feel that way.

He drove through the gate and up the red brick drive that wandered the lawn and landscaping he paid to have maintained. His stomach was on full-roil. Constance would be nervous about having the Slaters over. She loved to entertain, especially after a new acquisition or redecoration project, but was never confident an evening would go as she desired. Ryndell's job was to make that happen. When he pulled into the garage, he pressed the remote to close it and walked to the house's locked entry door. He knocked twice.

~ * ~

Mother used to lock the door, too. She said it was to protect Ryndell's stepsisters from men. Men had only one thing on their minds. Young Ryndell would be a scumbag man, soon. The door needed to be locked.

When he came home, he'd knock. Twice. Sometimes Mother answered right away, which was good. The longer he had to wait, the worse it was. Mother might be angry, and that meant a trip to the switch tree. Pick your switch, she would say. But Mommy, I didn't do anything. Pick your switch, or I'll pick one for you. No, Mommy. Please. She'd snap the switch off a branch. Take off your pants and undies, she'd say. Raining or snowing, it didn't matter. Fold them neatly or you'll get it worse. He had to grasp the rough-barked trunk, stick his fanny out and wait. Sometimes Mother did the switching. Sometimes it was one of his stepsisters, the girls Ryndell's stepfather left behind when he lit out. Wendy and Dora weren't as strong, but they made up for that with fervor. Delicious enjoyment. Dora, the older one, liked to bring the switch up from below, catching him full on his little nut sack. How could Mother do this? How could she favor Wendy and Dora over her own flesh and blood? Because they were girls? You're just a pint-sized man. I know how depraved you are, Mother told him.

If she didn't open the door, Ryndell didn't knock again. That guaranteed a trip to the switch tree. Sometimes it was minutes before she'd answer. Sometimes it was hours. Now and then, he spent the night in the garage, sleeping on the back seat of the Buick. In the morning, he'd go back and stand on the step, but he never re-knocked. Two raps were the maximum allowed. Just wait, young man. I'll get to you when I'm good and ready. He memorized the number of bricks in the wall. The number of nail heads on the overhang. Watched shadows creep across the concrete floor. Ryndell amused himself by counting and observing, attuned to the sound of the rattling chain lock, followed by the clack of the deadbolt. He'd shift on his feet, ready to step inside as soon as the dry hinges squealed when she opened the door. Get to your room was the greeting he'd hear, accompanied often by a slap on the head. The head slaps hurt, but not as intended.

~ * ~

Ryndell waited for Constance to open the door. If she was upstairs, it could take several minutes, but rarely longer. He was forbidden to use his key. She might be entertaining, she said. Might be sucking off the pool boy. Might be riding the gardener's big hard dick, Mr. Cuckold, she'd tease. He took it as teasing. He didn't believe she actually cheated, because he didn't want to. He waited, wondering which Constance would open the door. Finally, the bolt clicked and the door swung wide.

Constance was one of the most beautiful women Ryndell ever saw. She reminded him of that model-turned-actress, Lauren Hutton. Tall, willowy and blonde, with delicately chiseled character lines creasing her unblemished cheeks when she smiled. She was a woman who knew just how to dress. Always bought bras one cup-size too small to make her medium-sized breasts appear larger. Wore thongs or nothing to avoid panty lines while the clingy material she favored in slacks and skirts showcased her firm hips and thighs. Except when she was angry, which never occurred outside the house, her voice was a soft patter, like thick lotion waterfalling onto marbles. The night Ryndell met her, she kept hold of his hand when they broke from a slow dance. She sat with her arm draped over the back of his chair. Ryndell, who characterized his own looks as unfortunate, rode

192

waves of delighted disbelief when she made it obvious she thought he was intriguing. Inside of three months, they were married. That's when Ryndell the detective discovered he was foolish enough to be fooled.

~ * ~

"I told you the Slaters are coming over," she said, as though it were fact.

It was never good to cling to truth. "Yes," Ryndell said, bending to kiss her.

She swayed away. "I may have had something in my mouth you wouldn't want to taste, Rynnie," she said, pointing to the side of her face.

He obediently kissed her cheek. "What do I need to do?"

"I had the service in, so the house is clean." She sipped her tonic water on ice, all she ever drank except for a single glass of wine at dinner. "You're grilling steaks. Decide on the rest. Potato of some kind. There is fresh asparagus in the fridge. Salad. I bought a cherry pie, so you're off the hook on that." She turned to leave. "I'm sure you'll make it perfect. Mommy will be in the hot tub."

She'd taken to calling herself that, though she was twenty-eight years his junior. Ryndell made the mistake of confiding about his childhood, back when things were good between them. Before their marriage. Oh, Ryndell, don't hold back, she said. Letting it out is the key to putting it away, she told him. She stroked his head and actually licked tears from his cheeks as he recounted the horrors. Her face took on his grief, keen to share his misery and help him divest of his dysfunctional past. The fortified walls of his nightmares crumbled to harmless rubble with Constance heading up demolition. When he told her of the trips to the switch tree, how Dora took her turn whipping at his scrotum, Constance made him forget the pain, lavishing him with pleasure. She cupped him in her delicate hands and took him into her mouth. Moaned softly as he came, while waves of ecstasy supplanted memories of the searing pain that had once issued from his genitals.

Ryndell never planned to remarry. His years with Marge were a blessing. What were the chances another woman would want an ugly old brute like Ryndell? When Constance proposed, he found himself in a tumbledown of embarrassment. A beautiful young woman accepted him for what he was and spent months demonstrating it. How had he overlooked her feelings? He couldn't say yes fast enough. Pre-nup to protect his assets? Forget it. I love you, Constance. He always called her that, even though everyone else called her Connie. Constantly happy and in love with Constance. He lavished her with every attention, and she was so appreciative.

After their honeymoon, a subtle shift began. She started to expect. Demand. Let him damn well know if she wasn't getting what she deserved. How could this be? One afternoon Ryndell made a stand. He was in the kitchen, his laptop on the island, looking at speedboats, online. You're not wasting money on a fucking boat, Constance said. He couldn't believe what he heard. He held his temper and composure, explaining it was his money, not hers. His money from Marge's estate and the insurance. His money working as a senior detective, while Constance languished at luncheons and gatherings at the club. Not far into his soliloquy, a subtle smile pressed her cheeks. Had she caught him up in a joke? Was he going to wind up embarrassed? Oh God, Constance, I can't believe I fell for that, honey. But, her smile morphed to a sneer. Our money, she said. Community property, my love. She drew the word love out eight inches long, and slid it between his ribs like an assassin's knife. Half of the house. The cars. The investments and bank accounts. Your retirement. Half of it all, my love, her lips twisting the words to maximize the injury. "You just go and spend some of your half on a speed boat, my love. Then you know what? Half the speed boat will be mine, too."

Ryndell bellowed. No words, only sound born of insult and embarrassment and anger and sadness and dashed beliefs and smashed self-image. Bellowed like any beast when a trap sprung. A grizzly feeling the steel jaws. A boar, the snap of a snare.

Ryndell's rage washed Constance's face of any expression, except bewilderment. Or fascination. He took a step in her direction and the sneer was back in a pulse-beat. Sure, go ahead and put one finger on me. Come on, Dirty Harry. Make my fucking day, you ugly moose. Just one punch, one slap, one grab of my arm and I'll hire a lawyer and own everything, not just half.

Her leer gave way to a look he saw on con men he collared. Cunning. The look that says, you think you have me outwitted, but you don't have a chance in hell. He'd seen it in the Alonzo brothers' eyes, and Constance slammed him with the same look in the kitchen, that day. Cooking utensils hung overhead on wrought iron spokes, radiating like umbrella stays stripped of their fabric. "Choose your switch," she growled, pointing at the shiny equipment, "or I'll choose for you."

She didn't wait. She took a long stainless-steel spoon in her hand. "Your mother was right. You are a depraved fuck. I know what you wanted to do to me." She slammed the bowl of the heavy spoon into his upper arm and an electric sting radiated inward. "The fact you didn't do it doesn't change what you are." Another blow with the spoon, this one on his shoulder. He crumpled. It wasn't from the pain. Ryndell's nerve endings yelped; but at the same time, it somehow felt right. He'd wanted to harm her. To crush her. She was right, just like his mother. He was despicable. Ugly and depraved. And stupid enough to find himself in this situation. Trapped and humiliated. Capable of attacking a woman and deserving of the pain Constance administered. She hit him several more times. He took it. Cast his eyes down and let her flail.

When he heard the spoon clatter into the sink, he looked up. She smiled. The same smile Ryndell remembered from the first time they made eye contact at the country club's Tartan Ball. A smile so devoid of malice, he could almost believe the last five minutes never happened. "Now you know how it is," she said, her voice barely audible above the gurgle of the waterfall in her new living room koi pond. She winked, turned and walked out of the kitchen, her hips rolling provocatively.

Ryndell knew the ploy. It worked on suspects he questioned. Hell, it worked on everyone. Good cop, bad cop. Sweet and sour. Pain and pleasure. The human psyche is easy to manipulate, if you understand the technique. Constance could have written the book. She got and she gave. She hit and she held. Slapped, then gave him the best long slow lovemaking he'd ever experienced. The net result was he hated to love her and loved to hate her. But, he had to kowtow. That was her ultimatum. Dance to my music and the party continues. Otherwise, the band goes home and you lose half of all you have.

The hell of it was, he was thirty years closer to dying than she, and eventually Constance would inherit everything. He'd always treated her like a princess, lavished her with affection and money. So, was she just evil? Was she, herself, a product of the abuse/abuser cycle? Ryndell didn't know, but he knew it made no difference.

~ * ~

The Slaters arrived. Constance swept down the stairs in time to entwine her arm with Ryndell's, an instant before he opened the door. She was in deliriously-happy-doting-wife mode. She moved so Ryndell could affectionately shoulder-bump Phil. Constance cheek-kissed Phil and complimented him on his cologne. Ryndell bussed Jayne's cheek, then Constance took Jayne's hand, shepherding her to the new koi pool. Phil wanted to see it too, so the four of them stood and watched the palm-sized white and orange fish ply the shallow waters, ripples making their images pixilate like satellite TV on a stormy night. As Constance told it, Ryndell single-handedly installed the pool. What a wonder he is, she said repeatedly. Ryndell got off a couple self-deprecating asides to the contrary. Constance couldn't keep her hands off him.

Ryndell and Phil made the male exodus to the grille, out on the poolside patio. They sipped single-malt scotch and discussed pre-season football. The economy. They never talked about police work, off the job. After Ryndell turned the steaks, Phil buddy-punched Ryndell's shoulder. "I'm going to tell you something I never thought I'd say, Ryn. When you told me you were marrying a thirty year-old gal, I thought you were out of your goddamn skull." Phil chuckled. "You are the luckiest bastard I know," he said, smiling. Ryndell silently rephrased Phil's words. An unlucky bastard who let a wily young woman checkmate me. Much as he loved Phil, Ryndell was too proud and vain to let his friend know the truth. Ryndell smiled and clicked his tongue.

With the Slaters seated at the table on the patio, Constance walked into the kitchen and jabbed a knuckle hard into the small of Ryndell's back. He winced. "I can't believe you let the salads sit out nearly fifteen minutes.

And you never breathed my wine." Constance jabbed him with her sharp elbow. As they rejoined their guests, she clung to Ryndell like a drowning victim to a lifeguard. When she was seated, Constance forked a small bite of salad. "This is to die for, Rynnie," she said, smiling.

They never watched the movie the Slaters brought, some comedy spun off a *Saturday Night Live* skit. Instead, their talk flowed over diverse but predictable subjects. Vacations. The Slaters' concerns with their daughter heading off for college in the fall. Around 10:30, Phil said he was sleepy, which precipitated jokes about aging. Ryndell poured himself another whiskey. Constance extolled the virtues of a "seasoned" man, ultimately making Ryndell sound like a sexual dynamo. Phil seemed amused, but Ryndell thought Jayne's face registered a degree of embarrassment matching his own.

"How many of those have you had tonight?" Constance said, pointing at Ryndell's drink as the Slaters' car doors slammed outside. Ryndell could feel his insides shrink. "Uh? You going to be too drunk to get it up tonight, Rynnie? What if I require sex?" Ryndell didn't look away, much as he wanted to. Constance's fingers spilled from where her thumbs disappeared into the waistband of her slacks. Her jaw was on full-jut. Ryndell was a little boy, standing on the steps. She began to slowly shake her head. "What's the matter? Did Mommy hurt your feelings today when she had to punish you, little man?" She walked toward him.

His husky baritone barely made it to a whisper. "You treat me like you do, and expect me to make love with you?"

She grinned. "Who said anything about love, Rynnie? I hit you a couple times, today." She ran her hands down the outside of her thighs, crossed them over to the insides and brought them back up. Her thumbs and index fingers paired to form a heart-shape at her crotch. "I thought you might want to hit me back. Bang me hard. Right here," she said, breaking the heart to pat her pubic arch. Her grin widened, then she started for the staircase. "Pick up around here. I need time to freshen up." She paused on the first step. "Then, we'll see if you can live up to the billing I gave you."

Ryndell enjoyed order. There wasn't much to do. After the dishes and table linens were in their respective washers, he remembered his gun was unsecured, in his car. Constance forbid him to bring it into the house, so he moved his gun safe into the garage. He killed his whiskey and walked through the utility room.

The garage was his sanctuary. The walls were finished in cedar, covered with posters from auto races in places he'd never been. A big-screen TV rotated on its mount so he could watch from any area of the huge space. The floor was light gray, with black and white speckles, to contrast with the bright blue of his Porsche and the orange of his Corvette. Constance's silver BMW blended invisibly, which made him smile.

He reached under the driver's seat and pulled out his Glock. He slid the gun from its holster, pressed the release, and the magazine Jack-in-the-boxed into his hand. He checked to make certain the chamber was cleared.

His weapon was unloaded. Useless. That's how Ryndell felt. Gutted. Devoid of the power to take charge and resurrect the former Ryndell Klegg. Oh, on the job he was still a bull. The first to crash the door of a drug-house. The one who ran down twenty-something suspects, if it took blocks to do it. He was savvy about criminals he tracked and captured. In his professional life, these abilities made him a perfect law enforcement package. But in his personal life, he was a little boy battling a torrent of flashbacks while trying to stay afloat in a river of misery and humiliation. Forced to accept untenable abuse to earn occasional shots of bliss, and to preserve a lifestyle he could not bring himself to give up. He squeezed the cold, precise weapon in his hand. It smelled of oil and faintly of gunpowder.

Rydell slid the clip back in and chambered a round. A single bullet to Constance's head would end his misery. He started for the door, but only took a few steps. Shooting her would restore sole title to his fortune, but what good were riches in a prison cell?

The intercom crackled. "I'm waiting, Rynnie."

Ryndell opened wide and shoved the gun barrel against the roof of his mouth. The steel was cold against his tongue. The smell of gunpowder residue made his eyes water. He closed them and pictured the end of the hollow-point slug, less than an inch from his brain pan. He'd witnessed suicide scenes. He pictured what Constance would find when she rushed to investigate the explosion. Finger trembling on the trigger, Ryndell wondered what her reaction would be. Would she scream his name? Would a tsunami of guilt inundate her? Or, would her lips curl upward with the realization everything was now hers?

Constance was absolutely right. Banging her was way better than slamming a bullet into his brain. He pulled the muzzle from his mouth, picked up a cloth and wiped his saliva from the gleaming, angular steel. Ryndell pulled the clip, ejected the round and closed his Glock in the safe.

When he got to the entry door, it was locked. He knocked twice. It opened, immediately.

MONICA'S FALL

Monica looks down and realizes she's made a huge mistake. Thirteen and a half thousand feet huge. Two hundred-fifty bucks huge.

Until today, Monica thought only of otters as a cute fuzzy creatures paddling on their backs, using rocks to break open clamshells. Now, crouched in the open doorway of a De Havilland Super Otter, clinging to the cold metal of the plane's fuselage, it feels like fragile objects are shattering in Monica's stomach, two and a half miles above the checkerboard where humans play out their lives.

"We're almost at the jump zone," Kit, her jump instructor rumbles. His voice could make the speakers in her Kia buzz. Kit. Perfect name for someone so well put together. She's attached to him with two-inch webbed nylon belts, and every time they accidently jostle together, it feels like she's backed into Michelangelo's David. She never stood near the sculpture, but she's seen pictures. "Put your feet on the step," the chiseled Adonis says.

Monica looks down, realizing she's made a huge fricking mistake. The step, attached to the wing strut, seems two stories below. She obediently tries, but the near-hundred mile-an-hour blast buffets her foot from its intended target. Once. Twice. "What's the matter?" Kit intones. "Afraid you're going to fall?" He chuckles and she follows suit, though she's the butt of his joke. That only fortifies her resolve to get her Sauconys onto the damned aluminum step.

One foot finds its mark. The other is still windmilling when she feels Kit's anaconda arm cinch around her waist. "Time to hit it," he says. "Let go and roll out with me."

Oblivion. Monica is blind. Weak. She's a rag-doll in a hurricane.

She feels her cheeks undulating in the wind. She tries to care, but can't find the determination. Her arms flail. Kit grasps her shoulders. He's above her, riding her like a surfboard. Surprisingly sexual. Is it his position, or the thick crotch strap tugging between her thighs? I gotta pee. Lord, help me kegel through this.

Her senses settle. As they explained in ground-school, there is little sensation of falling. It feels like she's lying on a bed of air, with Kit riding her from behind, his body tight against hers. Kegel.

"Let's do a flip," he shouts. With that, he hammers his knees into the backs of her legs, forcing her to jackknife. He spreads his arms, and they somersault wildly. "Whoo-hoo," he whoops, and she involuntarily joins in.

Thousands of feet pass in too little time. "Time to rip it—brace yourself," Kit yells. The chute unfurls with a thunderclap and the straps cinch hard to squeeze the air out of Monica's lungs. Kit guides the chute to the field, where a crowd of well-wishers is clapping and cheering. On the ground, he gathers the canopy. "Well?" he asks, grinning.

"I think I'm falling in love," Monica replies. She notices Kit's smug smile broaden. "With skydiving," she adds. "Next time, I'll jump solo."

TAKING TROPHIES

Dalton Hill sat at the kitchen table, staring at the ad for a military collectables show. The very circumstance allowing him to go also yanked at his emotions. Two months earlier his wife, Leetha, died, ending Dalton's two-year stint as her full-time caregiver. When he noticed the ad in the Sunday sports section, it occurred to him nothing prevented him from making the trip up to Cleveland.

His rough fingertips brushed the stitches Leetha had skillfully sutured into the heavy linen tablecloth, and his eyes drifted from the circular. Embroidery floss. The words were like old friends. Anytime he called it thread, Leetha pursed her lips in exasperation and slowly shook her head, her pink scalp peeking through her thinning gray hair. "Embroidery floss," she'd cluck. He'd make his usual joke about dental floss, which always elicited another shake of her head and a soft hiss of air through her nostrils.

Dalton gazed back at the newspaper and a wave of excitement riffled through him. MILITARY COLLECTABLES. BUY. SELL. TRADE. The previous evening, Dalton enclosed a Luger P08 and a Walther P30 in bubble wrap and packed them into a cardboard box. Dalton took the Luger from a German infantryman he'd wounded. When that soldier died, Dalton kept the man's gun. Others viewed possessions of fallen enemy as trophies, and collected them like scalps. Dalton's Colt had been jamming, and the Luger's magazine was full. Having an extra firearm seemed prudent. Dalton's brother, Levi, gave him the more valuable Walther, just before he died. Dalton had no idea how Levi got the Walther, but he was certain Levi viewed it as a trophy.

A nice young woman at the library helped Dalton research the guns' value on the internet, and he was pretty certain he could come back home with the better part of four thousand dollars if he found the right buyer and negotiated well. That much money would easily cover a new zero-turn mower, something he'd wanted since he first saw Fred Gilmer's, the neighbor two doors down. Trying to remember how much Gilmer said he'd paid, Dalton raised his head in thought, and vertigo overtook him. Quickly lowering his chin, he braced against the table with his big calloused hands. The dizzy uneasiness surged, then dissolved into eddies of mild light-headedness. He'd first experienced the wooziness while changing the light bulb over his workbench; looked up to grasp the burnt-out bulb and nearly fell. I'll mention it to Dr. Phillips, next Tuesday? Careful to keep his head level, he stood to check what he'd written on the calendar. No, Wednesday.

The money the guns might bring was actually secondary. Dalton looked forward to being with other men who, like him, had seen action. A look was all it took to feel unity with another former soldier. Words were inadequate and unnecessary. Dalton kept his black scary memories behind a mental curtain. Sometimes, in dreams, sounds and vague blurred images escaped the shroud, but Dalton was always able to push them back behind the veil. He didn't mind hearing others' stories, if that's the way they needed to deal with their demons, but he never discussed what he'd seen and done to survive. It was his to live with and live down. Privately.

He pressed the newspaper flat on the tablecloth once more. To be held January 26, it said. He double-checked the calendar where he'd printed MILITARY SALE, looking over his half-glasses to keep his head level this time. Down through the lenses, now, 10 AM TO 9 PM. FOOD AVAILABLE. Dalton looked at his watch. "Better get going so I have time to stop at the cemetery," he mumbled.

He stood, tucked the sports section under his arm and scoured his memory for anything he needed to do before he left. A smile tilted the corners of his mouth. There was nothing. He'd fed his squirrels and birds, read the paper and washed his breakfast dishes. They sat in the plastic drainer next to the sink. He'd meant to dry them, but the radiant morning sunlight and dry winter air beat him to it. "You'll have that," was Leetha's favorite phrase. Sometimes it was her comment on the unexplainable.

Often, she used it to emphasize something humorous. But, she could also employ it to highlight her displeasure with something Dalton did or didn't do. He shrugged as he walked past the sun-dried dishes. You'll have that.

As he made the turn at the bottom of the basement stairs, Dalton stepped gingerly around Pepsi's bed. It comforted him to have it there, just the way she'd left it. Her favorite toy was where she dropped it, the last thing she did before he carried her to the car. He couldn't bring himself to move the ball, or even to touch its red rubber surface, pockmarked with the small craters her teeth left behind. He shook his head, thinking a heap of ragged towels and a chewed toy were all that bore witness to the pup's existence. Mrs. Thomason, from next door, was nice enough to come and stay with Leetha that morning. She'd offered many times, but Dalton took her up on it only that once. He believed Leetha enjoyed being with him when he ran errands. The day he took Pepsi to be put down, however, he was afraid it would upset her when the terrier didn't come back home with them, if she noticed. Leetha was pretty well out of herself by then. As it turned out, she never even mentioned Dalton's watery red eyes when he returned.

Sometimes days would pass without Leetha speaking a word. She only smiled, her lips pressed tightly together, one of her few conceits. Embarrassment over her crooked teeth restricted her facial expressions, even as her mind slipped away. But she was full of surprises, right to the end. Once, on their way home from the marketing, they saw a little girl tumble off her bicycle. "You'll have that," Leetha trilled, breaking weeks of silence.

The box holding the guns was on the bar Teddy built when he still lived at home and went to community college. Now he preferred to be called "Ted," and he and Rita only came in from Boston on Thanksgiving or Christmas, alternating years with her parents. This year, it had been Christmas. Dalton tried to make things as they always were, impossible with both Leetha and Pepsi gone. Regardless, he bought a half keg of Bass Ale for the tap in the old downstairs refrigerator. Bass was the best, according to Ted. Dalton preferred less pricey brews, but he wanted everything perfect when Ted and Rita arrived three days before the holiday. Of course, as luck would have it, neither of them could get the pressure set correctly on the CO2 tank. They had to let the pitchers set until the foam dissipated.

Dalton believed Rita fussed and made over him more than usual. She cooked the turkey while he and Ted drank beer and watched football. When Dalton told her the meal was as good as any Leetha ever prepared, Rita smiled and said, "You'll have that." Her eyes opened wide, she covered her mouth and turned nearly red as the stitches in the tablecloth. "Oh, Dad. I'm so sorry."

"No," he assured her, laughing. "That's fine. Miss hearing it." He put his arm around her, patting her shoulder the way he'd used to pat Leetha's. "That's just fine. That's perfectly okay."

He put on his parka and stepped into his rubber boots, loose on his size twelve feet, but too small to wear over his shoes. Don't need shoes, anyhow. He decided he'd close the steel fasteners later. Clasping the box with the guns against his side, he climbed the stairs and let himself out the back door. He twisted the knob. "The door is locked," he said aloud. He'd adopted this ritual to keep himself from questioning his memory. Once, he backtracked twenty miles to make certain he'd locked up. "Door is locked," he repeated on the way to the garage. "Guns in the box. Address is on the ad."

He pulled open the Crown Victoria's door. "Boots and coat," he whispered, dropping heavily onto the seat. He turned the key and pulled the gear selector into reverse, then realized he hadn't raised the door. He pressed the button on the remote and watched the door rise in the rear-view mirror. After backing into the turnout, he put the car in drive and checked to see that the garage door was closing.

Dalton noticed angry gray snow clouds now covered the early morning sun, though several yellow shafts still beamed through holes in the gathering shroud. Those openings soon closed, and by the time Dalton was halfway to the cemetery, the snow was falling and beginning to stick. When he drove through the gates at Ravenwood, the wind was blowing hard enough to form crusty white rollers with the inch or two that accumulated quickly in the squall. Coupled with the snow from the night before, the powdery covering was quilt-thick on Leetha's grave.

Anytime Leetha saw graves loaded with decorations, she always said, "Whoever's buried there was really well-loved." Even though Dalton thought such excess was foolishness, he vowed he'd do her grave up good if she passed first. He never dreamed he would have to make good on his pledge, because he'd suffered his share of respiratory problems. But once he retired on disability and escaped the welding fumes at the shop, he bounced back nicely. They called him in for reviews twice, and both times, his personal doctor wrote letters recommending against his return to work. The state doctor looked more at the paperwork than at Dalton, who had the leavings of a bad cold at his last review. "Lungs still a problem?" the young doctor had asked. Dalton coughed, phlegm cracking nicely. "Sometimes," Dalton replied. Sometimes, when I'm sick.

Dalton didn't feel bad about counterfeiting that bit of truth. Between the time he spent welding broken equipment in the repair shop at the D.O.T. garage and his hitch in the army, he'd given the government over thirty years of good, hard and often dangerous work. He lifted his hand from the steering wheel to trace the scar that began just below his right eye and ran like an extra smile line to his chin. During the war, his company was assigned to the big CG-4A glider planes. Each one carried thirteen troops and was supposed to land them silently in France on D-Day. Even during training, every touchdown was more or less a crash. The one that positioned them behind the German lines June 6th tore off the right wing and split the fuselage. He never knew what ripped his face open, but he packed the wound with mud to stem the bleeding, and fought for almost a week before a corpsman got a look at it. The gash only hurt if he ate, smiled or talked, something infantry did little of during those first days in the forests of Normandy.

When Dalton and Levi came home from the war, they were inseparable, sweating their days away at a brick factory up in Sugar Creek and carousing at night. Each bore scars testifying to their boldness in battle. The women Dalton met in bars seemed to think his scar made him look dashing. Reminiscing on those times with his brother, he recalled how they drank, gambled, and cleared out a beer joint or two. Levi always said, "Cross one Hill, there's another on the other side."

A blast of cold wind brought him back to the cemetery. Leetha's plastic tulips, brimmed with snow, looked like gaily-colored dessert glasses overflowing with sugary froth. Dalton slapped each against his pant leg. The snow dropped into the loose tops of his boots, adding to that which gathered during his walk from the car. It burned the exposed skin above his socks, and ice encrusted the buckles. Leetha used to remind him, "Buckle your boots." "Zip your pants." Fingering the front of his corduroys, he found he'd remembered to do that, at least. My feet'll warm up when I'm back in the car. He stuck the tulips back in their holders.

He lifted the two imitation grass mats and shook off the snow. "Whatever will you do with those?" Leetha scolded when he proudly unloaded his garage sale finds. He smiled and carefully returned two of them to rest between the twin rows of tulips.

He looked at the headstone.

Leetha Elise Hill

June 14, 1926—November 22, 2008

To the right of that inscription was another.

Dalton Felix Hill

March 4, 1929—

He stared at the blank space for several seconds, wondering what numbers would eventually appear there. He looked at the words, "Together Forever," incised on the top of the polished dark granite. That sounded pleasant, but he didn't put credence in the idea. Rita and Ted tried hard to get him to church when they were out for Christmas. "The older I get, the more time wears on those old superstitions," he told them. Rita's eyes bulged in surprise.

After glancing at the space reserved for the year of his death again, Dalton pictured Leetha in her favorite white blouse, back before her mind and her backbone gave out. Toward the end, she felt like a sack of fall leaves when he carried her to the bathroom or to bed. "How do you manage?" people would ask. He'd only smile. She couldn't have weighed ninety pounds. Dalton was seventy-nine years old, but he was over six feet, rangy, and strong as catgut.

He scanned the cemetery. The wind-blown snow swirled in gauzy layers that obscured any burials more than forty or fifty feet away, but those nearby had only a few wreaths and several grave blankets left over from

Christmas. None of the plots he could see were decorated as colorfully as Leetha's. He was certain she'd be pleased, if she had any idea.

"Got to be on my way, Lee," he said. "Going to sell those German pistols today." The irony made him grin. Leetha hated having those guns in the house, but Dalton viewed them as a savings account. Now that she'd passed, he decided to cash them in for a mower. Turning toward the car, he gathered up his collar against the stinging snow. "I miss you," he added, not turning back to speak the words. He didn't really believe she could hear him, anyway. Leetha used to say if she died first she'd look down and keep an eye on him. Trudging through the drifts, it amused him to imagine her watching from about the height of a second story window.

The engine was still warm when he started it. A hefty V-8 holds its heat in the winter, another reason Dalton favored them. He switched the heater to high, kicked his boots off into the passenger-side foot well and pulled up his soaked pant legs. The flesh above his wet white socks was tomato red and felt like it belonged to someone else. The hot air from the heater felt good, and the feeling started coming back, making his skin burn. He imagined Leetha peeking into the car's window from her second-floor vantage point. "You'll have that."

The snow was now three or four inches deep, and resisted the front tires. Despite Dalton's best efforts, the back tires spun furiously. He had four 50-pound salt bags in the trunk and they helped, but he lamented the passing of the Firestone snow/muds with tungsten studs he remembered from the 70s.

When he came to the stop sign at Wait Corners Road, he put the car in park and pulled off his socks, laying them on the transmission tunnel to dry in the hot blast of the heater. Driving barefooted in the dead of a winter storm brought a smile to his craggy face, deepening his war scar. He used to like to drive without shoes in the summer. "My lands, that's against the law," Leetha would scold. Sounded stupid enough to be a law.

Dalton met Leetha when she lived on her uncle's farm, which was five miles down Wait Corners Road from the cemetery, at the corner of Asmus Pike. She'd come out from Maryland for a job at the phone company after the war, and her father had arranged for his brother's family to take her in until she got settled. The farm had changed hands several times since, and was deserted the last time they drove past. Its surrounding acreage fell fallow, and trees and scrub overran the groomed fields. Leetha stopped asking to ride by, so Dalton hadn't driven past the place in years.

Should I go that way? He looked at the clock on the dash. Plenty of time. It's just as easy to take Asmus to Route 27, though he hadn't planned on it. Sometimes he wondered if he dwelled on Leetha too much. Did he love every minute with her? Certainly not. Did he miss her now that she was gone? Without a doubt. But, most things in life looked better in the rearview.

Dalton found getting a glimpse of the old farm strangely irresistible. He signaled, wondering who he thought might notice, and turned left on Wait Corners Road. The car's rear did a whoop-de-do, nearly sliding into the right-side ditch, but Dalton feathered the gas to find traction and got the big sedan tracking straight.

The blasts of snow reduced every object to muted tints of gray. Dalton found himself driving from telephone pole...to mailbox...to fence row, all of which were dim shadows in the blizzard. He passed Center Road. The next one he saw was Sparrow, which meant he'd somehow missed Ogden. Fearing he might not see Asmus, he doubled his efforts to pick out and study every tall object. Passing Denton Road, he decided to clock the mile to Asmus on his odometer, but soon realized his wheels were spinning too much for an accurate reading. He wound up stopping anytime he saw anything that might be a road marker.

He braked to examine something he hoped was the signpost for Asmus Pike, but found it was just another telephone pole. He pressed the accelerator and felt the big car begin to slide, its rear end whipping to the right. He took his foot off the gas, but that didn't seem to help. Riding a wave of panic, he wrenched the steering wheel left and floored it. Suddenly, it felt like a semi had rear-ended his Ford, and all he could see through the windshield was white. I must be in the ditch.

Awash in dizziness and about to retch, he slammed his chin against his chest to level his head. That helped, but there was a terrible roaring. The car was shaking violently as its front end listed sideways, like the bow of a sinking ship. When he realized his foot was still holding the accelerator to the floorboard, he lifted it and jammed down on the brake. The car continued its sideways fall to the bottom of the ditch, the force of the landing throwing Dalton painfully against the passenger door, where he took a good shot to the ribs against the armrest. *I forgot my seat belt.*

With the engine quiet, a soothing silence settled over him. His mind whirled madly in an effort to assess his situation. The glider crash crossed his mind. *Jesus, this is almost as bad.* He swiped at his face to test for blood. There was none. Nothing felt broken, but a sharp chill was creeping up his legs. He heard a gurgle and realized water was rising in the passenger compartment.

Terror shot through him like shrapnel. Gathering his feet, he vaulted straight up toward the driver's window, but pain engulfed his head and neck. *The window is closed.* With his vision narrowing to a small column of light, he fought to maintain his senses while he hung onto the steering wheel to keep from falling. He rubbed the painful spot on the top of his head, but it wasn't bleeding. He found the electric window switch, and a cold blast of snow and wind confirmed it worked. The box with the pistols was floating in the knee-deep water. Dalton grabbed it and hoisted it out through the window. He boosted himself, finding footholds, first on the seat, then on the steering column, and clambered out onto the driver's door.

Smoke slithered into the wind from the crevice between the hood and the fender. Dalton tossed the box toward the road and jumped after it, rolling like a paratrooper in the snow. Dragging himself to his feet, he stumbled a few steps to lean against a nearby post. He looked up and realized it had a sign atop it with "MUS" showing from under a frosting of snow. Through openings in the filmy veils of the blizzard, he could see a building looming in the near distance like an angular dark mountain. *My God, if this is Asmus, that has to be the farm.*

He tucked the box under his arm and started out, his first several steps bordering on a run. He drew up, forcing himself to pick his footfalls carefully. He felt a warm flush coming up his legs, but the sight of his bare feet reminded him his boots and socks were in the car, which lay on its side, half submerged. Fear stabbed at him. The warmth didn't make sense, but he could still put one foot in front of the other. *I can't fall.* Dalton focused every neuron on the execution of his steps, on staying upright in spite of the slippery footing, the heft of the box, and the howling wind.

When he reached the farmhouse, he discovered the front steps were no longer there. Tossing the box onto the porch, he put his hands in his coat pockets and did another paratrooper roll onto the waist-high porch. Hooking his elbow on the sill of the boarded-up front window, he dragged himself onto his feet again. The front door was ajar enough to show a sliver of darkness. Instead of bending to pick it up, Dalton nudged the box toward the door with feet that felt Novocained. The hinges were stiff, but his two hundred-plus pounds easily forced it far enough for him to slip inside. After pulling the box of guns inside with his foot, he used his shoulder to buck the door closed.

A powerful reality settled over him. He was standing in the very room where he sat with Leetha's Uncle Norbert and Aunt Elise in 1947. Word they were hiring brought Dalton home to Kentucky. He was seeking escape from the heat of the brickyard's kilns, and he had become weary of running wild with his brother. In the middle of Dalton's pitch to convince Norbert he was the man to hire, Leetha walked down the stairs, and the sight of her dammed his flow of words. Eggshell pale, and appearing every bit that fragile, Leetha seemed to glide down the steps. Her habit was to turn slightly at the waist—an attempt to hide the early indications of the scoliosis that would eventually bend and cripple her. To Dalton, the twist read as an endearing modesty. Now Dalton looked at the staircase, a decrepit ghost in what little illumination stole through cracks between the boarded windows, and remembered her small hand gliding smoothly down the banister. By the time he could regain his speech that day, the words came out in a jumble that reddened his face and made Norbert explode in laughter and say, "Leetha, meet our new hired man—Dalton Hill."

The room was empty now, but for scattered piles of leaves and several heaps of dusty fabric that once served as curtains. Tongues of wallpaper rolled away from the cracked plaster to wag in the breeze. They brought Dalton's attention back to the minor-key moan of the wind. In spite of the cold draft, he felt a strong warmth radiating from his legs into his torso. He looked at his feet, which were now an alarming grayish-white. It must be the light, because they feel just fine.

He knew it would be a while before someone spotted his car and came looking for him. Might as well sit down and get comfortable. In a corner across from the staircase was a chair-size gathering of leaves, and Dalton picked up one of the former curtains to drape over them. He kicked the box over to the leaves, then testing first to make certain nothing was hidden in the pile, he carefully lowered himself to sit with his back against the wainscot.

His feet felt cold to the touch, but the warmth coming from them calmed him. He unzipped his coat, but wrapped his feet in the curtain for good measure. He was tired. He remembered his Army survival training, that a soldier shouldn't fall asleep if he was cold. *But I feel nice and warm.*

He closed his eyes and listened to the wind, wailing like the engines on the C-47 Skytrain that pulled the glider aloft in 1944. The roar of the motors diminished once they'd cut loose, replaced by the soft rush of air passing around its fuselage, a quiet whoosh. He remembered how frightened he was, sitting with the others in the belly of that silent bird. Now, the wind's throaty chorus seemed to allay his concerns. He closed his eyes and wondered how long he'd have to wait for help. Leetha tried to talk him into a cell phone, but he wasn't much for new-fangled gadgets. Now he wished he'd listened to her.

He slept and reawakened several times. He didn't know how much time passed. He thought about checking his watch, but moving his arm seemed like so much effort. It would be hard to read in the dim light, anyway. Best to save my strength. When help comes, I want to walk out on my own. He nodded off, again. When he awakened, he thought he heard Benny Goodman's band playing, but it turned out just to be the wind.

"Dal? Is that you down there?"

His eyes snapped open. *They've come to get me.* "Who is it?" he called.

"Why, it's Leetha, silly. Who else?"

"Leetha?" He rolled his eyes upward and saw nothing but stringy cobwebs wafting in the draft below the ceiling. "Leetha? Can you see me?"

"No, silly. I'm still upstairs," she called. "Didn't you go to sell the guns?"

A wave of embarrassment crashed over him. "Ah, no. I...the car slid off the road."

"Slid off the road! Are you hurt?"

"No. No, I smacked my side on the armrest. Bumped my head, but I'm fine."

"You weren't buckled up?"

"I guess I forgot."

"As fast as you drive?"

"But I wasn't. It was slippery and hard to see. I...I was going real slow. But, once the car started sliding...I couldn't stop it."

"You'll have that," Leetha clucked.

"I missed the forecast. Were they calling for a storm?" he asked.

"I don't know. At least you're safe now. I'll be down. I'm just fixing my hair."

It's so thin, anymore, but she does all she can with it. "Take your time, Lee," Dalton mumbled, his head lolling against the wall. "I'll just be dozing."

Dalton dropped into sleep again, but awakened when he heard a noise, or thought he did. Regardless, he looked around. Leetha had to still be upstairs. He was just about to call out to her when his commanding officer, Sergeant White, hurried into the room. Dalton struggled to his feet and stood at attention.

"At ease, Private Hill," the sergeant said. "What are you doing here? Didn't you get my order?"

Dalton lowered his head. "No, sir. I guess I ... I might have—"

"You were asleep?"

Dalton rolled his eyes up to look at Sergeant White and nodded. "No excuse, sir," he said.

The sergeant smiled. "It's okay, Hill. The Germans are in full retreat. Fresh troops are on the way. They should be just up the road. I ordered everyone out to meet them." He clapped Dalton on the back. "It's okay, son. Go on ahead. They have blankets and hot soup. They're airlifting us out." He pointed toward the road. "Get started. I'll be right behind you."

Dalton snapped off a salute, started for the door, but remembered his guns and stopped, looking at the box.

"What's in that?" the sergeant said, following Dalton's line of sight.

"Guns, sir. A Walther and a Luger."

"You didn't get the directive? No taking trophies." the sergeant barked. Dalton began to nod, but the sergeant's laughter stopped him. "Everybody's collecting shit. Go on and get your soup. I'll bring the guns for you."

Dalton grinned and scurried for the door. He tugged a couple of times, and the hinges squawked as he levered it opened. He jumped down off the porch and began to run, as best he could. He wondered what kind of soup it would be.

STUPID LITTLE NOISE

A stupid little noise. Kept you awake last night, made you crazy all day at the office, and now on the drive home. Nobody else hears it. Your wife didn't say anything. Your employees might hesitate to mention it, but the guys at the gym wouldn't have let it pass. Big joke. "The hell, Paul, you got a motor in there? You swallow your wife's vibrator? Didn't know you two were into kinky stuff." No, none of them said a word about it while you swapped jokes and lies in the steam room. Oh, and inhaling atmospheres of hot water vapor? No effect.

Okay, only audible from the inside, but that's no damned comfort. A whirring kind of noise. Almost a purr, except a cat's purr is dry and crisp. This is a series of soft-edged rolling reports, like one of those scary, wet-feeling farts that make you wonder if your tighty-whities still are. Definitely respiratory. Nothing on the intake, but it spools up every time you exhale. If your Harley made such a noise, you'd figure it to be a bad exhaust valve. Expensive.

With the full coverage health care, cost isn't a concern, but mortality sure the hell is. And you know the first question Dr. Watson will ask. "When did you first notice this, Paul?" You're supposed to carry a diary? Your hands are full just running your business. Jotting down the day, date and time of every deviation from the norm your fifty-five-year-old body decides to take just isn't practical. And as with most people, your first reaction when you feel an ache, pain or anything abnormal is to ignore it and hope it goes away on its own. "Jesus, Doctor," you'll wind up saying, "I don't have a clue. Wednesday? Thursday?"

You test for it again. Inhale. Exhale. In the near-silence of your

Lexus's leather-clad interior, the wheeze, the rattle, the whatever-the-hell it is, sounds like an alarm going off. Okay, so turn up the stereo. Thirteen speakers. Janis Joplin begging, "Take another little piece..." No good. Still there.

What you need is a louder freaking car. Goddamn Lexus is too well sound-insulated. Where the hell *is* the engine noise, anyway? Four hundred damned horsepower, and the thing is quieter than an electric shaver. A muscle car. Yeah, that's what you need. You should start shopping around on the internet. Something loud and proud that will do zero-to-sixty quick as a sneeze. A car that will make enough noise to hide the goddamn rattling, farting, whirring, pitty-pat noise in your...

That's another unsettling thing. Where the hell is this noise coming from? Sometimes it seems it could be in your chest. Bronchial tubes, maybe? Upper lungs? Ouch, that's scary. Quit smoking cigarettes in...you can't quite remember, but it's been at least twenty years. Squeaky clean, now. Not so much as a puff. Guys on the golf course, some who never touch a cigarette, fire up cigars and offer them around. "Aw, thanks anyway. Nice of you to offer, but not today." That's what you say, but what a bunch of dumb asses. Walking around with big brown rolls of crap hanging out of their mouths. A turd clenched in the teeth is not the look you're inclined to go for. And they light up stogies at poker games, too. You asked a guy once, you don't worry about cancer? "Nah," shaking his head, "I don't inhale." Like hell! Everybody in the damned room was inhaling.

This morning, the noise seemed nasal. You wondered, could it be as simple as a stalactite of dried mucus? A damned rattling booger? Could you be that lucky? Blew your nose, then snorted in several huge lungs-full. The old reverse direction ploy. Nope. You even forced a mouthful of water out through your nose when you were in the shower, but that backfired big-time. A headline ran through your head while you choked and gasped— PAUL DETCHEN DROWNS IN SHOWER. How embarrassing would that be? You know you'll shoot through eventually, but your goal is not to go out in a way that will leave your friends shaking their heads, laughing and saying, "What the hell was that dumb ass thinking?"

Could the noise be coming from somewhere *between* your chest and nose? Back in the gullet someplace? Like one of those noises that drive mechanics crazy. The kind that could be in the rear axle, but resonates up the drive shaft and makes the transmission a suspect. All those pieces and parts snugged tightly together make the origin impossible to track down. Clear your throat. It isn't sore. Take a deep breath. No congestion. Voice is normal. The stupid little noise could be coming from your lungs, nose, or anyplace in between.

All right, just ignore it. Put your mind on other things. You make the turn onto Copeland, and stop at South Detroit. The playground on the corner, the one where you used to hit baseballs in the summer and run footballs in the fall, is vacant. A beautiful damned Friday, sixty-five or seventy, with mellow late-May sunshine and not a boy or girl in sight. Check your Rolex. Quarter to four. Goddamn mopes are all inside playing computer games or, worse, hacking into other people's computers. You blow a puff of air through your nose in disgust. Damn, the noise is still there.

The light changes and you continue down Copeland. The rise in the road is still there, but the railroad tracks that once rode the crest have long since been ripped out. Back in grade school, putting stuff on the tracks and watching the 'tons-of-train' effect was super cool. You had a penny almost two inches across before the big steel wheels sheared it in half. You pass Beverly, your old elementary school. Man, the times you had there. You wonder what your pudgy little sixth-grader self would have thought if he'd had any inkling he would drive past Beverly Elementary forty-five years later in a new maroon Lexus.

You get caught at the light at Anthony Wayne Trail, which usually pisses you off, but today you're joyfully wallowing in the comforts of reminiscence. The Trail was your favorite place to drag race, back in high school. Had a black 1960 Chevy Biscayne two-door with a small block V-eight and three-on-the-tree. You and Russ James worked odd jobs after school, and spent all weekend bolting hop-up parts on your cars. Dual four-barrel carbs, headers and hot cam setups. In the vernacular of those days at Bowsher High, your old Chevy would "shit and git." How long has it been since you last had grease on your hands? The light turns green and you jam the accelerator, but you can barely hear the powerful engine. The traction control kicks in and minimizes the wheel-spin, so you lift your foot. No sense wasting fuel when the damned engineers won't even let you lay a little rubber. Besides, the noise is still there, louder than your car, even when it's accelerating at full-tilt.

Copeland passes Toledo Country Club's fifteenth green, where you sank a twenty-footer and separated your friend, Doc Pellington, from two hundred of his dollars, last Saturday. Dave Harrison, one of the others in your foursome that day, decided to have a little fun at Doc's expense. Bad idea. "I think I know how you can get your money back, Doc," Dave joked. "Schedule Paul's wife in for an appointment."

"No can do," Doc replied, always ready with a comeback. "I have a policy against treating attractive women." Dave's wife is one of Pellington's patients. Old Doc, the king of subtle put-downs.

You bring your car to a stop where Copeland and River Road meet. When you were a kid, you and your buddies used to ride bikes past this spot to buy ice cream cones at Penguin Palace, a few miles down the road. Never in your wildest dreams did you ever imagine you'd one day own a house on the Maumee River. The road is lined with so many old-growth maple and oak trees, it's like driving through a tunnel of foliage. Large, well-cared-for homes hold the road at bay with their lush green lawns and colorful gardens, the same ones you could only marvel at from the seat of your old Columbia Flyer. In another quarter of a mile, you pull onto your wide blacktop driveway, and the weekend officially begins. A beautiful wife, a successful business, and a fabulous house with a fast ski boat docked out back. The life you've managed to pull together puts a smile on your face. How could it not? Everything's spectacular...except for that goddamned stupid little noise. Check again. Yep. Still there.

You press the button to close the garage door and walk inside the house. It's quiet as a shrine, the way it always is. Smells of vanilla, Jane's favorite aroma. The house is her domain, and she's done all the decorating. Friends refer to the place as her "crayon box," because of the bold colors she selected for the walls and furnishings. She has a flair for interior design, and the results are spectacular.

You make the swing into the kitchen, and you know something is very wrong. Jane is leaning against the granite countertop and her arms seem tensed, crossed beneath her breasts. Her head is tilted down. It's obvious she isn't looking at the throw rug or the hardwood, but she doesn't look up when you walk into the room. Did you forget something? Not her birthday. Not your anniversary. Were you supposed to go somewhere? She's wearing slacks and a sweater, so not to the club. Your counseling session? No, that's on Tuesdays. "What?" you ask her. Even to yourself, you sound like a whiny child.

She turns her head to meet your gaze. "I found a lump," she whispers.

The word hits you like a locomotive. "A lump?" Such a gifted response.

She nods. "After tennis. I was showering at the club. Here," she says, rubbing her index finger on the outside of her left breast.

"Are you sure?"

She tilts her head in a way that expertly conveys her exasperation with your question, which you recognize as the second stupid reply you've come up with in the last thirty seconds. "I'm sorry," you say, splaying your hands in a gesture of contrition. "Did you call your doctor?"

Her face softens. "He can't see me for two weeks," she says. "I'm on a list for cancellations." You cross the kitchen and gather her into your arms. She feels broken. She begins to sob. "I can't believe this is happening," she sighs. Her humid breath is hot against your neck. You rub her back, making small circles. For a moment, it almost feels as though the two of you aren't standing in the kitchen anymore, as though you're in some kind of windless freefall. You widen your stance for better balance and pull back to look into her gray eyes. You're certain she's trying, but she can't mask her fear. You wonder how your eyes read to her.

"Two weeks is too long. Should I call Doc Pellington?"

"Nick Pellington?" Her eyes widen. You can't decide if it's surprise, or something else.

"Yeah. He's in a group with an oncologist and a surgeon. It'll be a one-stopper. Your doctor will have to refer you, and that'll take even more time." You take her hands and squeeze them gently. "Am I right?"

"But Nick's from the club. We socialize with him. And Nina."

"Which is exactly why he'll see you right away," you tell her. Slipping your cell out of your pocket, you hold it like an offering. "We're friends. I can call him right now and he'll fit you in. Maybe even yet today. Friends at the club, maybe, but he's a doctor, and a damned good one." You raise your eyebrows and wait.

"I'm scared," she says. She begins to nod, almost imperceptibly at first, before her head bobs in full affirmation. "I need to see someone soon."

You wake your cell, punch up the phone book, and scroll to Doc's number. You press send and take a deep breath to calm yourself. You exhale and notice the stupid little noise is gone.

Acknowledgements

These stories have appeared in the following literary magazines:
Cigale Literary Magazine "Clicking"
Edge "Arrival"
Epiphany "Safe Harbor"
Litro "Reflection"
Microliterature "Speed"
Specter Literary Magazine "Crashing"

These stories have appeared in the following anthologies:
Voices From the Porch (Main Street Rag, 2013) Altering Terms
Daily Flash 2012: 366 Days of Flash Fiction (Leap Year Edition) (Pill Hill Press, 2012) Monica's Fall

About the Author

Christopher T. Werkman completed a thirty year career as a high school art teacher in 2000. He still paints, but his primary passion is writing fiction. He lives on a few acres outside Haskins, Ohio, with is partner, Karen and too many cats. He plays golf in the summer, indoor tennis all winter, and rides his motorcycle whenever there is sufficient traction.

Mr. Werkman has had over twenty short stories published in various literary magazines and anthologies. His first novel, *Difficult Lies*, was published by Rogue Phoenix Press in September of 2015.

Difficult Lies

Is Allan Vickery alive, or is he dead? After a blow to the head from a golf ball, Vic isn't certain himself. As it turns out, he's comatose and the things he learns while unconscious are life-changing when he reawakens. But for a man in mid-life crisis—struggling to keep his marriage alive while attempting to become a recognized painter and still succeed at teaching high school art—his new understanding becomes a volatile accelerant for issues that merely smoldered in the past. In the resulting inferno, Vic finds passion in the arms of a lover and riches in the world of high-stakes golf matches. Whether or not you play golf, you cannot avoid difficult lies in your quest to find the fairway to happiness.

An Excerpt

His musings came full circle. When he was comatose, Vic longed for his life in Toledo. Now, he hadn't even regained consciousness, and already missed Bascolm, Donald, Jason, and Loon's Lair. And his golf game. It would have been so great to stay and play golf, he thought. He could do that when he was comatose. His body was disconnected, but his perception in the coma was he could play golf—better than he ever had. He knew what that state of existence held for him, and he had no idea what lay ahead if he came to. He was sealed inside an unresponsive carcass. Everything was shut down. He couldn't find the switch to reanimate his body, but he couldn't find his way back out of it either. Of course, even if he could find his way back into the coma, would he wind up back with Bascolm and the others? Maybe that was like trying to return to the same place in a dream, after getting up to take a whiz.

Suddenly, Vic got the sensation he was falling; the cable snapped and the elevator dropped into darkness. His field of vision turned black, and he worried he'd lost his sight. Maybe the head-shot on the golf course blinded him. He strained against the urge to cry, but couldn't help himself. Goddamn! What the hell will I do if I'm blind? Teach art? Paint? Play golf? Not likely. How will I run? How will I drive? What the fuck will I do? It felt as though pins were poking at the sensitive skin around his nose and eyes. He wanted more than anything to reach up and rub his face, but his arms didn't work.

Then someone touched his neck. It didn't feel like any of the hands that restrained him earlier. These fingers were gentle and cool. They stroked his neck and slid up onto his cheek. It had to be someone who knew him, someone he was close to. Nobody better be touching me like that unless I know them pretty damned well. Angie, maybe? Something told him it wasn't her. Then he was suddenly overwhelmed with the feeling the fingers belonged to his mother.

"Mom? Is that you? Oh God, Ma, I think I'm blind."

"I'm not your mother," a voice from out of the blackness said.

"Who is it?" Vic asked, as surprised he could speak as he was embarrassed about the fact that he blubbered like a child.

The voice giggled. "I'm disappointed, Vic. You don't remember me?"

"I'm sorry. I remember your voice, but I can't put a face with it. And I'm blind, so I can't see you."

The voice laughed. "You're not blind, silly. I'm the one who's blind. Don't you remember? We spent a lot of time together the summer before you and Angie were married. Does that help?"

"Jillian?" Vic was thunderstruck. Was it possible? "Jillian Reefe?"

She combed her fingers through his hair. "Now I feel a little better. I'd always hoped you wouldn't forget me. But you never called me Jillian."

"Reefer," Vic whispered, overwhelmed with a wave of affection for this woman. He suddenly didn't care it was too dark for him to see her. It felt so good to be with her again; the blind girl who lived in the apartment across the hall from Vic during his senior year in college.

"Reefer, are you still smoking all that dope?"

"No, darling. I finally took your advice," she replied in her lilting voice.

Vic always thought Reefer's voice sounded like music, and he never tired of listening to her talk. When she was high, which was most of the time back in the summer of 1970, she'd tell him all kinds of funny stories about her crazy lifestyle. Vic remembered one, a story about her friend who had an old Cadillac hearse. The windshield wiper motor gave out on their way home from a war protest in Washington D.C. It was raining too hard to go on without wipers, so the guy found a piece of clothesline somewhere and tied it to the driver's side wiper, routed the rope through the vent windows, then tied it to the passenger's side wiper. They continued on their way at seventy miles per hour, with Reefer tugging the rope back and forth to sweep the rain away. Vic was never certain honest-to-God hippies even existed until he met Reefer. She was one of the first to arrive at Woodstock, and one of the last to leave. She sang and played her guitar in bars and coffee houses. The girl may have been blind, but she was fearless. Wonderful as her adventures were, however, they weren't as captivating as the sound of her voice.

"How's Ziggy?" Vic asked. Reefer's Seeing Eye dog's name was Zig-Zag, after the rolling papers, but Reefer always called her Ziggy.

"Zig died years ago."

"Oh, Reef. I'm so sorry. Shit, I should have done the math." Vic blinked against tears that threatened to overrun his eyelids. Being with Reefer again put him in touch with a raft of long-forgotten emotions, and the death of her big friendly chocolate lab turned them loose.

"No, no. It's okay. Ziggy lived a great life. I miss her, but the memories are good ones. I work with a cane, now. No other dog could replace Zig." She apparently heard him snuffle and wiped her fingers across his eyes. "You cried the first time we went out together. Remember?"

"What was the movie's name? That great anti-war flick with George Hamilton, right?"

"Um-hmm. *The Victors*. You cried when the soldiers shot Peter Fonda's puppy."

"That's right. You asked me to go see it with you because the manager wouldn't let Ziggy in the theater. Remember? You asked me to be your Seeing Eye dog for the day." He chuckled. "Man, nobody could get away with that shit now, barring a Seeing Eye dog."

"No. The world's a more enlightened place today. But I'm glad it worked out the way it did. We had a beautiful summer together."

A bit over five feet tall, with a curvy-cute body, Reefer wore sandals and tie-dyed frocks with scoop necklines back then. Her long, straight, dark hair accented her olive complexion. She wore beaded necklaces and tied feathers in her hair, which made her look like an Indian princess. Her single conceit was her discomfort about anyone seeing her eyes. She wore wrap-around bubble-lens sunglasses, and only removed them if she was alone, or if she was convinced it was completely dark. As close as they became, Vic never once saw her eyes. Although Reefer lived in an apartment right across the hall from Vic, they'd only exchanged hellos in the hallway or at the mailboxes until that summer. The June afternoon at the movies changed all that. Vic never spent time with a blind person before and was uncomfortable being with her, at first. He soon learned if Reefer needed help with something, she'd ask. She seldom did. Between Ziggy and her own self-reliance, Reefer seemed in control regardless of the situation. All through the movie, on that far-away summer day, she seemed to know what happened, and only asked Vic to explain what occurred a time or two.

When they returned to the apartment building, she invited him into her place for some wine, and later they went out for dinner at a Chinese joint. By the time they returned home, an early evening thunderstorm was building.

"I'm afraid of storms, Vic. Will you stay with me tonight?"

"I—I'm getting married in August," he replied, unable to hide his shock.

"But you're not married now. If you can't be with the one you love, love the one you're with," she said, more convincingly than Steven Stills himself.

"You're right, Reefer," Vic said, returning from his memories. "It was a beautiful summer. I've thought back on it many times."

"Me, too. How are things with you and Angie?"

"Ah, they're fine."

"Come on, Vic. It's me. You don't have to tap-dance." Reefer's musical voice melted his reluctance to tell the truth.

"Things aren't great, Reef. It started out so good. I love her so much. I always have. But she's not the girl I fell for back in college." Reefer stroked his cheek and said nothing. Vic imagined her cocking her head and dipping her chin, her habit when someone spoke to her. "I know people change over the years," Vic continued. "Hell, I'm not who I was back when you knew me in Bowling Green. But with Angie, the changes are so dramatic. She used to be so passionate. So happy. We used to play silly word games we made up as we went along." Vic decided that was a lame example of the weave of their life together before it unraveled, but he couldn't think of anything else that wouldn't take too long to explain. "Honest, Reef, she looks like she did the day I met her in the student union. Hasn't changed a bit. But it's like *Revenge of the Body Snatchers,* or something. Like somebody else moved in and pushed the woman I loved out."

There was silence. Vic couldn't even hear Reefer breathing. He was overtaken by the fear she'd gone and he was alone. Then her beautiful contralto came out of the darkness and literally gave him chills. "I understand," she nearly whispered.

"And, I can't believe I'm telling you this, but I've always wondered if it was all because of us."

"Us?" Reefer asked.

"Yeah. Punishment, sort of. You know, like I was unfaithful to her that summer, and this is what I get for it. You and I had a terrific relationship, and now Angie and I don't."

"But you never told her..."

"Oh, no. She doesn't have the faintest idea about us. No, I mean the karma thing. You know, yin and yang, opposite and equal. The fates evening up the score."

Vic felt Reefer's hand on his shoulder. She squeezed gently. "The universe doesn't operate that way," she said softly, with so much conviction he would have felt foolish if he asked her how she could be so sure.

"Anyway, the main problem right now is Angie and I have been apart. I got hit by a golf ball, and I've been in a coma. Unless you're wrong about it being dark, I'm blind." Again, he slipped toward the verge of tears.

Reefer kissed him on the forehead; her lips were as cool as her hands. She ran her fingers across his cheek. "You are not blind, Vic."

"Then why am I seeing black?"

"You're right, you're *seeing* black. You remember I told you I was sighted until I was six?"

"Yeah. Some kind of cancer? They removed it, but damaged your optic nerve."

"Yes. And I remember colors, so I know what black looks like. I can tell you for certain, if you're seeing black, then you're not blind."

"I'm not? So, what do you see? Gray?"

She giggled. "No, silly. I don't see anything. Hey, look at me with your nose," she said, giving the end of his a tweak. "What do you see?"

"With my nose? Hell, I can't see anything with my nose."

"There. That's what I see with my eyes. There's nothing wrong with yours. You need to open them."

"But they are ..." he insisted, before he felt her cool fingertips exert gentle pressure on his eyelids. Suddenly, he was looking at a light fixture on a ceiling.

VISIT OUR WEBSITE
FOR THE FULL INVENTORY
OF QUALITY BOOKS:
http://www.roguephoenixpress.com

Rogue Phoenix Press
Representing Excellence in Publishing

Quality trade paperbacks and downloads

in multiple formats,

in genres ranging from historical to contemporary romance, mystery and science fiction.

Visit the website then bookmark it.

We add new titles each month!

73930471R00130

Made in the USA
Lexington, KY
12 December 2017